TWO PLAYS

ARMAND GATTI

TWO PLAYS

The Seven Possibilities
for Train 713
Departing from Auschwitz

*Translated from the French
by Teresa Meadows Jillson*

Public Song
Before Two Electric Chairs

*Translated from the French
by Teresa Meadows Jillson
& Emmanuel Deleage*

GREEN INTEGER
KØBENHAVN & LOS ANGELES
2002

GREEN INTEGER
Edited by Per Bregne
København/Los Angeles

Distributed in the United States by Consortium Book
Sales and Distribution, 1045 Westgate Drive, Suite 90
Saint Paul, Minnesota 55114-1065

(323) 857-1115 / http://www.greeninteger.com

First Published by Green Integer in 2002
©1991 by Éditions Verdier
The 7 Possibilities for Train 713 Departing from Auschwitz and
Public Song Before Two Electric Chairs
were published in the three volume *Œuvres théâtrales*
(Paris: Éditions Verdier, 1991)
English language translation for
The 7 Possibilities for Train 713 Departing from Auschwitz
©2002 by Teresa Meadows Jillson;
for *Public Song Before Two Electric Chairs* ©2002
by Emmanuel Deleage and Teresa Meadows Jillson
Published by agreement with Éditions Verdier
Back cover copy ©2002 by Green Integer

Design: Per Bregne
Typography: Guy Bennett
Photograph: Photograph of Armand Gatti by Jacqueline Salmon

LIBRARY OF CONGRESS CATALOGING IN PUBLICATION DATA
Gatti, Armand [1924]
*Two Plays: The 7 Possibilities for Train 713
Departing from Auschwitz* and *Public Song Before
Two Electric Chairs*
ISBN: 1-931243-28-X
p. cm — Green Integer 51
I. Title II. Series III. Translators

Green Integer books are printed for Douglas Messerli.
Printed in the United States of America on acid-free paper.

Contents

INTRODUCTION

The plays reproduced in translation here represent the texts of the only English language productions in the United States of works by Francophone author, Armand Gatti. *The Seven Possibilities for Train 713 Departing from Auschwitz* premiered in English on April 20, 1988 in the Todd Theatre, University of Rochester, Rochester, New York, with Armand Gatti directing. *Public Song Before Two Electric Chairs* premiered on September 21, 2001 at the Los Angeles Theatre Center, in a *Courage* production, directed by Gino Zampieri, a member of the original production cast (1966, *Théâtre National Populaire*, Paris) and director of the Popular Romand Theater, Switzerland.

There are many reasons why these two plays are appearing together in this volume and why, out of the more than fifty plays written by this author, these are the two to have been produced in the United States. Both plays enter into the ever-present dialogue in Gatti's work between author and History and connect to some aspect of the author's personal history, a particular remembrance of that history, and an exploration of its multiple possibilities. *Public Song* was written in 1962, published at *Editions Seuil* in 1964 and first produced at the *Théâtre National Populaire* in Paris in 1966. It is based upon, though it does not reproduce the very American story of Nicola Sacco and Bartholomeo Vanzetti, poor Italian immigrants, anarchists and activists, falsely accused of a bombing in Massachusetts and executed after seven years in prison. Gatti's connections to this story are myriad. The execution and reaction to it are part of his earliest memories with his own anarchist father (Dante was not yet four). His name, Dante, was the same as that of Sacco's son. His father (Auguste) was living in Chicago at the time of the arrests and was nearly killed (prior to Dante's birth) for union organizing. The son of immigrant parents, Dante could have been born in the U.S. and was not only because of the attempt on his father's life. He was born in Monaco, still to parents of economic and political migration. Auguste ultimately died as a result of violent reaction to and oppression of the anarchist movement in Europe. These same elements: anarchism, union organizing, activism, immigration and exile play important roles in the writing and production of

Train 713 as well. In addition, this later play incorporates Gatti's personal history with other events of the first half of the twentieth century: the Civil War in Spain, the camps and resistance movements of World War Two, the aftermath of all of the above. And while this play is not a purely American story, it is based in a History in which American presence, physical and attitudinal, is paramount and its production in the U.S. changed the entire nature of the text.

Written more than twenty years apart, these plays reflect preoccupations, processes and approaches to writing, theatre, History (capital H) and personal history (small h) that continue to be the ground for the author's work. They are highly representative of that work, reproducing as well as similarities in subject and approach, a clear view of the scope of a major author's work. They also form the core of what might be called Gatti's "American plays," two of the three plays – *V Like Vietnam* being the third – where the United States, its particular view of and participation in the History of the Century are central to the structure and development of the play. This is most obvious in *Public Song* where the historical subject is objectively American. As you will see, however, this obvious ground in U.S. history is short-circuited by a refusal to "tell the story" and a structure which instead, interrogates a multiple, international and diverse view of the possible ways of seeing, telling and living the stories around that Historical event. *Train 713* too moves with the development of "possibilities," only one of which is American and an exiled American at that. The U.S. presence here, however, is more subtle, finding its expression in exploration of stories told by dominant U.S. forces, administrators and generals, but more importantly, in a particular (capitalist) way of viewing the future and its possibilities. *Public Song* works the concept of possibilities through the device of the "selmaire," versions of events as seen by individual characters or groups of characters. These "identifications" and replaying of events, real and imagined, are the reality of the play. The idea of possibility itself becomes the central figure in *Train 713*, each possibility represented by a group, rather than one character. Similarly, *Public Song,* while maintaining characters as carriers of personal history and possibility, assembles them in groups of location which then play out particular views of the events, their conflicts and possibilities. *Train 713* is the last of Gatti's plays to have named individual characters. These characters are, however, essentially elements of groups of possibilities – a less personalized way of posing the same questions of reality and perception posed by the earlier "selmaire" structure. In more recent works, characters give way entirely to groups defined in a variety of ways: ethnically, geographically, in terms of their relation to various institutions (the "psychiatrized" [sic]), as alphabets and/or languages… This approach lends itself not only to the author's long standing rejection of psychological characters, but also to his increasing desire to develop the dialogue between the languages of literature and science, to move between these domains and interrogate the possibilities raised in that juxtaposition.

The life and work of Armand Gatti are, at one and the same time, very well known and almost completely unknown on both the national (French) and international levels. Most analyses of contemporary comparative or French theater give at least passing recognition to his (early) work. Yet real knowledge of the work tends to end with the early 1970's. Subsequent mention, even in the frequent and often lengthy newspaper articles written about Gatti in recent years in France, tends to replace real analysis with vague reference to involvement in "cultural animation", or the "social" import of the work. Interestingly enough, this invisibility and vaguery of description accompanies the most active years of this author's career. In the last twenty-five years Gatti has written at least thirty plays (many in multiple versions) and film scenarios, made one major (and internationally prize-winning) film and four video films, one featured on French television. He has worked in nine countries and been invited to work in several more. At the publication of these works in English it seems imperative to introduce this author and the scope of his work as well as the nature of the work and a brief description of the process it involves.

"I was nearly born in America"

Dante Sauveur Gatti was born in Monaco on January 26, 1924 to Italian immigrants, Laetitia Luzona and Auguste Reinier Gatti. Auguste was an anarchist exiled from Mussolini's Italy for his politics. In the Chicago of the early 1920s he was attacked and presumed killed by Pinkerton agents working for companies wishing to be rid of union organizers. Only Auguste's presumed death kept Dante from being born an American. Laetitia managed to return home to the Italian Piedmont and eventually to rejoin a "resurrected" Auguste in Monaco in time for the birth of their son. Gatti's early play *La Vie imaginaire de l'éboueur Auguste G* (*The Imaginary Life of the Dustman August G*) is a dialogue with the possibilities of his father's life. Chicago and its place in that history is an essential part of a recent work, *De l'anarchie comme battements d'ailes (Of Anarchy as the Beating of Wings*, Editions Syllepse, Paris: 2001). Similarly, the long "cinematographic poem" *Ton Nom était Joie* (published in English as *Your Name was Joy*, in *50. A Celebration of Sun & Moon Classics*. Sun and Moon Press) is a dialogue of possibility with his mother and the Italian Piedmont from whence she sprang.

Conceived in Chicago, Dante spent his early years in the shantytown of Tonkin in Monaco and the Saint-Joseph district of Beausoleil, France, the working class immigrant district across the border, which provided labor to the glitter-world of Monaco. Both Gatti's self-identification as an "immigrants' son" and his near American origin play an important role in the particular approach to pro-

13

duction of *Train 713* in the United States as well as to both the writing of *Public Song* and its much later American production.

Gatti's father was a great teller of tales. Ranging from the literary to the heroic these tales were most often full of images of the coming Revolution ("I grew up thinking the Revolution was like Christmas; you woke up one morning and it had arrived. I lived in dread of sleeping through it, missing it somehow...", Gatti explains.) They often included stories of the voiceless and the powerless; historical wrongs like those done to Sacco and Vanzetti. Gatti would, in his own interrogative, multifaceted style, take up these stories again. Sometimes the writings examine the figures of the tales (Sacco and Vanzetti, Rosa Luxemburg), sometimes the base History for the tales, and always the juxtaposition of the History of events and the history of the voiceless participants in those events, the multiple versions of truth and fact... This is not retelling or reconstruction in a historical or realistic sense, but rather exploration of their possibilities, of the fragmented nature of the way History and the people and events it transmits perceive and are perceived. This "multilogue" with History continues to form the basis of his work even when the most traditional aspects of story (character, obvious plot) has long disappeared from it to be replaced by groups, multiplicity, fragmentation and the exploration of pure possibility. ("The important thing is knowing if Sacco and Vanzetti will die, once again, here, tonight.")

Auguste, who had survived multiple knife wounds at the hands of Pinkerton agents in Chicago, died from wounds inflicted by the police during a demonstration in Monaco, when Dante was thirteen. While yet in his teens Dante joined the French resistance and set off on foot to the Corrèze region of central France with nothing more than a backpack full of books (Rimbaud, Lau Tzou, Michaux, Rabbi Aboulafia...). A short time later he and his comrades were caught. Subsequent to interrogations in which Gatti responded to questions by reciting the poet Nerval and saying that his reason for being there was "to make God fall into time," he was sentenced to death. Reprieved by virtue of his youth, he was sent to forced labor in Germany.

Escaping from the camp, Gatti walked across Germany and France eventually arriving in Bordeaux and finding his way across the channel to join the parachutists of the British SAS (Special Air Service). (Ever thinking in terms of poetry, he compares his walk across Western Europe to Hölderlin's "walk to the sun"). As a member of the SAS he participated in some of the worst battles of the end of the war. The 1981 film, *Writing on the Wall*, interrogates, among other things, the meaning of his presence in the SAS when juxtaposed with the meaning of an occupying SAS presence in Ireland during the "troubles".

Following the end of the war and his near court martial for reacting against the poor and often brutal treatment accorded German prisoners (See Act VII, *Train 713*) Gatti went to Paris. He became a journalist for the *Parisian Libéré* and later *Libération*, *France soir*, and *Paris Match*, taking a "more French" name in the climate of postwar xenophobia evident in the Paris of the 1940s. All of his journalistic work and the poetry, theater and film to follow would be created and published under the name of Armand Gatti.

Some of Gatti's early assignments took him to former concentration camps to interview the "displaced persons" left in the camps with nowhere else to go at the end of the war. While his experience with the resistance and the camps is central to all of Gatti's work, this experience of the post-war camps is crucial to the writing of the play that would become *The Seven Possibilities of Train 713 Departing from Auschwitz*.

In 1954 Gatti became a foreign correspondent, eventually traveling throughout China, the Soviet Union, Algeria and Latin America. In that same year he was awarded the Albert Londres prize for journalism, France's Pulitzer, for the series of articles on wild animal training that would become *Envoyé spécial dans la cage aux fauves* (*Special Envoy in the Wild Animal Cage*). Many of the plays he would subsequently write would have roots in these experiences and travels.

1959 produced Gatti's last work as a journalist and the Fénéon prize for his play, *Le Poisson noir* (*The Black Fish*). From that time until the early 1970s, Gatti worked and was produced in the public theater in France. In France, the newly enlarged and heavily subsidized public sector was *the* venue for new theatrical texts, genres, performance styles and stagings during the 1960s and 1970s. Gatti became the single most performed living French language author of the 1960s.

In 1968 the Spanish government formally objected to what it assumed to be a production critical of the still living and reigning general (*La Passion du Général Franco*, at the Théâtre National

Populaire in Paris). The French government pulled the play from the program two weeks prior to the opening. This remains the only example of a play banned from a public theater in France. Subsequent to this event, Gatti left the traditional circuits of French theatre and began to move from an interrogation of the institution of public theatre from within to a broader interrogation of theatre as practice and genre from a variety of institutional and non-institution bases. He would eventually move to an almost total rejection of theatre, per se. This move paralleled a physical displacement/exile from France: six years spent working in Germany and with students in Belgium. Exile, self-imposed and other, and itinerance are another major element in Gatti's work. Although Gatti works continued to be produced in public theatres in France until 1971, Gatti himself withdrew from the "legitimate" French stage and has never returned to it. Upon returning to France in 1975 he continue to "wander" (the name of his current production structure is *La Parole Errante* – The Wandering Word) though much of that errance would be within France (Montbéliard, Isle d'Abeau, St. Nazaire, later, Marseilles, Avignon, Strasbourg). Gatti's trajectory would also continue to be international: Ireland, Canada, the United

States, Italy, Switzerland, Austria. The experience of the banning of *The Passion* and subsequent writing about the experience became the basis for a departure in practice to accompany the fact of his physical departure from conventional theaters. From the beginning, Gatti was an author of intentionally dispersed, non-linear theatrical texts and, by the late 1960s, of a writing inclusive of the groups of people of which it spoke. In the years following *la Passion*, both writing and practice increasingly incorporate the experience of their own making and that of the people and communities participating in creation. The years of self-imposed exile were years of exciting change, innovation and return to various forms of theatre, always maintaining a fundamentally personal but also broadly political connection to the author. While rarely the direct and obvious subject of Gatti's work, that work is always based in an intense personal experience and identification. It must, ultimately, be written, a piece of *écriture* (though it may be written on the body or with the alphabet of trees). This is not spontaneous, improvisational "agit-prop" theatre (though Gatti claims Piscator as a mentor of sorts). It is a perpetually changing, living theatre, based in both the experience of author and participants and a necessary written text. Gatti is ever ambivalent about the final product. He compares the book – i.e. the published, immutable text, fixing and imprisoning the word – to the concentration camp and the garbage can to the resistance, or liberated territory. This attitude parallels the move from traditional theatre with its emphasis on production and performance, to a process which becomes the reason for the effort and which de-emphasizes, or completely does away with performance. The underlying fable around which the project is woven must be a story of importance to Gatti's "dialogue with our century". During this period, Gatti's theater had become largely invisible not only because it functioned in alternative theatrical and literary circuits, nor because emphasis in the work had moved from product to process. Rather, it disappeared from the public eye because it began to speak not only of, but also through people rendered invisible and speechless by History (with a capital H) and contemporary society. Its political struggle is defined within social and historical patterns of exclusion, marginality and alienation attempting to give critical and poetic voice to marginal groups and to their equally marginalized histories. Although Gatti no longer explicitly rejects the publicity of public stages, public funding and publication, in practice his invisible subject, subjects and means of production erase much of his work from contemporary view, a fact which does not go unacknowledged in the various projects. In *Train 713*, all of the characters, with the exception of the representatives of authority, are blind; an ironic commentary on the very different invisibility of marginalized groups, of this theater and of power. During this period, Gatti would also continue to explore a variety of media and means of expression, both separately and, increasingly, in combination. Video, the use of daily and weekly published work journals, written work by the participants, poster workshops and expositions associated/dialoguing with the work are languages which continue, in ever differing ways, to structure and inform Gatti's work.

Well known for more than a decade, in the course of the subsequent two decades Gatti and his work became unknown, or better, mis-known. As he continued to work, write and believe in the Word in all its manifestations (written word, action as associated with engaged thought...), the way he went about creating changed. The projects were removed from the traditional circuits of production, then, more gradually, from circuits of consummation. No longer available for traditional spectators, readers or critics, this theater reconstructs itself within various "communities" and attempts to remember a discursive community based on exchange of (social) experience. The work centers on a storytelling dialogue between historical situation and/or character, and the stories of the participants. Both historical characters and participants tend to be forgotten by History – workers, immigrants, street kids, concentration camp prisoners, anarchists, resistance fighters and revolutionaries from the "wrong" wars, street sweepers, maids, nurses. This is not historical theater, but rather a reconstruction of the multiplicity of social history based on a constant interweaving of past, present and future, of History, story and possibility. The interweaving of story and History is not only a reconstruction of social memory in all the fragmentation of the contemporary society in which it strives to survive; it is also a rendering of it as visible and vocal. These new chronicles mix the "real" and the "imaginary," the told and the telling without hierarchization, allowing the one to question the other. Gatti takes the whole of his century to be the ground of his work and of his life. The objective veracity of personal history is less

22

important, less real, than the reality it enjoys in the dialogue with History. In the various projects, participants' stories become part of the text, dialogue with the text, with Gatti's own stories and with each other. Ultimately they take on the invisibility and silence created by the larger, louder and more visible Stories of our century. The traces left by the tellers of different projects vary. They appear as whole segments of the contemporary story interwoven into the historical character, as video-taped telling juxtaposed with conflictual or seemingly disconnected staged portrayal, as song, as narration, as image, even as character. In any event, the telling is a joint if dis-jointed process of historical reconstruction. The result carries the prints of these voiceless tellers in all their jarring discontinuity and contradiction. The title of one such project is indicative of the ongoing dialogue with History – *Nous ne sommes pas des personnages historiques* (*We Are Not Historical Characters*) – and of the way Gatti's work progresses and develops throughout the 1980s and 90s.

Public Song is a play of the "in" years when Gatti was widely known and performed in the public theatre in France. Produced at arguably the most influential of the public theatres in France, it was, nonetheless, highly criticized for its unorthodox treatment of History, its fragmentation, its use of space. It also already raises the questions of voice and perception that would become increasingly central to both writing (écriture) and production as Gatti's work progressed. It is a prime example of the ways in which history (small h) dialogues with and has the potent potential to transform History (capital H). The three versions of *Train 713* come at the end of an itinerant period in Gatti's work during which he developed a process which would be more important than any product (i.e. final production) and which invariably included those involved in said process. In the years separating the final version of *Train 713* from its publication in English, Gatti completed a personal cycle of immigration, exile and return.

Although Gatti continues to work and be involved in projects outside France, he has been based and worked primarily in France since the establishment of *La Parole Errante* (The Errant Word) in 1986. Housed in the old Meliès studios in Montreuil-sous-Bois, in the *Maison de l'arbre* (House of the Tree), this "International Creation Center" functions as office, studios and "think tank" for the various projects of Gatti and his associates. Appropriately off-center, this working class suburb of Paris and the regional governments with which Gatti works reflect the real constitution of the nation and its people much more than the capital itself. They also reflect the tenor of a life's work. Continuing to emphasize the concept of writing in all mediums, his recent work emphasizes the association in artistic creation of the languages of writing, theater, painting, video and cinema in the "public forum" of his work with specific populations.

Notes on *The Seven Possibilities*
for Train 713 Departing from Auschwitz

Train 713 had three beginnings, in three national
contexts, three languages, among and with three
different publics. The third and final version of the
train was produced at a private American university, in English, with student participants. *Noah's
Arks*, the train as it was known in Toulouse, was
created in the heart of what could be considered
the preferred public and participant population for
Gatti's theatre, *les lou-lous*. They combine, in their
social existence, the multiple exclusion of this
theatre's ground: immigration, ethnic difference,
linguistic incompetence in the dominant language
and poverty. This public continues to embody the
matter of Gatti's theater today. In their public space
one finds the voice to accompany the alphabets of
exclusion, which make up the train, which fill the
arks. This link between public and text remains am-
biguous as always. Exclusion is never simple, never
simply other, but it does represent an understand-
able base upon which to build.

In Vienna, it was not primarily a marginal public who would create the train, but rather young bourgeois theater students. Here the most obvious link, the thread to be woven, seems to be History itself, a physical proximity to the stories and paths followed by this train and so many others. This is a public history often hidden away but present in the sites, in the names, in the people themselves, in everything that is said and all that is not. And this is a city, country and History very present in the story of Train 713.

Train 713 recounts by means of continuous fragmentation the story of groups of former prisoners abandoned to die in Auschwitz at the retreat of the German army and subsequently shuttled around Central Europe in search of a haven. The characters suffer from multiple and contradictory exclusion. They are members of those groups chosen for the ultimate exclusion of the camps, their labs and crematoriums: Jews, Gypsies, Revolutionaries, X-Children. Excluded from even the larger group of prisoners sent on to Buchenwald from Auschwitz on the basis of their ultimate infirmity, at the liberation, they are excluded from the "Great Convoy" of former prisoners being returned to their homes. These displaced persons have no country to take them in. Once again they are excluded by ethnicity, by politics, by their very existence. The play is constructed on two levels: that of the "real", both the historical real, that which did indeed happen, and the realistic, the day to day reality of such a convoy; and the level of the imaginary, also two-fold, that which could have been and has a realistic base, and that which is not realistic and is played out on a figurative/symbolic level. This multiple layering, which becomes even more complex when staged, sets up a dialogic structure questioning the very conditions of exclusion and otherness, even within pre-established marginality. In *Train 713* the constant of exclusion is particularly evident in the text, whereas in other works it may be more obviously present in production. Here the initial situation is based on already multiple exclusion. The characters are historical outsiders: the Jews of the ghettos – the literal/physical ghettos of Poland, but also the figurative ghettos of much of western Europe; the Gypsies – nomads, accepted nowhere, at home nowhere; female Spanish Republicans – unusual in their political participation in a culture which relegated women to non-active back-room roles, foreign in their struggle against dictatorship, ultimately exiled in dcfeat; International Brigadists – fighting against their own countries' expressed wishes, often having fought against countrymen, outsiders in the land for which they struggled, exiled from home because of that struggle; children, almost exclusively Jewish, both excluded and implicated by age and ethnicity, usually excluded from life itself in the camps for those same reasons. These are the "pipel" of whom Eli Weisel writes, children used in every imaginable way, whose survival depended on exclusion from self, on total loss of identity – no name, no origin, no definitive gender. Even the bureaucrats, the administrators of the convoy are members of marginal groups made more so by the war – a Ukrainian woman, a German from the Volga – like the students who played them, participants in a dominant power structure while tied historically to an outsider history, foreign on the very soil of its making and confronted with very different possibilities.

And in the United States? Upon what basis could a public and a public space of the Gattian variety be established? Ultimately it would be on the basis of both of the preceding versions – exclusion and History. How can one speak of exclusion when the participants are self-selected from among the students of a private university tending to reproduce and affirm a certain upper class detachment? How can one compare young people who expect to take their place among the elite of the nation if not the world, and may well do so, with the invisible peoples of History? These were Americans and, as such, part of the perpetual immigration which is this country. They were, whether they recognized it openly or not, whether they were aware of it or not, eternal outsiders in their own country, excluded by the very form of their domination. Their multiple histories represent so many stories of exclusion, of exile, be it self-imposed or forced. And this may be all the more true for those attracted, for often unclear and poorly formulated reasons, by this project.

The eternal outsider comes together with a certain History tied to the fable of this project, tied to the stories of the passengers on the minor convoy which would be Train 713. But the fact that one was of Jewish or German or Italian descent, even the fact that ethnicity and class had destroyed one's family, was not enough to engage in the dialogue required by this experience. It would be necessary to recognize that this History, in all its ambiguity, in all it brings by way of complication in the daily life of the good American citizen, belongs to us as much as to the Austrians who were both passengers and agents of this train. Once again, exclusion is never simple, univocal or unidirectional. Multiplicity and fragmentation are the means by which this theater examines the plurality of its voices. *Train 713* stopped in Rochester after stops in Toulouse and Vienna. It carried its own story as well as the stories for which it was the vehicle, and the History circulating with it. The text translated and reproduced here, and the convoy which both ended and began in Rochester, integrates these stories and completely new possibilities. In Rochester the participants worked on their own realities. They learned karate as a possible physical language for the train. These possibilities did not enter into the final dialogue. The train did take on a bass rhythm, the musical rhythm of a bass guitar. Both the music and motion of the train were conditioned by karate but decided by other evolutions. This train became a convoy of blind people, of the visually handicapped. Handicapped in being, without the vision, which allows continuation of life, of existence in the world, blind in the view of others, they are nonexistent and invisible. And these blindnesses became in turn so many quests for sight, so many ways of living in this world become invisible. Noah's arks, the seven possibilities of the train, became totems, interlocutors of the forces of the possible.

In a rectangular, white space, only the black benches for the spectators, the black rails traced on the ground and the images of the train and its symbolic cargo made an impression on the eye. The four walls covered in white carried this train and its alphabets drawn in black. These symbols became possibilities of sight, ways of seeing, which, in performance, took on the paths followed, in red. In the space, other than the spectators' seats, there were nothing but four white train pieces. Two of these, platform cars placed at the two ends of the playing theater, made up the other playing spaces of this triple staging. This was a space and a decor which would give free rein to the movement of the train, to the broad gestures of the blind characters, to the evolving interpretations of the text. At the same time, the staging required the actors to have a heightened consciousness of the space in a way the characters' blindness could only exacerbate. The staging forced the public to become aware of it as well, since this public would play the role of geographical formations and obstacles around which the train had to pass. This flexible space didn't change during the performance, but did take on other allures and function at different levels. Realistic close up, when the train circulated, the space became the countryside to be crossed, empty signifier whose proper and weighty meaning awaited the multiple and internal visions of the different groups. At the same time, the space entered the realm of the fantastic since the imaginary was always present in this triptych and invaded the entire space at times.

This decor and staging created three theatrical spaces: the dynamic, the mechanical-musical and the graphic. The dynamic space was the central space of the train in motion, of the journeys, the visits, the meetings. The realistic space, one step removed, this is the space of the historical fable, of the passage of this train and these passengers that no one wanted across a Europe that could not see them. The mechanical-musical space of the mechanic and his locomotive was the origin of the rhythm, which provoked the rhythm of the feet, which made the train advance. An imaginary space motivating the realistic space, its motivation would be called into question at every moment. The graphic space of the controllers and their report was that of the rigidly spacialized journey of the seen but not lived. Once again imaginary, this was the space of optical vision, of that which creates for itself a complete vision and which sees everything on the level of the Big Picture and is blind to all the particulars.

This staging divided and unified the representation of the mechanical, the graphic and the dynamic just as the text does for time, stories and possibilities. This constant movement between the whole and the part gives the impression of a living tapestry where the occupation of the space becomes a weaving of the fixed (graphic) image on a base of the (dynamic) image in motion by the mechanism of the constant (musical) rhythmic image. The rhythm was also triple, and was woven from the beating feet of the passengers and the guitar of the musician on the canes of the blind in motion and the drumming hands of the seeing mechanic. This performance advanced on the rapid, medium and slow rhythms of the locomotive, of the train. It breathed to the rhythm of the canes of the blind in search of vision.

Train 713 is a dense and complex text. In one sense it is perhaps less so than some other Gatti texts, but in another it is more so simply because its historical ground *seems* more concrete. There is a fable that can be traced, that can be followed just like the convoy follows the rails, and like the graphic image which created itself on the walls in production. But at the same time, it is a text that destabilizes and that does not allow one to take things too literally. While presenting characters and groups who have stories, it refuses a simple psychological identification and requires a conscious public, which accepts the risk of the participant and therefore refuses the facility of a detached comprehension. This complexity demands risk on everyone's part and makes concessions neither to History, nor to the public, nor to the possibilities of the imaginary. This demanding destabilization is at work in every aspect of the play. It plays in the language, which runs the gambit from the most realistic to the most poetic, and which refuses naturalism while using it in order to create dialectic of language. It is in the anecdotal, in the story told that shocks because it is horrid and at the same time provokes laughter, however little. Passengers who accept the risks of *Train 713* find themselves grappling with this logic of the unbearable and questioning their own place in this system.

THE 7 POSSIBILITIES
FOR TRAIN 713
DEPARTING FROM AUSCHWITZ

CHARACTERS

Jewish Group:
The possibility of the Book
MOISHE STERN, SARAH ELIEZER

Gypsy Group:
The possibility of going back up the Danube
RITA DONAU, KORRI, DJANGO

Spanish Group:
The possibility of the dog for the blind
SOLEDAD BAUER, CONCHA PARIS

Brigadist Group:
The possibility of assassinated political language
TANTI BACI, RANDAL

x Child Group:
The possibility of childhood in Auschwitz
PIPEL 19, PIPEL 21

Soviet Controllers Group:
The bureaucratic possibility
GALINA ROUBLEIVA, FOLK STOTSKY

Mechanical Group:
The possibility of the locomotive
THE MECHANIC

ACT I

The place where trains arrived at Auschwitz having become a departure space immediately after its liberation by the Red Army. The liberated K.Z.s who will be found on these quays are nearly all (at least what's left of them…) the sick and infirm abandoned during the terrible evacuation of the camp for another camp (Buchenwald), farther from the Soviet advance. Grouped by nationality, the K.Z.s waiting to be evacuated to Odessa where the hospital boats of their countries of origin should repatriate them. Leaving those who, for different reasons, the war has stripped of any claimable nationality, those already excluded from peace: Jews, Gypsies, ex-international brigadists, republican Spaniards, and the x children… who the camp left without identity (and without tongue). They are part of the Great Convoy. Satellite of this great convoy, to which are promised those who carry further yet this exclusion within exclusion: Train 713. It carries nothing but the blind, and their companions.…

It is the night before departure with the last passings on the quay and the first arrivals of the different groups. In the distance, the sound of cannon fire, the front is still nearby. In the beginning, PIPEL 21 *from the group of the blind* x *children relieves his dysentery near the locomotive space.* PIPEL 19 *joins him. After a moment* PIPEL 21, *with a half-rodent, half-toad step, hearing a rat's squeal charges off toward a flatbed car. The* MECHANIC, *in the process of preparing his locomotive for departure, sees* PIPEL 19 *defecating against a wheel. He chases him off yelling, as if the fact of being blind would keep him from hearing well.*

MECHANIC: Rot, the camp is full of it…. No need to add more to the rails… This, here, is the locomotive … The locomotive of convoy 713. Understood?

PIPEL 19 *seeks refuge under a boxcar.* PIPEL 21, *having arrived in front of the platform car, gives a cry of joy. He has just found his rat, the Besht.*

PIPEL 21: Besht … You will be the besht in the great journey… Look … You can look… You will change the world… Not like the others … And now listen… The sea, we have never seen it… But we have invented it… The camp, you, me…

42

This mud … The mud of the camp is deeper than the sea… It is deeper … since the evacuation of the kapos, before the arrival of the Red Army, it has filled with swimmers… These dysenterics… These typhics, come to relieve themselves… They sunk in slowly. The only thing floating, in spots, their ugly rictus … It's not a freezer like in barracks forty-five where they all died together… You can go there… you won't find anything for you… They understood everything and they are all smiling… They go on, hard and dry under the watchtowers having understood everything, and smiling still without knowing why… The swimmers, they resurface… It's not the first time… Everyone says that then their sight expands… It's the opposite of the blind. It is even exaggeratedly expanded… That's what all your like go bite … I don't like the way you smell then … It's not a pipel smell … The pipel died on the gallows, and when they were hanged, they were too light to weigh on the rope and they continued to look at God's creatures, like you, when the hanging was over. A pipel at the end of a rope has always been the horrible solace of God's creatures, the rotten tooth wrenched out, the bad weed burnt, one less hole for kapos…

honor reconquered in some way… The poor honor of the deportée… Touch this sea of mud which surrounds us for a few more hours. Touch it with the two kernels of light planted on your head. Touch the barbed presence of the two trees that grew there. Beneath them, there are no dead birds to be torn apart with your teeth. But there is a Christmas tree with fake toys, fake stars and the gallows with real pipel hanged only a few weeks ago, with real stars on their chests. Only the place where roll was called at Auschwitz could invent that. Rat, it is with the vision of the things from before that we will make this journey. Me, almost surely. So you, inscribe the two trees of the roll call. What your eyes take, we will carry with us. It will share with us the terrible encounter of memory deported with the rails. The fir is a tree for toys, the gallows too. Remember the Dutch kapo's boyfriend… He was twelve, he could have denounced all God's creatures to the officials in the square before taking an hour to die at the end of his rope. There was even a voice to cry out amidst the greatest silence: God is dead… And you, the Besht, you know because you were stuck in my sweater. Photograph them with your rat's brain: they are

44

going to leave with us, the two trees... They will be set on each kilometer of rail crossed... You know, each day more I lose contact with shadows and lights... If vision returns... When it returns, my sight, I know there will be the Christmas tree and its fake toys watching the gallows of the hanged pipel and between the two, you Besht, inventing them.

During this time PIPEL 19 *comes forward, hopping. He knocks* PIPEL 21 *over and takes his rat.* PIPEL 21 *responds immediately. Fight between the two blind* PIPEL.

PIPEL 21: Besht! ... He's my rat.

PIPEL 19: He's mine too.

At a moment when PIPEL 19 *seems to have the upper hand he cries*

PIPEL 19: Stop! He must have left.

PIPEL 21: The Besht?

PIPEL 19: Yes.

45

The fight stops.

PIPEL 21: If he is lost there will be one less blind person taking the train in a little while…

He hunts. PIPEL 19 *who smells the rat nearby grabs it and runs. Arrival of the controller,* FOLK STOTSKY, *preceded by the beam of his lamp.*

FOLK STOTSKY: You're early… Join your group (Jewish Group, right?)

PIPEL 21: Who are you?

FOLK STOTSKY: Soviet Authority, accompanying to Odessa the convoy of the blind.

PIPEL 21: May we touch?

He touches FOLK STOTSKY'S *uniform with his hands.*

PIPEL 21: You all have the same wool… I'll only leave with my rat.

FOLK STOTSKY: There is not yet a provision for rats in the Soviet sanitary transports.

PIPEL 21: I'm staying with him.

FOLK STOTSKY: The Auschwitz camp is still too close to the front. Handicapped as you are, you will be at the mercy of the least return of fire.

PIPEL 21: That never bothered me. I am for the return of the flames. They settled my father's accounts on the very day of his arrival. Unfortunately his rotten cock had already left me his obscurity.

FOLK STOTSKY: Don't feel obliged to play the fascist. As of now, we've turned that page.

PIPEL 21: Neither Jew, nor fascist… X child… according to yesterday's census. All with the same gaze, Pipel, and (still) a number: I am blind Pipel 21.

FOLK STOTSKY: Pipel 21 you must join the group of the X children… over there…

He tries to push him in the supposed direction of the x children. PIPEL 21 *struggles.*

PIPEL 21: First, my rat.

FOLK STOTSKY *takes a grip on the* PIPEL *and immobilizes him, all the while speaking to him gently.*

FOLK STOTSKY: The journey is long, we will have to put up with one another. You will not be the only blind ones on this convoy.

Distant voice of PIPEL 19 *mocking* PIPEL 21.

PIPEL 19: For 21... We're the ones who have the Besht.

PIPEL 21: Let me go, I want to join my group.

PIPEL 21 *is not released.* FOLK STOTSKY *leads him out of the playing space. From as far away, but in an opposite direction, the voice of* DJANGO *the Gypsy.*

DJANGO: Wherever you are Queen, hide yourself. They want to arrest you.

RITA *appears. She has the obvious look of a hunted woman. She looks all around. A light is pointed at her,* COMMISSAR GALINA ROUBLEIVA'S. RITA *cries out*

RITA: Wait!

She quickly puts on a balaclava

GALINA: Have you lost your group? What are you hiding under that balaclava?

RITA: The microbe that puts holes in cheeks.

GALINA: I see… You're a Gypsy?

RITA: Yes.

GALINA: The microbe has been declared among the blind as well?… Join your group for sanitary inspection otherwise you won't leave.

RITA: Where?

GALINA: That way.

She starts her in the right direction.
FOLK STOTSKY *reappears. He announces to the commissar:*

FOLK STOTSKY: Controller General Folk Stotsky... Inspection of the convoy complete. We are ready to leave.

GALINA: Commissar Roubleiva. We are going to make this journey together. I am Ukrainian, and you?

FOLK STOTSKY: German from the Volga (or what's left of it)

GALINA: The demands of war... (Forget!) You can begin to bring all the groups scheduled for departure together here. Watch out for the Spanish women, they come from a neighboring camp where they held a liberation strike to get a dog for the blind. They didn't get it, they're likely to start in again. To compensate, in this very spot, they gave three dogs to the Gypsies who had lost their sight in the experiments of Doctor Mengele (on the run!). The dogs were cooked in a nettle soup, and the Gypsies ate them. As for the pipel, they are children without family who only survived because they served as women for the kapos. One never knows with them if it's a question of perversion, of revolt, or of despair.

In any case, they are the sickest of the convoy's sensitivies.

FOLK STOTSKY: I just saw them.

GALINA: The former brigadists from the war in Spain are the calmest. Even though their leader, a German who was not blind, committed suicide the day after the liberation of the camp. The Jewish group is, as always, deeply divided – as many confrontations as individuals. At their head, those who uphold the notion that the cars of our convoy are the letters of the alphabet in search of the Book. What is the book made up of? Of ambushes amongst themselves, and of shots taken at point blank range. An entire typography.

FOLK STOTSKY: After the trials undergone in the camp, anything is possible.

GALINA: As for the Gypsy group... uncontrollable, ungovernable, here it is.

*The Gypsy group, whose two women are wearing
face masks, enters lead by* KORRI.

KORRI: Korri, companion… The distribution of canes for the blind is where?

FOLK STOTSKY: Form a waiting line… You will be the first.

GALINA *talks to* DJANGO *who is not wearing a face mask.*

GALINA: You don't have the microbe that eats cheeks?

DJANGO: The one that eats the light of day is enough for me.

Arrival of the Jewish group in two parts. First STERN *accompanied by* SARAH. FOLK STOTSKY *leaves. He's going to get things moving faster.*

SARAH: Why do you want this journey to be yet another trial…

STERN: I had only to touch the characters of this train with my hand, and they are letters. To all evidence we inhabit the letter Iod (that of the reproach to God).

GALINA: In the Ukraine it is forbidden for a Jew to be prosaic. Nonetheless it is from that that they draw (or should draw) their strength.

STERN: In the Ukraine the Jewish world is backwards. It isn't strength that it needs, but truth. But where is its truth?

ELIEZER, *suffering from dysentery as well, seeks to join the group of the Book.*

ELIEZER: Rebi where are you?

STERN: I recognize your voice Eliezer.

SARAH *goes to get* ELIEZER.

SARAH: I am the companion of the Blind of the Book.

STERN: Can the characters of a Book be blind at the moment they set out…

GALINA: You mean: can one be a Jew and blind?

STERN: As Jews, we are not blind.

GALINA: So what are you at this moment?

STERN: A preparation for reading.

GALINA *throws her hands in the air.*

SARAH: Maybe it would be better to prepare for the journey awaiting you behind the eyes of the locomotive.

ELIEZER: It's the same thing.

FOLK STOTSKY *returns. He supports – and occasionally carries – the two Spanish strikers.*

FOLK STOTSKY: Was it you who called a liberation strike at the Tatenberg camp?

GALINA: What sort of thing is a liberation strike?

CONCHA: Refusing fate.

GALINA: You refuse it often?

CONCHA: It's not over yet, however things may appear. In any case how it appears is no longer our concern, we must look elsewhere.

GALINA: You swallowed your entire ration of vitamins all at once this morning.

SOLEDAD: Do you know her? She is Concha Paris. She's the one who served as model for the effigy of the Spanish Republic.

FOLK STOTSKY *sets them to wait near the Gypsy and Jewish groups, then goes to look for the bags. Arrival in the playing space of* PIPEL 19. *He asks:*

PIPEL 19: The starred group?

ELIEZER: Here… oblique left in relation to your voice.

PIPEL 19 *snickers.*

PIPEL 19: I'm only asking so that I can stay far away.

The group of the book shrugs its shoulders.

STERN: A pipel?…

SARAH: They are Jewish, intolerable, criminal, de-generate, and all that in one body – that of inno-cence.

PIPEL 19: Are you talking to my rat, Mama?

He goes toward her. She screams. He jumps in the direction of the scream. PIPEL 21 *arrives and hurries over in turn.*

PIPEL 21: He stole my rat.

PIPEL 19: It's mine.

PIPEL 21: Not today.

PIPEL 19: Come and get it.

They go for each other again. GALINA *intervenes and stops the fight with two arm locks.* PIPEL 19 *runs off.* GALINA *says to* PIPEL 21:

GALINA: You are starting your trip badly.

SOLEDAD: It would be better not to leave Auschwitz before all our rights to existence are officially recognized.

GALINA: Stay in Auschwitz? Do you know what they call you in the report? Incurable nationalists. It is not only in body and mind that you are ill, but in nationality. While we're on the subject…

She opens her report and asks:

GALINA: Rita Donau, is she among you?

KORRI: Who's that?

SARAH: You don't know her? She is a Gypsy. Self proclaimed Queen. (But a murdering queen…)

DJANGO: Who never stopped saving lives.

SARAH: With rare cruelty.

DJANGO: You'll never give up your prisoner mentality.

KORRI: Rita allowed our whole tribe to survive.

DJANGO: In any case, she's the only one who dared intervene for a horse (mine) the day they put the deportee's hat on his head… under these watchtowers.

GALINA: The committee of the liberation of the camp is asking for her. I have no idea what she might have done.

DJANGO: Deportee stories don't interest the Gypsies.

ELIEZER: What are we other than a deportee story?

DJANGO: That's your problem. Not ours.

KORRI: The lice are always the same. Before, during, and after deportation. The constabulary too.

DJANGO: You wanted to imitate us, it didn't work and it continues to not work for you.

CONCHA: What does it mean to imitate a Gypsy?

58

DJANGO: To understand nothing about anything.

STERN: Rest assured, on this platform, to understand nothing, you are not alone.

SOLEDAD: There are the Spaniards as well.

Snickers

PIPEL 21: The deranged children, they understand everything.

Arrival of the brigadists. They try to joke about the situation.

TANTI BACI: What your eyes are incapable of seeing! A blind macaroni. Here for the entire journey: Tanti Baci, ex- (and still) Garibaldian.

RANDAL: What even the eyes of the blind can see! An American. Randal of the, as ever, Lincoln Brigade.

The MECHANIC enters to explain.

MECHANIC: I am your mechanic. The great convoy left without those who have no specific nationality – or who find themselves in suspense in some way ... meaning, you.

General disappointment.

MECHANIC: With cars 1, 3, 7, 12, 15, 22 we will form a minor convoy which will be leaving immediately. It will be reserved solely for the non-seeing and their companions.

The blind try to touch him. Most of them are doubtful.

SOLEDAD: *That's* a mechanic?

MECHANIC: Enough to drive a locomotive with a double light to act as his sight.

CONCHA: How can you distinguish a real one from a fake?

TANTI BACI: Experience will tell.

GALINA: First we are going to proceed with verification and give you a cane which will serve as your identity during the journey. Each one corresponds to the matriculation number which, in theory, you cease to be as of today.

MECHANIC: This will be convoy 713. Remember it well.

FOLK STOTSKY *arrives with the canes. The two liberation strikers lean on him. The canes are distributed in an atmosphere of unease, the noises from the front seeming to get closer.* FOLK STOTSKY *asks the two Spanish women first.*

SOLEDAD: 14763 – Spanish in matriculation… (German by marriage). We have stopped our strike but we maintain our demands.

CONCHA: We come from the Ravensbruck camp, transferred to Tatenberg. For me, it's 14698. Our matriculation numbers are consecutive. We were directed toward Auschwitz because our whole group began having eye trouble at the same time.

SOLEDAD: Concha and I are all that is left of the group.

GALINA: In Odessa you'll find your sight again. There are excellent specialists on the hospital boats.

SOLEDAD: For the moment we see one for the other.

CONCHA: But if a dog could see for both it would be better yet.

FOLK STOTSKY: The Gypsies!

KORRI: Z3989

FOLK STOTSKY: The companions have a right to the medicine kit. It is under their responsibility. If the contents disappear on the black market you will be penalized according to the criminal code of the country we are crossing.

KORRI *receives the medicine kit.* RITA *distances herself as if suffering from an indisposition.* DJANGO *explains.*

DJANGO: Dysentery... Couldn't you give me her cane?

FOLK STOTSKY: What's her number?

DJANGO: A Z and something else, like all of us.

FOLK STOTSKY: And you?

DJANGO: Z4071

> FOLK STOTSKY *gives him his cane, and goes toward the brigadists.*

FOLK STOTSKY: International politicos.

TANTI BACI: 73 549

RANDAL: 73 551, almost the same.

FOLK STOTSKY: American? ... You'll be able to ask your consul in Odessa to admit you to the floating hospital.

ELIEZER: And the Jewish group?

GALINA: An organization (JOINT) will, no doubt, take care of you.

FOLK STOTSKY: Your numbers?

STERN: 90 981

ELIEZER: 185 460

SARAH: A 87004

Instead of the cane like the two others, SARAH *receives a medicine kit.* GALINA *tries to read the matriculation number tattooed on the arm of* PIPEL 21 *who refuses.*

PIPEL 21: Not me, I'm an X child... I don't want a name...

STERN: You still have a race.

PIPEL 21: No.

DJANGO *who, in the meantime, has taken a walk to the place where the dysenterics relieve themselves, intervenes.*

DJANGO: You are not a Gypsy… You are not a constable… so you are a Jew.

PIPEL 21: I hate all three.

ELIEZER: That, alas, is not new.

SARAH: Don't pay attention to him, that's the only way to make him stop.

PIPEL 21: You, I piss on you, Mama!

ELIEZER *aims his cane at him, makes him trip.*

ELIEZER: It's better than denouncing (as you did) the brave Dutch kapo on the day he blew up the Auschwitz power plant.

PIPEL 21: You've got that wrong… The pipel of the Dutch kapo didn't say a single word. He was denounced by all the creatures of God's sacred name – like you.

GALINA: Who was that pipel?

ELIEZER: An X child. He was eleven years old.

65

PIPEL 21 *tries to bite* ELIEZER *while* PIPEL 19 *creates a diversion by screaming out.*

PIPEL 19: Hanged on the gallows before all your repressed prayers…

STERN: God was absent that day, and that is really the problem.

FOLK STOTSKY *has grabbed* PIPEL 21 *around the waist and reads the matriculation number on his arm.*

FOLK STOTSKY: 160 989

He gives him a cane. PIPEL 21 *suddenly brandishes it.*

PIPEL 21: Don't fight, Pipel. It's a weapon they're giving us.

FOLK STOTSKY: To defend yourself against space – not to attack.

The MECHANIC *in turn grabs* PIPEL 19 *who offers no resistance.*

MECHANIC: A48 706

PIPEL 19: And the weapon?

He receives the cane.

PIPEL 19: That's it?

Intervention by GALINA *who has decided to take things in hand. As cars are added to cars, the two Soviets and the* MECHANIC *will transport and attach each blind person's bags to them.*

GALINA: We have reserved a car for you. There will even be toys inside.

PIPEL 19: A sham…

PIPEL 21: Or a fraud, Grandmother. They're the fake, toys of the Christmas tree from the place where roll was called. We know them.

PIPEL 19: We'll be alone in the car?

FOLK STOTSKY: Of course.

PIPEL 19: With our rat?

GALINA: We'll have to find an appropriate order to fit him.

PIPEL 21: The rat doesn't need any order, but needs holes to feel calm.

FOLK STOTSKY: Car number 3 is full of holes.

The Pipel group together with their rat form Car number 3.

GALINA: Car number 12, Spaniards!... Forward...

Instead of coming forward, the Spanish women go farther away. RANDAL *is the one to ask:*

RANDAL: This train must be made habitable.

FOLK STOTSKY: It is. We also have our car. Number 1.

RANDAL: I'm alluding to the economy... Some Soviet controllers have known since their most tender youth that it would change the living conditions...

GALINA: What are you asking?

RANDAL: The creation of a modest bank.

MECHANIC: What is he saying?

RANDAL: Far West style... I have a miner ancestor. He comes from the gold mines of California. The bank and the mine are like husband and wife.

GALINA: You want to start a bank on the little convoy?

RANDAL: It could be the sign that peace is going to return.

GALINA: Going into the Soviet Union to found a bank, even on rails, that risks prolonging the journey.

The Jewish group introduces itself.

STERN: The time has come to make survival (our lot) a pilgrimage toward the Book. Will we know how, each time, to recognize the letters of the alphabet?

ELIEZER: And if leaving Auschwitz behind us we also leave the Book – What will Auschwitz be for future centuries, if not the burned Book...

SARAH: Which Book are we talking about?

STERN: You are sighted – and we are non-seeing. And because you are sighted, you mix everything together. Without Book, there is no God. Without God, there is no more Just Man. Without Just Man, there is no more Jew. We are the people of the Book.

FOLK STOTSKY: Why not? Car number 7... You will certainly find other alphabets there. They will comfort your searchings.

The two blind Jews group around SARAH *and form Car number 7.*

GALINA: Is there anyone who would like to make music?

KORRI: The Gypsies. Music is their way of being in paradise (by eating the apple).

GALINA: Car 22 has been provided for you.

The Gypsies group together and form Car 22.
DJANGO gives his cane to RITA.

DJANGO: Take my cane. Before this evening, I will have made two more grow from the very boards of the train.

GALINA: Car number 15, the brigadists.

Very disciplined, the brigadists form Car number 15 immediately.

GALINA: The travelers of Car number 12, have you decided?

SOLEDAD *refuses.*

SOLEDAD: I've already had my share of boxcars in my life. Impossible to add one more.

To FOLK STOTSKY who goes toward them, CONCHA explains:

CONCHA: She is Sol Bauer, the wife of Helmuth Bauer, the German communist leader.

FOLK STOTSKY: All the more reason why we should take care of her.

CONCHA: But he was deported.

FOLK STOTSKY: The deported are also on the verge of winning the war.

CONCHA: But not the ones from Siberia… A German today is much more likely to enter a camp than to come out of one.

SOLEDAD: And if, what's more, he is a communist representative.

STERN: Maybe, in order to group all the impossibilities under one skin you have to add the Jew to the German and the communist.

The pipel add their bit.

PIPEL 19: You're forgetting the pederast, Great-Grandfather…

PIPEL 21: The blind homo is even better.

FOLK STOTSKY: Enough! That situation is not provided for in any of the pages of the report we are to turn in to Moscow concerning this transport.

GALINA: If it is not provided for then it does not exist.

SOLEDAD: My husband was nevertheless arrested by his own friends (his comrades...)

FOLK STOTSKY: Who is that?

SOLEDAD: My man... I met him in Madrid in the burning University... I thought I could follow him everywhere in the world... It stopped in Moscow.

GALINA: Our report also stops in Moscow.

SOLEDAD: But not Helmuth Bauer put, who knows why, into a camp, who knows where, in the area of the White Sea... After his arrest, mine... Cage cars for prisoners... Stolypine trains for the camps of the great Siberian north... Four years, then return to Moscow... Three times as many Stolypine trains as on the way there, with other anti-fascists, but without my man... Helmuth, a price on his head in Germany and disappeared in Siberia. Yet another Stolypine and another Stolypine. In the one that started off once again toward the West, Helmuth was absent... I was there... the accumulation of incomprehensible journeys... the arrival in Poland which we must now cross again in the opposite direction... So it was the NKVD who turned us over to the Gestapo... On the Brest-Litovsk bridge... The market, the fair, of German communist representatives. And then Ravensbruck... Then Tatenberg... then Auschwitz... Six years from one to the other. And now, you would like to demand a new departure for the East of me? No. I am from the country of orange groves, I don't want to tremble with cold in the frozen wind which must continue to blow on the Brest-Litovsk bridge any more.

TANTI BACI: Careful of the report, comrade.

FOLK STOTSKY *gets mad. He pushes* TANTI BACI *in front of him.*

FOLK STOTSKY: The report is my business, do you have something to write in it? Commissar Galina Roubleiva and I, we are not your enemies. Our Car number 1 is the car of objectivity. The report we must turn in to the Ministry of Transports will in no way be a story of rats, of banks, or of alphabets in search of a book – rather an analysis... How to live oneself as a steam engine, at present, across Europe in the process of liberating itself...

GALINA: ... or yet how to be a mechanic today.

MECHANIC: Me, I drive – only – My interlocutors: wind, water, fire, earth. Not a ministry. My possibility on the journey being prepared is purely mechanical.

GALINA (*To* SOLEDAD): So what have you decided? The departure strike?

SOLEDAD: Yes, and I ask the solidarity of all the blind.

TANTI BACI: The war is not over. Maybe it would be better to leave before it catches up to us.

CONCHA: In any case, your Helmuth, you will only find him out there.

SOLEDAD *breaks down.*

SOLEDAD: What's the use? I see less and less.

MECHANIC: What do we do?

GALINA: Warm it up and we're off.

Once more to SOLEDAD:

GALINA: We have the reputation of making people happy in spite of themselves. We will submit to that one more time. Come on! Let's go.

The two Soviets grab her and set her in the middle of the others where she will form, together with CONCHA *and their bags, Car 12. The* MECHANIC *announces the departure. He sings.*

MECHANIC'S ANNOUNCEMENT

The escaping blows
will rhyme with the pulse
of a giant animal. They
measure its strength
The steam will become traction,
the locomotive, countryside.
And we, conscience of the century.

LOUDSPEAKERS: Direction Brest-Litovsk... Imminent
   departure.

Alert. Panic in the cars.

FOLK STOTSKY: Careful! Don't spread out.

GALINA: Get out of the cars in order and lie down in
   the trenches.

FOLK STOTSKY: You are in no danger. Just a recon-
   naissance plane...

They are all lying on the ground. The MECHANIC
circulates among them as if he were going to dance.

MECHANIC: There is no more aviation with the black cross. It dropped all the crosses on the ground. It no longer has a cemetery to promise in the sky.

End of the alert. They take up their places from before except for TANTI BACI *who approaches* SOLEDAD.

TANTI BACI: I am a friend of Helmuth Bauer. Madrid Front. International Brigade liaison.

SOLEDAD: You came by the Brest-Litovsk bridge too?

TANTI BACI: No.

SOLEDAD: You knew him where?

TANTI BACI: Here.

SOLEDAD: What are you saying?

TANTI BACI: He represented the brigades in the camp underground organization.

SOLEDAD: Impossible.

TANTI BACI: Anything is possible in a camp 2500 kilometers square. After the great departure of the kapos, he was responsible for the typhus and dysentery barracks.

SOLEDAD: You see, I was right to stay. Stop!

MECHANIC: We're leaving!

SOLEDAD: Stop! Stop!

The train officials come running.

GALINA: What is going on?

FOLK STOTSKY: Her again…

GALINA: She must be calmed… Companion!

SOLEDAD: I don't want Helmuth to see me blind.

SARAH *arrives with her medicine kit.* GALINA *immediately prepares a shot.*

FOLK STOTSKY: Don't be afraid. In the boxcar, no one will come to see you.

SOLEDAD: Helmuth is in Auschwitz, I have to stay…

GALINA *gives her the shot.*

SOLEDAD: Someone stop the train!

She is put into the car. Everyone returns to their place. Departure. This first journey is made facing front.

STERN: Leaving the camp with no emotion… Nothing… Emptiness.

ACT II

The convoy advances across the Polish plain.
SOLEDAD *tries to pick up the conversation* TANTI
BACI *had started with her.*

SOLEDAD: The one who knows Helmuth Bauer?

TANTI BACI: Tanti Baci, International Brigade.

SOLEDAD: Where is he now?

TANTI BACI: On the ghostly eve of the liberation, he
   got up, so they told me, alone amidst the dying.
   He lifted his fist and sang an International even
   more alone than he. The first day of freedom, he
   was dead. Alone.

SOLEDAD: Far from the women's barracks?

TANTI BACI: At the place where he sang for the last
   time, fist raised.

RANDAL: Bauer was always an anachronist. Symbols,
   we're full of them.

CONCHA: We too. (This is Concha Paris speaking to you.)

TANTI BACI and RANDAL: Tonight we are speaking to the survivors of assassinated political language.

Slow down.

LOUDSPEAKERS: Katowitz! Indeterminate stop.

Immediately military anthems can be heard. The commissar, the controller, then the MECHANIC run in all directions, then suddenly:

FOLK STOTSKY: Get down all of you.

STERN: We're no longer going to Brest-Litovsk?

FOLK STOTSKY: Stand at attention!

DJANGO: What for?

RITA: Jackal, don't you hear the anthems?

End of the anthems. The MECHANIC starts doing pirouettes.

MECHANIC: The war is over.

He runs to GALINA. FOLK STOTSKY *to him. They roll
on the ground.*

GALINA: The war is over.

FOLK STOTSKY: We have won the war!

DJANGO: What's this all about?

They are all motionless – as if petrified by the news.

MECHANIC: That's all the effect it has on you?

RANDAL: What does it change for us?

MECHANIC: Oh! Come now!

GALINA: Embrace! Dance! Jump!

*Only the pipel do anything, they rid themselves of
the rest of their dysentery, pants down, on some of
the others' feet, sowing total confusion. Only the
Jews have joined together, crowded one against the
other; they are crying.*

MECHANIC: The end of bombed rails. The end of ferrying people and goods. Do you realize!

CONCHA: You don't just invent joy like that.

DJANGO: You have to be Russian to do that.

FOLK STOTSKY: You should have a part in the common joy.

GALINA: Unless you're an enemy, today it's a duty.

SOLEDAD: We have lost the taste for celebrating.

DJANGO *goes looking for the instruments.*

DJANGO: We are going to try to invent it. Don't let it be said that Django the jackal was bypassed by History yet again. Anyone here from Vienna?

STERN: Alas!

DJANGO: Viennese spectacles have the reputation of being the most joyous.

STERN: When the rebis drag themselves on the ground...

SARAH: ... and the women burn their wigs on the Taborstrasse in order to have the emancipating joy of parading themselves shaved.

ELIEZER: A wig is unhealthy ... But the joy, for a hilarious crowd, of cutting into a beard, that's something else... All the more so since a beard will grow again.

FOLK STOTSKY *applauds.*

FOLK STOTSKY: That's humor.

ELIEZER: Jewish.

MECHANIC: Do you think that Jewish humor is appropriate?

Demonstration by ELIEZER *doing the number of he who bends iron rods and then has himself run over.*

ELIEZER: Prater Street! Me the strongest Jew of my time, I climb onto a stage covered with Jewish flags before bending steel bars and before being driven over by the wheels of trucks. No longer a question of knowing how to live when one is Jewish, but rather if, as a Jew, it is possible to go on living.

Laughter.

STERN: First answer.

ELIEZER: It begins with the name.

STERN: A Jew in a commissariat in Vienna.

ELIEZER: The name for a Jew is an unhappiness which precedes even his birth. So, each Jew has a name.

STERN: When he arrives in Vienna, he has two.

ELIEZER: Two family names joined by the word "RECTE" (true).

STERN: Or by the word "FALSE" (false). No one knows (especially not he) which of the two names he has a right to.

ELIEZER: The parents, what is more, have been married by the rabbi. Independent of the always transitory truth represented by marriage, it has no legal value.

STERN: If the husband is named Joanovici and the wife Abramov.

ELIEZER: The simplest case, because in general it is much more complicated.

STERN: The children of this marriage will be called Joanovici false Abramov.

ELIEZER: Unless they are named Abramov recte Joanovici.

STERN: Let's say that one or the other is preceded by the first name Moishe ben Moishe, which would lead one to understand that he is his own son...

ELIEZER: Why not after all?

STERN: …he will automatically, in order to facilitate its pronunciation in the police stations, amputate any part likely to need explanation. And he becomes simply Leo.

ELIEZER: Note that, the cut being brutal, he will feel himself onomastically nude for entry into the cold labyrinths of civil process.

STERN: So he'll add to this first name one or two letters which will clothe him adequately for the commissar. He has now become, Leon.

ELIEZER: But the first name needs a family name: Joanovici false Abramov? Or Abramov recte Joanovici?

STERN: Things being as they are (and the hours spent in the police station being what they are) he simplifies and takes a pseudonym which risks reminding the commissar of something.

ELIEZER: And here he is becoming Leon Trotsky without ever having been.

Demonstration by the pipel and their rat.

STERN: He doesn't know that, this way, he qua-
druples his chances of persecution, and maybe
even of a secret blow to the back of the head
with the butt of a pistol when he's hardly out of
the station.

ELIEZER: Unless he corrects (partially) the approxi-
mations by false birth dates.

STERN: With the help of the pogroms, they are rarely
right because they're always part of burned ar-
chives.

ELIEZER: A police commissar and his station gain
time by knowing for sure that…

ELIEZER and STERN: A Jewish name is objectively
false in advance.

STERN: So they invent names that allow them (they,
the commissars) but not always the Jews, to find
themselves.

ELIEZER: And that's even worse.

STERN: But it's the only solution, because it creates a situation which is so bad it can only get better.

They smile then continue their demonstration in the midst of the others.

SARAH: How does it get better?

PIPEL 19: Let the Bescht dance …

PIPEL 21: He's opening the era of rats on two feet.

The two singers of the Jewish name continue.

ELIEZER: The Jew can, with such a name, go walking in the street among a facetious people who, to amuse themselves, will make him wash the street and the sidewalks with caustic soda.

SARAH: With the obligation given the person with an objectively false name to clean the streets with buckets of caustic soda…

STERN: … and a toothbrush for scrubbing.

SARAH: So started the story of Jewish humor in Vienna. It spread to all of Europe.

STERN: To have entire streets washed with a toothbrush: the Viennese are fated to spectacles which make one laugh.

Interruption. The pipel disappear behind the wheels of a boxcar.

PIPEL 21: The rat's packed his bags.

FOLK STOTSKY: Don't you think that it's just a little difficult to evoke a victory day?

STERN: Not with a toothbrush … Here!

He shows his toothbrush.

STERN: I saved it through all the transports (those of the past and those of the future).

ELIEZER: Since for a show, showing a toothbrush isn't enough, we'll dance around it.

He shows his toothbrush to the characters of the convoy who start dancing around him singing the "Blue Danube Waltz".

MECHANIC: Even soaked in humor, your joys are sad.

FOLK STOTSKY: Especially on a victory day.

ELIEZER: The victory will do without.

LOUDSPEAKER: Train of the repatriated – Boarding, direction Odessa. Inspection formalities and customs at the border between Poland and the Soviet Union.

MECHANIC: Since everyone must have drunk a great deal carry your canes in front of you where they can be seen. They are your identity. And that will facilitate your entrance into the new rail division.

They all, with their canes well in view, line up behind the MECHANIC. Only the commissar and the controller remain apart.

SARAH: Which of the journey's possibilities?

THE JEWS: Jewish.

THE GYPSIES: Gypsy.

THE SPANISH WOMEN: Spanish.

THE BRIGADISTS: Brigadist, even if they are contradictory.

THE BUREAUCRATS: Bureaucratic.

THE PIPEL: Or even lost child…

SARAH: … Will tell you why this train must disappear.

KORRI: A blind person who has survived the camps, that doesn't exist.

EVERYONE: So do we exist?

MECHANIC: While we're waiting, prepare yourselves to come up against your own image placed at all railroad crossings.

Suddenly the block of possibilities disbands.

TANTI BACI: The Spanish woman has attempted suicide.

RANDAL *hurries over to* KORRI.

RANDAL: Hurry! The medicine kit.

KORRI *tries to slip away but* RANDAL *succeeds in catching her, takes her box, opens it.*

RANDAL: The box is empty.

SARAH *is the one who brings aid to the Spanish woman from her kit.* SOLEDAD *is lying on the ground.* CONCHA, SARAH, ELIEZER *and* GALINA *are near her and trying to revive her.* FOLK STOTSKY *goes after the Gypsy group.*

FOLK STOTSKY: Who did you sell it to?

KORRI: On Victory Day it was only normal.

DJANGO: We had to build capital.

94

FOLK STOTSKY: All you can think about is capital on this train. Do you have an ancestor in the gold mines of California too?

DJANGO: No! You are wrong on every level. What is important is the cross on the box – not what's inside.

KORRI: What is a pharmacy for if not to give life. The cross is a sign that there is piety among us – even if you are all miscreants.

FOLK STOTSKY: You will add the application of the law to piety. All that will be entered in the report.

In the other group CONCHA *cries:*

CONCHA: She's reacting! She's reacting!

Movement of the Gypsy group toward the one around SOLEDAD. *First* RITA *corners* DJANGO.

RITA: Don't ever do that again.

KORRI: There is no risk of doing it again. Everything has been sold.

DJANGO: They are the ones who kill daily on the cross and who put the Gypsies in the bad situation of making the nails.

Around SOLEDAD.

SARAH: She's regaining consciousness.

FOLK STOTSKY: You have only friends. You must live.

The pipel haven't moved. They are sarcastic.

PIPEL 19: Useless.

PIPEL 21: It already smells like dead meat.

FOLK STOTSKY *goes after them.*

TANTI BACI: You must live this time, comrade Bauer.

RITA: You must live.

ELIEZER: You must live.

STERN: You must live.

SARAH: You must live.

RANDAL: Soledad Bauer, I promise you a dog.

CONCHA: Orange. Stay in the garden, even if it knows nothing but winter.

DJANGO: Sol, little note of music, you must sing now.

Little by little SOL *gets up. And although very weakened, in order to respond to the deportees surrounding her, she sings.*

SONG OF THE ORANGE

The orange groves are dead
like one day in April
the people of Spain
And the fruits on the branches
continue their fruitly
delirium

97

A delirium in search
of a gaze
And it is toward this
that the blind
of the Tatenberg camp journey.

MECHANIC: Let's go!

ACT III

Departure from Katowitz to Smerinka beyond the Soviet border, on the road to Odessa. After a moment, stop.

GALINA: Stay calm. We are maneuvering to attach two additional cars.

RITA: Who is in those cars?

DJANGO: Go see, Korri! It just may be the blue devil.

KORRI *leaves the convoy and looks on, horrified.*

KORRI: It's well-dressed people.

DJANGO: Judges or policemen?

KORRI: It looks like both at once.

DJANGO: Alert to the non-seeing.

STERN: Who is in those two cars?

FOLK STOTSKY: Italian diplomats coming from Rumania, going to Odessa.

TANTI BACI: Are they blind?

FOLK STOTSKY: No.

TANTI BACI: Then we don't want any part of them..

STERN: No to the sighted!

EVERYONE: No to the sighted!

MECHANIC: Who's in command on
these rails?

CONCHA: You, but then there'll be a strike.

FOLK STOTSKY: Again!

GALINA: You missed that in the camps. And now you're catching up. What is a blind person's strike? Starting to see?

MECHANIC: Never yet seen that.

PIPEL 21: I can lend you my glasses.

Silent departure until arrival in Smerinka. Stop.

MECHANIC: This is Smerinka. You are now on a garage track. You aren't bothering anyone. Not even the diplomats who can be attached to a different convoy.

STERN: You said we were in Smerinka?

FOLK STOTSKY: Don't forget to form pickets lines and to send us your union representatives when you feel that the time for bargaining has come. Goodbye.

STERN: The problem lies elsewhere.

He goes away from the group. STERN *very upset, tries to recognize the space around him with his cane.*

STERN: We are in Smerinka... Its former specialty, blind singers. There are no more. They all ceased being blind on the very day of the great meeting which brought them together in Kiev a few years ago, under the gaze of the red icons which then filled the countryside. Before them, still today, the alphabet should enter in silence. The greatest pogroms in history happened here.

SOLEDAD: We're already in the USSR?

GALINA: For the past week.

DJANGO *worries.*

DJANGO: (This is not the moment to go on strike…)

TANTI BACI: And we haven't changed wheels for the new rail division?

GALINA: This seemed to make no more impression on you than the victory. You were all asleep.

RANDAL, *even more worried.*

RANDAL: Why did we stop? Being in the country of socialism changes (even if we are blind) our view of things. Who is still (or ever was) for the strike?… No one?… We can start up again immediately… Mechanic!

102

The MECHANIC *tries to draw the attention of the blind to the opposite quay.*

MECHANIC: Look at that convoy on the quay facing us.

CONCHA: What is it?

MECHANIC: Animal cars.

KORRI: Women! Women!

TANTI BACI: Women?

GALINA: Ukrainians, like me.

SARAH: Like you?

GALINA: Yes but they left the fields devastated, the schools closed, the offices destroyed, all for the bread of the invader – and they caught the sickness.

SARAH: They are the ones who guarded us in the camps.

FOLK STOTSKY: Not all – but all participated in the Nazi war effort. Whence their deportation when they had barely returned home.

STERN: Now, the strands of barbed wire are closing around them.

DJANGO: Too bad! By the sound of them, those are young, solid bodies, not yet degraded like the women of our convoy.

KORRI: Poor Jackal! For all you can see of the women of your convoy.

CONCHA: Take that!

She inflicts him with blows of her cane. She hits TANTI BACI *at the same time.*

TANTI BACI: The war is over comrade.

GALINA: Not for them and it is sad for me. We came from the same wheat fields.

SARAH: As far as wheat fields go, they specialized in the art of the common grave for Jews.

PIPEL 19: With the same sadness as yours, commissar?

GALINA *rushes after* PIPEL 19 *who gets away. Protests from the group of the alphabet.*

GALINA: He offended me. I don't allow… He merits immediate punishment.

FOLK STOTSKY *chases* PIPEL 19 *under the boxcars. Immediately the group of the alphabet begins to argue in his favor.*

STERN: The pipel are made to carry that portion of evil that exists on this train. In some way they were predestined for that. It is a sacred calling to take for one's own the evil of a community. All the more so that all of these communities on wheels no longer have fixed points of reference. The idea of evil is displaced at all times. It becomes as unknowable as that which is good.

ELIEZER *adds.*

ELIEZER: Lack of knowledge which obliges the pipel to invent evil there where it doesn't exist.

FOLK STOTSKY *comes out from between the wheels of a boxcar with* PIPEL 19.

FOLK STOTSKY: My fist, just like the pipel, can have two meanings. You are depraved. With you one can only discuss by striking. The harder it is, the more convincing it is… it can also mean: you insist on provoking. You are irresponsible but you may risk a lot and make me risk a lot as well. It is the latter that I choose.

With a blow of his fist he sends PIPEL 19 *rolling to the ground.*

STERN: No!

PIPEL 19 *picks himself up and goes toward* STERN.

PIPEL 19: Stern!

STERN: Yes.

PIPEL 19 *gives him a head butt to the stomach which doubles* STERN *over. He then goes looking for refuge with* FOLK STOTSKY *whose hand he kisses.*

SARAH: It's impossible!

ELIEZER: He has found the provocation worthy of himself.

Now it is FOLK STOTSKY *who becomes* PIPEL 19'S *advocate.*

FOLK STOTSKY: Each speaks in his own way.

The convoy of the Ukrainian women takes off again.
SOLEDAD *starts to run behind it.*

SOLEDAD: The death convoy is going to leave … Here the possibility of the blind women of the Tatenberg camp… You are going into a country where it will be impossible for you to free yourselves from the cold. You will dance against perpetual motion, and the world will close in on you.

TANTI BACI *starts to run behind* SOLEDAD.

TANTI BACI: Here the possibility of internationalism,

even if it invents itself (just like your convoy) against the grain of history.

PIPEL 21 *runs behind* TANTI BACI

PIPEL 21: Here the possibility of childhood... So many years to say what?

The MECHANIC *runs behind* PIPEL 21.

MECHANIC: Here the possibility of the mechanic. Only the train doesn't look back...

PIPEL 19 *runs behind the* MECHANIC.

PIPEL 19: Here again the possibility of childhood... What do we do other than look back? You are like us, lost in the dance of love.

ELIEZER *and* STERN *start running after* PIPEL 19.

ELIEZER: The Siberian camps are without indulgence. Here the possibility of the alphabet.

STERN: You are also searching for language. It reigns elsewhere, in another world where it has yet, for all that, to take on a glorious aspect. We know now of what – and why, language wants to die.

FOLK STOTSKY: Let's go! I just received precise instructions by radio.

FOLK STOTSKY'S *announcement ends the call of the possibilities. The death convoy is now far away.*

SOLEDAD: Must we disband? That is our image without us, passing before us.

GALINA: A piece of us, gone off toward a winter that knows nothing of us.

While convoy 713 is reforming, GALINA *sings the manual of Russian grammar.*

MANUAL OF RUSSIAN GRAMMAR

The oak is a tree
The rose is a flower
The deer is an animal
The sparrow is a bird
Russia is our homeland
Death is inevitable

FOLK STOTSKY: We are leaving again backwards in order to catch up to the Great Convoy which waiting for a favorable moment, has just been— sent into hibernation. In Odessa, no ship could take its passengers.

RANDAL: But there is the American hospital ship. I must take the shortest path leading to the USA.

FOLK STOTSKY: The shortest is through Siberia.

RANDAL: Indeed.

FOLK STOTSKY: Our goal has always been to tie up with the Great Convoy, whether it goes to Odessa (or not). We will go into hibernation in order to join up with it.

KORRI: What does that mean, hibernation?

GALINA: That you must be protected from the great cold. A convoy stopped on the steppe by ice, that's the end of all the travelers of Convoy 713.

LOUDSPEAKERS: Direction Minsk! All Aboard...

The convoy leaves again going backwards. The
MECHANIC *sings.*

SONG OF THE DIFFICULTY OF BEING

Oh war not yet burned out
It's hard, it's long
To be a locomotive there
The locomotive drives onward
The locomotive weakens
The locomotive cries
The locomotive starts up
The locomotive starts up again
and hunts for the rail
Oh war crossed again belatedly
Rail cut so as to lose
All trace
And
Driving on
(to go where?)
Wounded with a thousand griefs
Which cross the universe
With a thousand sobs
Which hide it
It can't desert
Can one desert the future?

Now, only one primary direction before us: the north.

PIPEL 21: Tenth day of the coming reign of the Besht. This train is only made of images. Images of others who, looking at us, invent our fear.

PIPEL 19: For ten days, the Besht has been erasing them... Steppes, forests, lost villages, river, eternity...

PIPEL 21: But there are those who, with the complicity of the rails, remain; car 3, car 7, Car 12, Car 15, Car 22 – and above all, the locomotive.

PIPEL 19: The rat declares war on Convoy number 713.

ACT IV

The pipel take over the imaginary space of the train, traveling north.

PIPEL 19: Declaratrion of war on train number 713.

PIPEL 21: Communique number 0. The two lamps of the locomotive drive us. Like two eyes. The pipel of train number 713 must appropriate it for themselves.

PIPEL 19: Not to be forgotten… It was Josef the kapo without ears who saved the pipel, today nineteenth in the dynasty of the blind. Josef could easily see that the pipel was losing his sight. He closed his eyes to it. In a way, he never opened them again… he was cut down at the liberation by the people of this convoy, today, with eyes just as dead as his. To the memory of Josef the kapo…

PIPEL 21: Communique 0, addenda. For the moment (even if I know it's shot) for what's most important, I can still see a little. Communique number 0, addenda states that living inside the rat's gaze, it is necessary to die there and be resuscitated in order to put down the things the two lamps of the locomotive say about things.

PIPEL 19: Visit to the front of things heard which surround the Besht and his declaration of war.

PIPEL 21: Eyes of the Besht. Infomation service. Car number 7. What are the enemy noises doing? They are eating.

PIPEL 21 *isolates Car number 7 where the group of the alphabet plays the situation realistically – the sharing of the food.*

ELIEZER: We are more interested in reasons than in things: is that bad?

STERN: Writing, no more than nature, can not be taken literally. The evidene is too superficial to be true. In all things, we must discover a meaning which, through use, will become sacred.

SARAH: Can we eat just once in this train without going off in a pilpoul that will leave us without night?

STERN: Against whom do you hold it? The creator? Or the creature?

PIPEL 19 *isolates Car 22 which goes to take its place near Car 7. Its occupants play the situation realistically.*

PIPEL 19: Inside Car 22, the noises eat sunflower seeds in the gaze of the Besht.

DJANGO: The important thing is not knowing the history of bread, it is eating.

KORRI: At home the newspapers announced the sale of the Gypsies in the public places. One day, in Bucarest, there were, by the heirs of a judge, two hundred families to be sold.

DJANGO: With my horse I was part of a lot of five families at once (with easy payment terms, it's true).

RITA: This Danubian delta has never been happiness.

DJANGO: It wasn't better away from the Danube. In order to distinguish us from others they would cut off an ear. The left, in Bohemia, the right in Moravia.

PIPEL 21 *isolates Car 15 where the Garibaldian and the American turn to a game of chess whose figures are made with bread crumbs.*

PIPEL 21: Car 15. Game of chess with figures made of bread crumbs they deprive themselves of in order to be able to play what is left of internationalism foundered in the Rat's gaze.

RANDAL: With money everything can be resolved. If we succeeded in founding a bank right here three quarters of the problems posed by this train would no longer exist.

TANTI BACI: A bank?

RANDAL: And even a little saloon next to it with a portrait of Karl Marx as welcome. We could play *chemin de fer* there.

TANTI BACI: Otherwise called baccarat… It is not a question of place. It is a question of patent.

PIPEL 19 *stops Car 12 in line with the others. Same as for the preceding groups.*

SOLEDAD: Each day sight lessens to the point of being only a fog in which silhouettes move.

CONCHA Each day, I become blind again but expect anything.

SOLEDAD: Already in Ravensbruck, a blind person had to present the perfect illusion of sight, under pain of being selected for the current session.

CONCHA: A terrible story, but for me, illuminated entirely today by the help of others.

SOLEDAD: I was able to hold out for a year in that fog of silhouettes with the eyes my sister women lent me. Here, on this convoy, I have lost that gaze.

PIPEL 21: To see or not to see, what is the importance? This evening the mind of the rat sees the controllers struck and rolling on the ground – and the mechanic boiling in his firebox.

In the version of the Pipel's imaginary space, the controllers and the mechanic are assassinated by the mind of the Rat. In the realistic version, they are lying down smoking rolled tobacco while waiting for the signals to allow the train to enter the station.

PIPEL 19: Soon a station… Do you hear what the loudspeakers are saying?

PIPEL 21: No.

PIPEL 19: They say to us, "Nothing to be done in the station, pipel. You already have your part of mud and of cadavers…"

PIPEL 21: It's hard to be a pipel.

PIPEL 19: And then it doesn't last long.

PIPEL 21: And the Besht whose gaze at war is the death ray answers: if we kill all the screaming shadows of this little convoy, we will be masters of the space. At this hour, the eyes of the controllers are nothing more than poorly extinguished fires, and their hearts bank like a swinging door. The night images of the X children devastate the bureaucratic version.

PIPEL 19: I salvage the inevitable traces of blood the mechanical version leaves behind it, and make sausage of it so that the two Spanish women die. They are too sad. They only dream of the great rival, the Dog, whose gaze will devour that of the Rat.

He smears the faces of the two Spanish women with his hand. After a moment they lie down always according to the same basic idea. Simultaneous, the imaginary and reality are ignorant of each other.
PIPEL 21 *is on the group of the Alphabet.*

PIPEL 21: The Jews look too much like the Besht... All the more reason... Knowing who one is striking... Smash the mold... One... two... That's taken care of.

*The group of the alphabet lies down according to
the same idea as before.*

PIPEL 19: Hard to differentiate between the Gypsies.
The eyes of the Besht must penetrate the vagina
(incubating space of the Rat) of each time their
queen. All the recognized intelligence of the
camp – Jewish, French, Czech, Polish, Hungarian, Greek, Ukranian, German doctors – cut,
trimmed, shuffled, scraped, amputated, slashed,
scratched, tore the vagina place of the rat. And
the whole camp without knowing it, but twisted
with the desire returned by the presence of
death, thus made love to these queens – a love
whose least trace it had lost within itself – and
from which it felt at the very moment it found it
again, definitively castrated. Engulfed head of the
Rat having no longer anything but its back feet
swinging in the void to direct with jerking blows
the horrible orchestra of the camp.

*Same with the Gypsies as with the other groups.
Great cry of* PIPEL 19 *taken by an epileptic seizure.*
KORRI *wakes up suddenly.*

KORRI: The sacred evil. The pipel is having a seizure.

120

PIPEL 21: The war of the Rat isn't over... Ever... It is doubling itself... The train... the double of the other... Chain reaction.

All of the assassinated people from the pipels' dreams wake up and group around PIPEL 19 *shaken by violent jerks. Sarah arrives with her medicine kit.* GALINA *doctors him.*

STERN: Our compassion for the pipel!... They carry all the evil of Convoy 713.

RANDAL: Where are we?

SOLEDAD: To smell it, it must be another death convoy.

SARAH: To see it too.

The new convoy is an interminable series of animals being deported. FOLK STOTSKY *tries to be reassuring.*

FOLK STOTSKY: It must be the Berlin Zoo being moved. The most beautiful one in the world... We all have a right to beauty. That's why the zoo moves around.

STERN: It's a sign. Noah's arc – yet again.

Superstitious, DJANGO *crosses himself.*

DJANGO: Maybe my horse is in this convoy… he wants to catch up with me.

CONCHA: What's that?

FOLK STOTSKY: A camel. And that's a bad sign. In the German Soviet Republic the lungs and spleen of a camel brought as much as 245,000 rubles during the famine, almost the price of an entire herd. On the Volga, a camel announces famine.

DJANGO: What was I saying?

The brigadists end up mixing in with the others, while still not interrupting their chess game.

CONCHA: Do you hear? There are even dogs.

FOLK STOTSKY: Those are the water dogs who were to set off the mines in front of our advancing troops. At each attack there were hundreds pounded, pulverized, on the steppe or in the swamps…

SOLEDAD: I must have all of them.

FOLK STOTSKY: Calm down. The convoy is starting up. Do you hear?

RANDAL: Horses again! You can't mistake those whinnies.

KORRI: And all the Gypsies are going to cry.

ELIEZER: Those are seals! You're confused.

Hearing ELIEZER, DJANGO *addresses the sky.*

DJANGO: Jesus! A little restraint! It wasn't for people like that that you came to die on the cross…

KORRI: Even with the filth and the dust that you can't see, those are horses.

The MECHANIC *brings explanations.*

MECHANIC: In front of us there is another convoy to which this one will be attached. Tens of thousands of horses: draught, race, foals, nags and the dead they unload next to the tracks.

STERN: Our image: it has caught up to us… Even if we can not see, we are inside it.

GALINA: Leave it on the rails – and go get registered. You have arrived in the Minsk welcoming camp, where you will hibernate.

TANTI BACI: For warm blooded animals it isn't always required.

MECHANIC: You are here in Minsk in an historic station, the first in the world. And the train will go no farther.

STERN and ELIEZER: We refuse.

They all group together facing the controllers and the MECHANIC.

EVERYONE: We all refuse.

FOLK STOTSKY: Your refusal would be believable if you had a country likely to receive you.

RANDAL: We have America.

FOLK STOTSKY: You maybe, but the others?

ELIEZER: We have Israel.

FOLK STOTSKY: That hasn't existed for several centuries.

GALINA: Today it's Palestine and I assure you that the people there have no desire to see you… You have no country to take you in.

DJANGO: We have the whole Danube.

MECHANIC: No neighboring country, even if you cross it from time to time, wants Gypsies. They haven't wanted any part of you for centuries now.

KORRI: In Rumania we were protected by slavery.

FOLK STOTSKY: You call slavery protection? Unfortunately for you. There is no more slavery in the liberated territories.

DJANGO: Oh well, too bad! That would have allowed us to have a country!

SOLEDAD: With Franco, at home it's simpler.

The two Spanish women strike their sticks to imitate the sound of a machine gun.

PIPEL 19: And even simpler yet for the pipel: it's clearly among people that they have no place.

GALINA: The victorious powers are thinking. They are trying to give you an intermediate nationality as displaced persons. They are going to create an immense market where even the belligerent countries can buy those who fit their immigration laws... So, socially you are handicapped. Handicapped in sight to be precise. Which excludes you in advance from any immigration request. This is the Minsk camp. Contrary to other countries, only foreigners (seeing or non-seeing) have a right to it.

FOLK STOTSKY: In transit of course.

MECHANIC: The administration is absent, you will see.

GALINA: But present in each person's comfort.

MECHANIC: The cooking is good. Any locomotive mechanic who has passed this way will tell you.

GALINA: Only one occupation: learn to wait. Now that peace has returned that ought to be easier.

DJANGO: Even in peace a stopped Gypsy doesn't exist. Walking and breathing are the same thing for him.

FOLK STOTSKY: The Gypsies are invited either to be part of the orchestra or to be cured of the microbe that eats cheeks, or both.

The Gypsies seem to allow themselves to be convinced. Immediately the pipel intervene.

PIPEL 19: The Gypsy companion doesn't have the microbe.

DJANGO: Because she's cured. Who wants to get in the way of healing on this convoy?

PIPEL 21: The face mask is to hide her.

KORRI: How do you know? You can't see anything…

DJANGO: A blind voyeur. That's going a little far.

PIPEL 21: The Besht knows.

DJANGO: What?

KORRI: Stop this childishness.

PIPEL 19: We are his espionage service.

RITA: Make them be silent – they poison everything.

PIPEL 19: Make the Gypsy companion let those who see, see.

FOLK STOTSKY *interrogates* KORRI.

FOLK STOTSKY: Is it true?

He takes off her face mask.

FOLK STOTSKY: It's true.

KORRI: It was for the hibernation.

FOLK STOTSKY *goes toward* RITA.

FOLK STOTSKY: And you?

RITA *puts* DJANGO *in front of her.*

RITA: Defend me Jackal.

DJANGO *takes out his knife.*

DJANGO: Watch out! No one touches the Gypsy women.

RANDAL *attempts a diversion.*

RANDAL: The problem is that we are all lacking women which sometimes leads to misunderstandings.

FOLK STOTSKY: The railroad administration has provided no answer to intimate problems and to that one in particular.

GALINA: I'm a woman… So?

With a kick she knocks the knife out of DJANGO'S *hand.*

129

GALINA: Do you have something to say?

DJANGO slips away.

DJANGO: Yes, I ask to be part of the orchestra.

GALINA: Go talk to the central administration.

She picks up the knife which RANDAL has already put his foot on, closes it and hands it to DJANGO.

GALINA: You lost this.

DJANGO: Me?

GALINA: You need it to cut bread with (only bread). As for the face mask, nothing forbids it. It is even recommended during the periods of great cold which lie ahead of us. For the moment, all around you is the giddiness of autumn. The forest will give you dead leaves waist high, plus trade in mushrooms and blackberries.

RANDAL: Interesting (very interesting!).

FOLK STOTSKY: You who have always been mislead by History, here you are authorized to enter by the main gate.

SOLEDAD: Camp gates, that's already known to us.

FOLK STOTSKY: The camp is nothing other than the first station in the History of the Railroads. You are there.

RANDAL: Trade with the peasants from the area, is it possible?

MECHANIC: Not with money but with barter.

Some organize by group to make the rounds of their new camp. The movement is interrupted by the cries of PIPEL 19 *who is seeking the protection of the authorities. Behind him* KORRI, *who, has taken his blind person's cane, showers him with blows.*

PIPEL 19: Controller...

FOLK STOTSKY: What is it?

PIPEL 19: The companion took my cane.

KORRI: He stole my face mask.

FOLK STOTSKY: Again!

PIPEL 19: It's not true. The Gypsies set an ambush for me so they could take the dog away.

CONCHA: What dog?

PIPEL 19: A Red Army dog, one of the ones who jumped on the mines.

DJANGO *arrives in the playing space with a dog.*

DJANGO: Guess what I'm bringing? ... He hasn't much meat under his skin, unfortunately.

PIPEL 19: He's mine.

DJANGO: He'll eat your rat, imbecile... Be smart for once.

RANDAL: What are you going to do with him?

DJANGO: Me?... Rita Donau managed to have one roasted every month. With that she put the salvage kapo at her feet. And that meant social progress for all the Gypsies.

RANDAL: I'll buy him.

DJANGO: There is a law in the camp that puts dogs under the control of the Gypsies. Whatever the arrivals were, all submitted to it. Even the SS respected it. They left the care of their kennel to the Gypsies.

PIPEL 19: If the American buys my dog from you, I'll kill him.

DJANGO: No useless words. You stole this dog. It's yours. I steal it from you. It's mine. Right? Besides I'm going to teach you to be a man... Korri bring the dog to the American. He wants to offer it to the widow, over there...

SOLEDAD: Me?

DJANGO: Question of humanity... The money... I don't want any. And now, Pipel, don't ever find yourself at the end of my cane because then it will strike.

KORRI *brings the dog to* RANDAL *who then takes it to the Spanish women.*

RANDAL: In memory of the combat in the University of Madrid, comrades... With a dog you are real blind people now.

TANTI BACI: What will you call it?

CONCHA: Dog.

STERN: That's a bit short. The prophet Habacuc accustomed us to better in regard to dogs' names.

CONCHA: How else would you call it? It's the name of one (and maybe two) constellations.

SOLEDAD: With him we are going to enter History and discover with his eyes the first station in the History of the world.

134

They almost all go out following the dog in the discovery of the Minsk station as if it were a procession. RANDAL *is detained by* KORRI.

KORRI: In exchange for the dog, Django wants to make you a deal… You bring the start up funds, and he, three mares from the German army lost in the forest here when the front broke. Blond, voluptuous, blue eyed. They want only one thing: to leave the USSR and go back to their ruins in Bavaria. We take them in hand and protect them for the entire crossing. We'll make a killing. It's a deal for everyone. If you think that women are lacking on this convoy, now is the time…

RANDAL: We have to stay within the bounds of legality… true legality … not Gypsy.

KORRI: It changes every day… We cross so many borders.

RANDAL: Finagling is your weakness. We have to give ourselves the possibilities of barter. It will bring in more and we'll stay legal.

*The group of the dog has completed its tour in
History. They return, what's more, to music as*
DJANGO *proudly brandishes a violin.*

RITA: Let those who have no eyes listen. The Jackal
is now an official person.

ELIEZER: A marching band's matriculation number
has been delivered to his cane by the central
administration.

DJANGO: The instrument which scratches the sky
with its strings has been given him. No more
stepping on his toes under the pretext of your
being blind. Understood. And now the Dog
thanks the Jackal.

THE SONG OF THE DOG

You are an invention of the dog.
We too, his blind, the first.
Thank you for being so numerous
in the view that he has of this convoy.

RANDAL: This isn't California, but almost.

MECHANIC: In the camp of the historic station of Minsk locomotives are anguished women and dogs become the vision of men.

STERN: Here, the Germans call themselves Austrians, the Austrians call themselves Italians, the Rumanians too ... The Poles call themselves Americans, the Hungarians call themselves Basques, the Spanish call themselves French (sometimes Mexicans) and the Georgians consider themselves Greek.

SOLEDAD: Here, a woman with a contralto voice calls herself a Hungarian general.

FOLK STOTSKY: Here, the Russian guards are all Mongolian.

RANDAL: A multinational. We can't let such richness go by. We are in the first station of History, we must found the first bank car here.

ELIEZER: The necessary supply funds, where are you going to find them?

RANDAL: By doing a show.

137

STERN: We have already given proof of our incapacity at that.

RANDAL: We didn't have the help of the commissar and the controller.

GALINA: Us? Careful. That might turn against you. We are here to make a report – not a music hall.

TANTI BACI: Who's paying?

RANDAL: The Germans who call themselves Austrians, the Austrians who call themselves Italians, the dogs who call themselves men, and the transvestite women who call themselves generals of the Magyar promotion will pay.

FOLK STOTSKY: With what?

RANDAL: With the excess food the camp administration gives them… As long as it's decent, we'll make money from it. How? With an American show like on the East Coast.

DJANGO: We could put the three mares in it. They must know how to sing.

GALINA: What's this?

DJANGO: Without a woman (a real one) an American show makes no sense.

MECHANIC: I only know one real one here: the locomotive – and that's my woman. No one touches her. Gypsy law for me too.

RANDAL *cries out.*

RANDAL: He has found the scenario for the show.

The groups applaud. The MECHANIC *gets mad.*

MECHANIC: What scenario?

The groups knock him over and announce.

EVERYONE: The locomotive, prey to the contradictory loves of the rails on which she slides – show invented in the Minsk camp by the blind of Car number 1.

FOLK STOTSKY: Not number one…

GALINA: Number one is us.

EVERYONE: Then, show invented by the blind of Car 7, Car 12 … Car 15, Car 22 …

STERN *exults, he breaks away from all the other blind people who are dancing around the* MECHANIC *brandishing their canes.*

STERN: The letters of the alphabet!

The controllers try to get the MECHANIC *back.*

GALINA: You're mistreating him.

FOLK STOTSKY: We'll no longer be able to leave.

PIPEL 19: That's what you want, isn't it?

The controllers take the MECHANIC *into their protection.*

RANDAL: Train 713 has become a State. It is taking its first steps at this moment.

The blind form a locomotive supposedly looking at the MECHANIC.

ACT V

The locomotive (played by everyone), the garage track of the first Station in the world. Across from it the MECHANIC. *He would like to get even. The locomotive will form and unform itself according to the groups and their dancing.* RANDAL *is the showmaster. He immediately introduces the group (the Gypsies) meant to be part of the orchestra of the camp.*

RANDAL: Representative of so many wounded countries, the blind salute you with an American smile on their lips. By meeting here, in Minsk, in the first station in the world, we have left the Danube, line of fortune and of life in each Gypsy hand. This evening a blind Gypsy hand (and its liquid music) will trace it for you.

He introduces DJANGO. KORRI *and* RITA *join him and place their canes on the same line as he.*

KORRI and RITA: There are three of them.

RANDAL: Three Danubes?

KORRI and RITA: Just what's necessary to make the
    Gypsies of Minsk laugh and cry,

RANDAL: What's that?

KORRI and RITA: The song of the three parallels.

*They inscribe three parallel lines all around the
    show space with their canes, and sing.*

THE GYPSY GROUP: Which is the oracle line
wishing to be
parallel to the Danube

The one traced, going back up,
by the Gypsy wagon?
The one, getting down from
the loco of 713?

RITA: The loco has its two
eye-lamps in front

KORRI: The wagon has
    only one behind
    that the least bump
    closes forever

143

DJANGO: The two women of the Danube

KORRI: The woman street singer

RITA: And the woman opera of iron

KORRI: We are one

RITA: And we are the other

DJANGO: The sickness of the rails for all

RANDAL: Lost in the camp of Minsk…
    The woman opera is sad.
    Is she in search of the Book?
    The library of the first
    station in the world is closed.

SPANISH GROUP: Only the controllers' report
    with hammer and sickle
    gave her asylum
    in atonal tomorrows
    from having sung.

RANDAL: What to do? What to do?
    Can a locomotive

drive into a Book?
What becomes of her if she does?

*The locomotive at the hour of Judaism. The Jewish
group breaks away. Hassidic dance.*

JEWISH GROUP: The locomotive crosses the Talmud
And the rails take hold of her
like in the time when
one sought to know if
one could, on the Sabbath day
eat a lain egg.

Swinging of heads.

ELIEZER: The Shammai school: one can eat it.

STERN: The Hillel school: one can not eat it.

JEWISH GROUP: It is written that one train
hides another.
It is written that one sin
brings another with it.
Anyway, that's what makes
the locomotive advance.

SHOWMASTER: Toward what? Toward what?

ELIEZER: The rail doubts the locomotive

STERN: The locomotive doubts the rail.

SARAH: For wanting to precipitate the
   redemption, the Besht,
   (the real one, not the rat) is punished,
   his powers are taken away.
   What is left to him? What is left to him?

STERN and ELIEZER: So he recites the alphabet
   with a fervor such that
   all his knowledge is returned to him.

THE JEWISH GROUP: The infinite is not in man
   it can be found in words.
   Those we pronounce – already
   pronounced by Jeremiah,
   pronounced by Isaiah.

SARAH: If with twenty-two cars
   which are the twenty-two letters

of the alphabet, the locomotive
doesn't know where she is going,
whose fault is it? Whose?

ELIEZER and STERN: Which distancing from country
to country is the guilty one?
Which distancing from rail
to rail, and again to rail?

SARAH: Our rails have changed
in geometry.
They are going to meet.
Without ever knowing where.

RANDAL: Stop! Change the spacing.

While the locomotive reforms completely, the
MECHANIC *rushes at it and hits it.*

MECHANIC: I knew it. My locomotive can't run on
any old rail, at the mercy of any old geometry.
Something your alphabets can't understand: it's
a conjugal issue between her and me. Do you
want my opinion?

He sings.

Beyond the bombings
nights spent, between a train
of explosives and another of gas,
we drove you, locomotive,
on two parallel irons.
Beyond the border crossings
the deviations, and the stops,
today on the steppe
we cry out to you from station to station:
Dance universe, oh my locomotive!
Screaming steam, sacred song,
you and I, convoy rhythm
the pulse of blood on earth.

TANTI BACI: The analysis of the situation which is
only possible with a political language capable
of feeling the weight of each vicissitude of these
loves is missing.

*He throws himself into a wild foxtrot. The brigadist
group breaks off from the others. The locomotive
faced with political language.*

RANDAL: There's the subjective locomotive.

TANTI BACI: And the objective locomotive.

BRIGADIST GROUP: They stamp each other
without ever meeting.

TANTI BACI: Run lights! Another
geometry yet!
The parallels tie
like the knot of a tie.

SHOWMASTER: They can.

BRIGADIST GROUP: On
How many spacings
of contradictory geos
subjective or objective
the locomotives
must they advance?

*Terrorist raid by the two pipel. The locomotive
breaks apart. Falls. The* SHOWMASTER *tries to
reassure.*

SHOWMASTER: It's nothing, it's the rat's scene.

DJANGO: What rat's scene?

SHOWMASTER: A pipel improvisation on the theme
of derailment, most likely.

*Confusion. The rat hunt is organized. The pipel end
up disappearing into their hole. The* MECHANIC *threat-
ens:*

MECHANIC: You are going to end up on the rails,
between the rails and the wheels. Crushed.

*The locomotive forms up again, but the Spanish group
stays outside. The canes strike the three blows.*

SPANISH GROUP: Spirit of the enshrouded republic,
are you there?

*The pipel come out of their hole to scream at the
top of their lungs.*

SPANISH GROUP:
We are only fiction,
we are no more than the idea
we make for ourselves of
Spain in exile in
the first station in the world

with vision, that of a dog,
to decipher one night
each twenty-four hour day.

The locomotive regroups around the two Spanish women.

RANDAL: You are going to experience live, the loves of the three parallels.

DJANGO *begins strumming a few chords. Whistles from the controllers.*

DJANGO: Careful! The show is taking a bad turn.

RANDAL: It is even going to benefit from unforeseen collaborators.

LOUDSPEAKERS: The citizens of Train 713 are called to appear before the main gate of the station.

SARAH: We're there... What do we do?

RANDAL: Send the finale.

EVERYONE: Only the locomotives
  cry in the night
  tears of clarity

Arrival of FOLK STOTSKY *and* GALINA, *very upset.*

GALINA: Against the wall, hands in the air.

RANDAL: I protest.

FOLK STOTSKY: Now's not the time.

TANTI BACI: What happened?

CONCHA: Is it serious?

FOLK STOTSKY: Attempt to restore capitalism on Soviet territory. No more, no less.

The former locomotive from the show is divided stage right, stage left. In the middle DJANGO, KORRI *and* RANDAL.

GALINA: Each citizen of the cars of Train 713 is being sought for questioning.

STERN: Is it collective or individual guilt.

FOLK STOTSKY: The investigation will tell.

DJANGO: We are ready to answer. The cars are perhaps guilty, but not us.

FOLK STOTSKY: Already, we have noticed in one of the stopped cars a supermarket for exchanges with peasants from the area … How is this car stocked?

GALINA: There would also seem to be a bordello car – hence commerce in human persons.

FOLK STOTSKY: Even more serious (according to statements) a butcher shop car with three stalls.

RANDAL: To set up a butcher shop is to hasten our return to normal life.

GALINA: We are already informed that huge horse steaks cooked in forest mushrooms are served there.

RANDAL: At prices challenging any competition.

TANTI BACI: It has washed these faces of their concentration camp stigmata. You're not against that?

RANDAL: The bank on four wheels has been able to gain strength.

DJANGO: In the interest of all…

FOLK STOTSKY: Do you work there?

DJANGO: Me? Not today.

STERN *would like to separate himself.*

STERN: I ask that Jews and non Jews alike not be in agreement with them… They have killed animals that were in the Minsk convoys. And by doing that they have destroyed something in our convoy.

SARAH *goes after* STERN.

SARAH: They have only killed the world you live in.

STERN: So, what are you doing among the Jews? You threw yourselves into the trains of animal deportation at night. You cut throats, bled animals.

DJANGO: So they'd be kosher.

STERN: And you carried them away for profit.

RANDAL: A little sooner, a little later... You're not going to reproach us for eating and for feeding those who were, for a long time, deprived?

DJANGO: We don't have anything against the animals we eat. On the contrary... I could tell you about my horse...

SARAH: Don't always look for someone more stupid than yourself when you want to speak.

FOLK STOTSKY: While the investigation is underway, games are forbidden, illicit commerce is forbidden, prostitution is forbidden. Clandestine slaughtering is forbidden.

SOLEDAD: Are you train controllers? Or camp guards?

FOLK STOTSKY: No provocations.

GALINA: We are here to take you to a land (if it exists) which will accept you. And not to be subjected to the affronts of the most wretched among you.

SOLEDAD: So, I'll rephrase the question...

FOLK STOTSKY: I repeat: no provocations!

SARAH *addresses* SOLEDAD.

SARAH: The situation is serious, don't compromise it definitively.

DJANGO *believes the time has come to clear himself at* SOLEDAD'S *expense.*

DJANGO: The controllers are right. You are a calamity, even for me who called you my little note of music. You compromise me...

SOLEDAD: I would do without to an extent that you cannot imagine... Just as much as the camps where my man (Helmuth Bauer) disappeared.

STERN: Why make others undergo the trials which have overwhelmed us?

SOLEDAD: Like all religious people, you are a reactionary, Stern... Before the end of the journey, in order to stay within your logic, only misfortune can come to you (if it happens that there is an end to this journey). Archaics like you are condemned.

SARAH: Threats? ... We won't allow it. Especially not from a German (by choice...) What do you have to say to a Jew, after everything that has happened.

SOLEDAD: I'm leaving the convoy (with my dog).

CONCHA: You leave the convoy if you want. But without the dog.

GALINA: You will not leave the convoy, you are under our responsibility.

SOLEDAD: And you think, you, that you can stop me.

GALINA: Yes.

SOLEDAD: You all have the minds of false victims. Minds which project us each day into a worse world than that of the executioners.

PIPEL 21: What are we doing in this historic station?

FOLK STOTSKY: You are evicted from this place. All the citizens of Convoy 713. We are forced to leave.

PIPEL 19: Where?

GALINA: In the opposite direction.

ACT VI

The train now drives on toward the Rumanian border. CONCHA PARIS *announces:*

CONCHA: Soledad Bauer has committed suicide. She engraved a message on the walls of the boxcar. (You can read it with your fingers.)

MESSAGE (off): Helmuth, my only love, I should tell you goodbye... I had decided in this convoy to talk to you once a day. To tell you anything. Wherever you may be, I kept you alive each day. You were alive in me, with the secret hope of feeling myself alive in you. But there is no History within which to feel alive. The one we were chasing is ended. There is only the wind in the trees the length of the iron rail ... Farewell from the hand with the dog's vision not as a replacement view of things, but finally a different view. To the lamps of the locomotive to which the blind deportees are subjected, it was necessary to respond with other eyes...To make of the defeat of sight a victory over things. The refusal of all (or the incapacity to accept it) has made it so that the lost vision of things remains in suspense like all the lost battles of this century. For all the voyagers of this train who (in spite of divergences that I may have with them) are my comrades, I don't accept it. I ask my compatriot Concha Paris, the face of the Spanish Republic from before the defeat, having become blind, to keep for all the possibility of the vision of a dog for the non-seeing. If she loses it she will die (and they will all die), not like me in a few moments but like all things which only have a mechanic (and his machine) to say they are sighted. Helmuth, (you again!) all this, I learned from you. Your (political) language in time of trial was already that... It will henceforth always be mine... Signed, Soledad, wife of Bauer.

The journey continues without a word to the Rumanian border.

LOUDSPEAKERS: Sighetul Marmatiei, indeterminate stop. The station master informs suffering passengers that an aid center for the countryless is functioning in the old buffet. It is run by the Two Sublime Old Men.

FOLK STOTSKY *walks the length of the convoy.*

FOLK STOTSKY: You have time to visit the city. The border is closed (I have no way of saying for how long) to convoy 713.

STERN *tells the pipel while all the citizens of convoy 713 disband in groups:*

STERN: We must go to the Sublime Old Ones (they are two rabbis..)

ELIEZER: Jews are always in solidarity.

PIPEL 19: And the old are always mentally deficient. If we go there they will cry and lament over these oh so poor children who have suffered so…

PIPEL 21 … and who carry the sum of evil in suffering on earth… So much the better, after all, we'll be able to make some money. Not much, … but, with feelings it's always little.

The entire group of the alphabet presents itself in the playing space. They remove their shoes to enter. The pipel go and sit down in front of them, but keep their shoes. By turns, they will explain.

SARAH: At the aid center for the countryless, two old men on their last legs received us. They were as scarred by the passing time as us. They nonetheless offered us a crate of grapes for the sick on the convoy. What's more they emptied their pockets to give to the American's bank (to which we are contributors now) a fund of Rumanian money. By nothing but their presence the sublime old men impressed the pipel; they stayed with our shoes on the doorstep.

PIPEL 21: The place was naked, stripped – there was nothing to make off with.

PIPEL 19: To tell the truth (even if it always creates problems): We didn't dare…

ELIEZER: One of the rebs said: we are a disappeared world. What remains may be the hidden sanctuary of the kingdom of the Spirit. If we forget it, the saintliness of this century will remain God's secret.

STERN: Then I said: that is why we are searching for the Book… We are an alphabet gone in search of it.

PIPEL 19 *stands up to join in the conversation.*

162

PIPEL 19: From before the door we cried out to re-lax the atmosphere: God's secret is the locomo-tive. No one laughed.

He sits back down among the shoes at the entrance.

STERN: And the reb who had the youngest voice… we are still a pure premonition, the melody of his eternal call… We are also the sign of his pass-ing in the forest of forgetting. I wanted to ask: whose time, the Canticle?

ELIEZER: The one whose voice was no more than a breath… We are aware of being implicated in a story transcending dynasties and empires…

STERN: And again: … We are in fact unraveling the course of an eternal story. Even carriers of the misery of beggars and vagabonds, we preserve the respect of the spirit.

ELIEZER: I'm the one who said: I'm against it. This story is our shame. In the Book where our al-phabets should come together, there are only stricken names.

SARAH: The reb nevertheless responded: there are always names that survive being stricken.

ELIEZER: I responded in turn, I cried out ... but on the pages torn out, one loses even the memory of the Book.

PIPEL 21: We said nothing. In all that only the shoes were of interest.

PIPEL 19: We could exchange them for the tobacco leaves of the Rumanian peasants.

STERN: I tried to calm them by asking if the blank page was the freedom of the Book? Or the great beyond of the Book? But the two patriarchs swept away the question.

As they talk, they show the greatest joy and jump higher and higher.

ELIEZER: We are God's stake in human history.

STERN: We are the aurora and the challenge.

ELIEZER and STERN: We are the challenge and the proof.

SARAH: Moishe Stern remembered the Hassidic new year in the camp, the gladness of the common prayers and the gladness…

STERN: (I emphasized the gladness)

SARAH: of the celebrations of the feast of the Law. So this aid center for the countryless whose windows were of nailed boards grew to the dimension of prophesy.

THE JEWISH GROUP: Sanctity swept away utility. Loyalty swept away success. Wisdom swept away information. Prayer swept away discourse. Tradition swept away fashion. And the meaning of life became once again: perfecting the universe!

PIPEL 21 *disappears a pair of shoes.*

PIPEL 21: We still didn't say anything.

ELIEZER: Then yet they asked: if death rests outside the Book? of what can the Book be the illusion?

SARAH: And again: you are in the process of living the vigil around an absent Book.

STERN: … with our dead between the pages.

The pipel make another pair of shoes disappear.

PIPEL 19: Us, silence and sewn mouth.

End of the audience with the sublime old men. The group of the book has no more shoes. They hunt. SARAH *is soon intrigued by the waists of the pipel.*

SARAH: We are going to pray that our shoes may be returned to us.

STERN: Discussing with the eternal for a pair of shoes, what a risk!

PIPEL 21 and 19: That's true.

SARAH: Nothing worrying the Creature ought be spared the Creator (blessed be).

Suddenly she takes away the two pipel's canes which she then sticks in their faces.

SARAH: Pray..! … in gladness (as Stern said).

PIPEL 21 and 19: Who? Us?

SARAH: To jump is to get closer to the Creator…. All together!

SARAH and the PIPEL: God (may your sacred name be blessed) give to your creature the pair of shoes which will allow them to go forth, as quickly as possible, to accomplish good.

They jump. The shoes fall.

SARAH: A miracle! … Put your feet in them, Stern. Don't always be down to earth.

STERN *finds his shoes.*

STERN: Truly!

ELIEZER: What could we do with such a miracle?

STERN: Accept it.

Intervention by the MECHANIC, *very unhappy. He addresses them all.*

167

MECHANIC: I must beg you to not empty the coal from the tender anymore… Without coal we can no longer leave… From now on, I will shoot buckshot and firebrands at the first to approach.

CONCHA: What's the harm? No one wants us. We are rotting where we stand. There are some who try not to rot. The coal is for cooking. The hot water for washing.

DJANGO: You know what has to be done if we are to leave? Drying up the water provisions, and making the firewood provisions disappear, the barriers against the snow, the crossings to make fire. The cars on garage tracks must be reduced to their ten wheels. The locals will be so fed up that they'll pay us to leave.

Entrance of GALINA *and* FOLK STOTSKY

FOLK STOTSKY: Everyone on the ground!

ELIEZER: Again!

They obey and form a long line.

FOLK STOTSKY: Those who steal straw and light fires with stolen wood – step out of the line.

They all step forward toward FOLK STOTSKY, *including* CONCHA *and her dog.* FOLK STOTSKY *throws his hands in the air.*

FOLK STOTSKY: Even the dog!

GALINA *joins* DJANGO *who hasn't moved.*

GALINA: You, are you the only innocent one?

DJANGO: Always.

GALINA: And the goose of Rakhovo, what was that?

DJANGO: We didn't steal it. We pretended to.

GALINA: And why was that?

DJANGO: To get a little cash. The station master with his Polish accent bought it from us.

GALINA: And before the train pulled out, you had sold him the same goose six times.

DJANGO: Only three times, the fourth time we stole it from him to give back to its owner.

KORRI: It was the station master who said six times.

DJANGO: He wasn't honest in the deal. He took advantage of our infirmity.

GALINA: I must add with sadness that by following the advice of the Gypsy from Car 22, you have won. We have obtained transit though Rumania. Transit only.

Applause. Whistle from GALINA *to stop them.*

GALINA: Let's go, one more time.

PIPEL 19 *throws himself at her feet.*

PIPEL 19: Stop! …

KORRI: Tie him up! He's having a seizure.

She jumps on the pipel. They fight.

STERN: We tie no one here.

FOLK STOTSKY *goes after* KORRI. *The struggle ends.*

STOTSKY: That is not among the attributes of a companion.

PIPEL 19: Car 22, the Queen of the Gypsies.

PIPEL 21 *comes to reinforce.*

PIPEL 21: Rita Donau in the convoy.

RITA *tries to flee.* SARAH *intercepts her.*

KORRI: The Queen is on her own path: the path of the Gypsies. Who does that bother?

RITA *offers no resistance. She allows the face mask to be lifted by* SARAH.

SARAH: Do you recognize her?

RITA: If you had recognized me when we left Auschwitz you would have lynched me, I know. Today, it's too late.

CONCHA: There is still no prescription for kapos.

RITA: I came down the Danube with you. But a Gypsy only really exists when she goes back up it. Here I am, even without prescription.

TANTI BACI: You must be given credit for a certain courage.

Attempt by the pipel to dash away. The controllers stop them. DJANGO *takes out his knife.*

DJANGO: I have already given warning (therefore I would not be guilty). Whoever touches the Gypsy female will pay in kind.

RITA: Jackal, let me.

She takes the knife away from him and puts the blade to her throat. The controllers try to cajole her.

FOLK STOTSKY and GALINA: No!

STERN, *who isn't in on* RITA'S *threat, asks:*

STERN: Why did you stay among those from whom you had separated yourself during the trials?

RITA: Misfortune made me like you.

ELIEZER: Misfortune is not meant to unite.

SARAH: What do you mean to do with that knife to your throat?

RITA: Invite you to a great meal of rediscovery.

RANDAL: So you took it out to cut bread?

CONCHA: Do you think that we will come?

RITA *ends her threat.*

RITA: Of course. The ants have always criticized the grasshoppers but have always envied them.

Night. They camp. The transition is made with the song of the Gypsies.

SONG OF THE GRASSHOPPERS OF A LAND GROWING COLD

Here we are, grasshoppers
of a land growing cold
For them for a long time
the future is past
For how many days yet
will their destiny play out
on the Danube
carried as it is
by the dead horse
like one of the four white, red, black, tan horses
of the Apocalypse
Where did the story exist
entrusting to the Gypsies, a river
to their children, the sight of the horse
with the same paths
where pass by thousands of years
all the itinerant families

ACT VII

They are seated beside the tracks. And they wait.
PIPEL 19 *goes and sits down near* CONCHA *and tries
to take the dog from her.*

PIPEL 19: He's mine.

CONCHA: You aren't going to go on like that all night?

SARAH: He doesn't want to let it go… one morning,
you'll wake up without him.

CONCHA: Needless to say he is guarded by the words
Sol engraved on the wall of the boxcar.

She pushes the pipel toward DJANGO *who, in turn,
pushes him toward* TANTI BACI

DJANGO: Even on a railroad track, we can't have quiet
anymore.

TANTI BACI *distances the pipel who goes off and
attaches himself to* SARAH'S *breasts.* SARAH *fights
him off vigorously. Fight into which* ELIEZER *thinks
he is intervening with severity.*

175

ELIEZER: What I am hearing is only an error in accentuation on a poorly written sentence, I hope…

SARAH: What does he really want?

STERN: Always the same thing.

SARAH: And what's that, the same thing?

STERN: He is asking if he is loved.

RANDAL He's crazy.

ELIEZER: In that case, we need to know why that seems so scandalous to us.

RANDAL: That is exactly the kind of question we don't ask ourselves anymore – at least not in that way.

CONCHA: Or else that is just not asked.

RITA: Especially on the border of a central European country.

Appearance of PIPEL 21

KORRI: We know.

PIPEL 21: That's the third time that someone has come into Car 3 to trample the toys they gave us. Do you remember the Christmas tree at Auschwitz? That's what is being trampled.

DJANGO: Toys have nothing to do with the Gypsies.

RITA: Yes, I remember well, they were fake toys.

STERN: Where does the sale of the toy stop? Where does its wandering begin …?

PIPEL 21: They did what they could as toys. Why destroy them?

RANDAL: Is there a guilty party? If so, he should be penalized according to a vote by raised hands, like in the march of the 49ers toward the Far West.

ELIEZER: We're not talking about the same West.

MECHANIC: And who would the guilty one be?

ELIEZER: That is the entire question.

MECHANIC: So let him speak.

ELIEZER: To say what?

KORRI: That it's time to dump the pipel in the first asylum we come across.

PIPEL 21: The Besht saw who wrecked Car 3.

MECHANIC: And who was it?

STERN *tries to break the tension.*

STERN: For the menu of Restaurant Car 713, the consumers have decided not to cease devouring each other for a period of twenty-four hours. This humanitarian feast goes into effect beginning now.

He strikes three blows like in the theatre. In a totally unexpected response, the x *children start a Cossack dance. They all get caught up in it.*

STERN: If the rats dance it is a sign that the cat is not there.

FOLK STOTSKY: Don't be mistaken, I'm always there.

In turn, he throws himself into a whole series of acrobatic steps that GALINA interrupts.

GALINA: We are leaving one more time.

The game stops. Preparations for departure.

CONCHA: When I'm told we are going to leave, I always have the impression that a barrier is going to come down in front of the locomotive.

TANTI BACI: You have the dog now.

RANDAL: He can lift his leg with no problem on all barriers, which, struck by the poor hygiene he imposes on them, will draw back, horrified.

TANTI BACI: There should be no more problem.

CONCHA: Only the insufficiency, grown larger every day, of our reality poses a problem for me.

TANTI BACI: We still have the one given us by the borders.

CONCHA: Of the passage between Rumania and Yugoslavia, I only retained the rain falling inside the car – and I only thought about the impossibility of making fires at the stop… that we'd have to skip the meal… The dog too…

RANDAL: You are changing possibilities, Concha Paris. It is the one (and I'm happy for you) of the dog now.

CONCHA: That of the dog's gaze, more like.

Suddenly PIPEL 19 *begins to scream imitating*
STERN

PIPEL 19: Restaurant Car 713. If anything bad happens to the dog, end of the striking menu, the Besht will devour you all from the inside – from ass to teeth.

KORRI: What's eating him?

RITA: Another pipel.

PIPEL 19: Yes, another pipel.

Suddenly the loudspeakers.

LOUDSPEAKERS: Train for displaced persons: departure postponed.

CONCHA: What was I saying! The barrier has fallen.

GALINA: The stop is likely to be prolonged. Yugoslavia only allowed transit and Hungary wants nothing to do with us. A responsible and dignified behavior is asked of all. Don't stray. Bargaining is going on now between the Soviet authorities, under whose responsibility you now are, and the Ministry of Transportation for the new Hungarian government.

DJANGO: All that for us?

RANDAL: There is an American in the convoy, don't forget.

DJANGO: But blind, like us.

GALINA: The results will be communicated to you at any moment. A distribution of Hungarian pork, said to be impossible to find since the declaration of war, would seem to predestine them to be good.

RANDAL: You believe in predestination, Garibaldi?

TANTI BACI: Obliged to because of the always moral comic strips of the Little Anarchist of Milan and of his soap opera rebel. A Decembrist Russian (my hero then) and who, in a way, is still following me today. He was a deportee in Siberia that the Czar had condemned to having his eyes burned with a red hot iron... During the entire serial he couldn't see. But the final episode said that two tears had fallen from his eyes when he thought he had seen Blessed Russia for the last time. At the moment when the red hot iron was applied to his smoking eyelid, the tears had saved one eye.

SARAH *looks at the Garibaldian with emotion.*

SARAH: Thank you for your words Tanti Baci... We went toward Siberia, even if now we are going away from it the tears accumulate, the red hot iron of the events marks us, but you, for the whole convoy, you keep hoping.

TANTI BACI: A measured hope. For the moment the sight which returns with the last number of the series is lacking.

RANDAL: And we don't know in which station newsstand to get hold of it…

CONCHA *returns with her mess kit.*

CONCHA: You wouldn't have felt or heard the dog go by? I gave him a little freedom.

KORRI: He was still here a little while ago.

PIPEL 19: For animals who appear and disappear you must address yourself to Car 22.

DJANGO: Something in my ear says someone's looking for me.

CONCHA: What are you saying?

DJANGO: That I am always butting up against the same international: that of the homos.

PIPEL 19: The homos, that's us…

PIPEL 21: But not when you say it like that.

Charge of the pipel. Confrontation with DJANGO
immediately stopped by FOLK STOTSKY.

FOLK STOTSKY: Where is the Spanish woman's dog?

PIPEL 21: Ask the Rakhovo goose.

PIPEL 19: It's a classic case.

DJANGO: Someone's trying to offend me ... and I am
offended. I gave the mutt to the Spanish women.

RANDAL: I'm the one who gave it.

DJANGO: You, bank, it's in your interest to be quiet...
If I offered the mutt it was so he would do his
job – and not so he would go running off looking for adventure – with whom? I have no idea
– maybe with a ram.

FOLK STOTSKY: What are you saying, Gypsy.

DJANGO: Exactly... Like all homos... Even if, in Hungary, the rams have twisted horns, I am offended.

Laughter from some. Exasperation from others.

RITA: Jackal, you make me laugh.

CONCHA: In your place, I'd abstain.

KORRI: What does she have to say? She's even drier than her cane.

GALINA: What do you have against her cane?

KORRI: I'm speaking as accompanying nurse.

Laughter to protest the title KORRI *is giving herself.*

KORRI: We get woken up at night by the flea-bitten bagpipe... We can't tell anymore if it's snoring or barking...

CONCHA: One or the other, in a more intelligent way than all the other flea bags in Car 22, their nurse companion and her empty box.

DJANGO: The Gypsies are being insulted.

He takes out his knife once again. RITA *interposes herself.*

RITA: Who do you want to strike? The speed of the train? She doesn't exist. Besides, she sees nothing.

DJANGO: Me neither, that's no reason.

SARAH: A whore who has named herself queen isn't hard to see.

DJANGO *goes after her, generalized melee with the blind people's sticks.* RANDAL *tries to calm his associate.*

RANDAL: Django! A horse who bolts is always bad.

DJANGO: Don't you worry about horses, that's not your field.

TANTI BACI: If anyone harms the Spanish woman, he can consider himself crippled for the rest of his days. My word as a Garibaldian.

DJANGO: It's the Rat I want.

PIPEL 21: You are hunting the Rat because the Rat is the only one to see. The mechanic has known that for a long time.

MECHANIC: I will tolerate neither comparison nor competition with a rat.

RITA *to* GALINA

RITA: What are you waiting for to get involved? The third world war?

Brutally GALINA *puts an arm lock on* RITA *and pushes her out of the circle of confrontations.* RITA *fights back.*

ELIEZER: We are already united by misfortune. What more do you want to confront?

PIPEL 21: The toothbrush to clean the rats... That's what's missing for you, isn't it?

STERN *falls into the language of the others.*

STERN: Shame on you, invert!

PIPEL 19: To see you, that's better than being an escapee from the prayer for the dead.

SARAH *tries to disperse the rising distress of the convoy.*

SARAH: A convoy is always full of waiting madness. Don't let it out.

STERN: What are we defending on these rails?

GALINA *hurries over, warning:*

GALINA: Another convoy, like the Ukranian women's. It is entering the station...

They all turn in the direction of the convoy.

TANTI BACI: It's not difficult to recognize.

EVERYONE: A death convoy.

STERN: Because it is us... It is us once again... Put your ear to it. Hoarse breathing ... Stray coughs... Mucusy words... to ask for what? Water, again water, water again. A demand which cannot be mistaken… Asphyxia is mounting inexorably as in a lost submarine. Do you hear? They are fighting… Touch the doors. Underneath… Liquid excrement… Smell… Listen… Who has never heard a hand scream torn on the barbed wire of the window of a boxcar?

CONCHA: Is it the train that survived all of ours? The ghost train?

STERN: Not ghost! With very real men inside… speaking a language, German.

KORRI: We should sing. That's the best way to answer them.

STERN: Where are the assassins?

ELIEZER: Everywhere and then? Rebbi, it is impossible to untangle.

STERN: When the Red Sea closed on Pharaoh's soldiers the angels began to sing. And it was the wrath of God. Creatures (my creatures, they too) are perishing in the waves and you sing! The death of a human being, do you know what that is?… Here it's worse. It is about a degraded human being.

KORRI *sends an exorcism with her hands.*

KORRI: The Gypsies whose eyes were collected are not there to see.

ELIEZER *to* FOLK STOTSKY

ELIEZER: Say something.

FOLK STOTSKY: A certain distance is necessary. Yesterday, you… today, them… Tomorrow, us.

STERN: And the next day, their fall is on our heads.

RANDAL: Maybe (very respectable!) but today, for us, vengeance! It's fair.

STERN: Did we come this far to reconstruct the camp?

SARAH *tries to calm* STERN

SARAH: No one is reconstructing anything ... The war is over. You are making there be no end.

STERN: They are victims at this moment ... Any victim is innocent.

SARAH: Stay with the people of the train, Rebbi. Don't go flying off on your yet unwritten pages.

PIPEL 21: There are too many kapos who survived.

RITA *understands the allusion.*

RITA: May ulcers and the blue devil eat out your insides, abortion!

STERN: We are being engulfed at this moment by all we have kept safe.

ELIEZER: Rebbi, I can not agree completely with what you are saying.

CONCHA: A strange double game is being played here.

They all go overboard. PIPEL 19 *succeeds in taking* STERN'S *hat.* STERN *smiles as if he had been expecting it for a long time.*

PIPEL 19: We are going to put up for bid a spy's hat … so one can pass unseen at synagogue.

STERN: One is always a bit of a spy when one goes in search of the Book.

KORRI: He said he was a spy.

SARAH: He did not say that!

KORRI: He just said it.

To SARAH:

DJANGO: He's one of theirs, that's what he said.

SARAH: He said he was a journalist at a Yiddish weekly. That's all.

ELIEZER: You are crazy.

FOLK STOTSKY: Don't exaggerate, you… As for the others, if you want to know the depth of my thoughts, I wash my hands of it. You alone carry responsibility for your words.

DJANGO: May the Jews be judged on the vivisection room and its starred doctors, before whom passed the Gypsy women.

RITA: Now's not the time, Django.

KORRI: About our stomachs, he has no right – but about his horse, he may.

DJANGO: That will give me back my sight! May the Jews be judged on my dead horse.

SARAH *grabs* DJANGO

SARAH: Big bag of rotten chestnuts … you take yourself for a judge with your look of an alcoholic constable.

DJANGO *goes to strike with his cane.* FOLK STOTSKY *stops him.*

FOLK STOTSKY: It's in your interest to stay calm, you!

DJANGO *resists.* FOLK STOTSKY *grabs him and tries to take him out of the hot spot.* DJANGO *fights back all the while continuing to talk about his horse.*

DJANGO: My horse knew the tambourine, the dance... He could line up five numbers one after the other. From walking his hunger in the camp his brain became striped... Like a deportee's outfit.

FOLK STOTSKY *immobilizes him on the ground.*

FOLK STOTSKY: Are we calmer now?

DJANGO *continues nonetheless.*

DJANGO: That amused everyone but me... My horse was a Gypsy, he wouldn't allow it. He rose up on his two legs... A secondary officer emptied a whole load into him. Today, in the name of all the Gypsy horses, I have the right to ask for fire from heaven, right here... And we will all have sight.

RITA: Django, stop!

DJANGO: You are the one asking me to stop? That horse, only I crossed the earth with him.

ELIEZER: The Romanche hell will decide about your sight and your horse. But not about us. We are the search for the Book and not a lamentation on the madness of days past.

DJANGO: The horse gone mad had a jacket and the striped hat, like you.

SARAH: With your jackets, your hats, your tambourines, and your fixed numbers, you are now what you never stopped being, blind people, but also poor charlatans. All of you.

FOLK STOTSKY *thinks he has found the best way to appease the situation.*

FOLK STOTSKY: Excuse me, but I will have to make a bad report on your activities as companion.

SARAH: And why is that?

FOLK STOTSKY: It is your group which is leading the craziness on this convoy.

The group of the book is struck dumb by this intervention. The others applaud FOLK STOTSKY. STERN *tries to dominate the applause by pointing to the parked convoy.*

STERN: May the fire of unwritten words be upon you if you don't bring provisions and comfort to these men... They must be given water... Thirst, as we know, is the worst.

RANDAL: You say anything that comes into your head!

TANTI BACI: Stop playing brothers of mercy. It's almost a provocation.

DJANGO: What did Django say! The prophet of 713 wants to tie us to the worst.

SARAH: Listen to them, Stern... Nothing in your life as a Yiddish journalist predisposes you to martyrdom.

196

CONCHA: Don't you sense that he wants that above all. This impression of emptiness that he creates around himself, that is his way of being.

STERN *addresses the soldiers in the death convoy.*

STERN: Brothers! May you be rewritten according to the words of the Book.

TANTI BACI: A very bad book.

ELIEZER *in fear kneels and strikes the ground with his fists.*

ELIEZER: He has become goy!

STERN: Who blasphemes?

STERN *tries to come back toward* ELIEZER, *he catches his feet in the pipel who, feeling him on top of them, push him.* STERN *falls. The pipel exalt.*

PIPEL 19 and 21: The first victory of the X children at war! …

First stones thrown. They are not aiming at any particular person. These are the first gestures of the liberation of all the camps being taken up again, as if it had become urgent to take them up a second time. Even if a few stones eventually reach one of the characters. It will never be a lynching (at least avowed), but rather some blind people who, in a moment of great tension (and even of hysteria) seek to express themselves. SARAH, *who sees, runs to look for protection.*

SARAH: Misfortune is upon this train… commissar, commissar!

KORRI *who can also see intercepts her. The two women hit each other with the medicine kits.* ELIEZER *yells in the direction of* STERN *who is trying to get up.*

ELIEZER: Rebbi! The dead have charged you with a mission impossible to accomplish… Live, Rebbi!

He tries to get back to the spot where he supposes STERN *to be in order to protect him.* STERN *falls, hit.* CONCHA *is verging on a nervous breakdown.*

CONCHA: Justice! .... Justice – but what face is she wearing? We don't know anymore.

RANDAL: A kapo pays. It's the law... We are beginning again the liberation of the camp... We are once again finding our gestures of that day.

ELIEZER *takes flight. The others, after hesitating in several directions, go after him.* SARAH *has taken the advantage over* KORRI *who remains whimpering in the playing space.* FOLK STOTSKY *and* GALINA *intercept* SARAH.

FOLK STOTSKY: What's going on?

SARAH: The same thing as what happened to the Soviet troops outside Warsaw when they refused to give battle.

GALINA *gives* SARAH *a tremendous slap.* SARAH *flees in turn. The two controllers come up in front of* KORRI. *The* MECHANIC *joins them.*

GALINA: Serious?

FOLK STOTSKY: Maybe not, but the remaining medicine kit has run off – unless it too has committed itself to the logic of the camp.

MECHANIC: I'll take care of it.

He goes looking for the runaways. Suddenly STERN *begins to move, then gets up. He advances slowly toward the place where the* MECHANIC *just spoke.*

STERN: Rabbi Bounam wrote "The Book of Man". The book was to contain all of creation, but in only one page... Each day, he would rewrite that page ... Each night, he would put it to fire...

STERN *tries to smile, suddenly crumples.* GALINA *leans over him.*

GALINA: It is the end... We are in a riot situation... Above all catch them... They must not be far.

They leave. RITA DONAU *who had hidden herself reappears. She goes toward* KORRI, *helps her up, then turns toward* STERN.

RITA: What happened?

KORRI: Maybe it's the war continuing.

RITA: Hey! Alphabet… You are from no country. Me neither. One must be found for us (however inhuman it may be) if only to have the right to the stone that others throw at you…Hey! Alphabet…

She takes off her shawl and covers him with it. The MECHANIC *brings in the two brigadists with their canes pointed at their backs. Having arrived in front of* STERN, *he makes them touch the body, then tells them, while returning their canes:*

MECHANIC: One dead for the moment. Some wounded maybe… Good work.

RITA: If he had not been called a kapo would he be dead?

RANDAL: I didn't say that he was subjectively a kapo… I said objectively.

TANTI BACI: If we had listened to him, the Fascist soldiers who put all of Europe in fire and blood would have been freed. It would have been a failure of justice.

MECHANIC: What justice?

TANTI BACI: The one we have been fighting for for half a century.

MECHANIC: You must not have the same one as the Jews.

KORRI: A question of possibilities…

FOLK STOTSKY *and* GALINA *bring in the seditious ones, each from their side.* RITA *says one last thing to* STERN.

RITA: Here you are an alphabet free from everything and from everyone, now.

FOLK STOTSKY: Serious events have just taken place. There has been the death of a man. An investigation is open. You will be heard first as witnesses. All of you. The file will be transmitted to the military powers. Some of you will have to appear before the war council (after having won it). What sadness!

GALINA: You are going to bury him.

RANDAL: In the ditch?

GALINA: No! In the nearest cemetery. If there is no cemetery, invent one, you're used to it.

ELIEZER, then SARAH *returns. For the first time* SARAH *weakens. She bends before the evidences of the Book.*

SARAH: Alone and poor ... are the signs of the Just Man ... before what repose? Rebbi, dead through signs. The living part of us with you.

ELIEZER addresses the others.

ELIEZER: Since our departure it has been, from city to city, a story of burned books, of tongues torn out, of mouths cut off... Who holds in hand the book whose letters dissolve?

SARAH: Who welcomes the disarray?

SARAH approaches the body. ELIEZER is led there. GALINA, SARAH and KORRI organize the burial. STERN'S body is placed on a sack to be carried to earth. They all sing.

203

SONG OF THE SIGNS WHEN THEY DIE

Rebbi Moishe Stern
Rebbi in what repose?
The time has returned
of lamentations from on high
Gleaning
Crushed ears
All begins again
Rebbi!
Rebbi in what repose
will you find again
at the horizon of so many autumns
spent in fatality
and the circle of lynchings
the traces of the Rebbi
who looked for himself
through the words of the Just
today cut down.

*Departure of the cortege of the blind for the putting
to earth.*

ELIEZER: For those who seek it here
　　language

reigns elsewhere
in a world completely other

SARAH: The name of the Messiah precedes the Mes-
siah
The Word precedes Creation.
Before acting, God speaks.

ELIEZER and SARAH: The Verb introduces man
into history. Not the contrary.
Rebbi just to the end
beyond the evidence.

The cortege has stopped. ELIEZER *says a final
farewell.*

ELIEZER: The lullaby most often sung in the ghetto
nights tells of the Reb teaching the letters of the
alphabet to his students. "… When you are
grown, you will understand how much these letters contain of tears and pain."

The controller and the MECHANIC *return to the
abandoned playing space. They speak through a
megaphone to the characters of the burial.*

MECHANIC: Hungary agrees to transit, on the condition that there be no stops, not even in Budapest for reprovisioning.

FOLK STOTSKY: Set your friend beside the road with a note asking someone to take care of him. We are leaving immediately.

SARAH *writes the note.* STERN *is abandoned. They all return and prepare to leave. The* MECHANIC *insists on warning them.*

MECHANIC: A bit of advice before we leave... From now on, wherever the train passes, expect it to be assaulted. At that time don't stand near the doors. We will respond with jets of boiling water. Otherwise we might as well stop the journey at once. In mountainous regions, with a certain surplus weight, the locomotive can advance no further.

SARAH: By whom will we be assaulted?

FOLK STOTSKY: Survivors like you. One thousand five hundred Jews since the end of hostilities have been, where we are going now, killed in the pogroms because they were trying to regain their peacetime homes. Returns are always difficult.

SARAH: A new diaspora begins.

ELIEZER: Where are we going now?

MECHANIC: Don't you see the Beschides across from us?

RANDAL: Difficult for us to respond even if they are mountains.

FOLK STOTSKY: They ought not be unknown to you.

GALINA: First step in their direction, Ostrawa.

SARAH: A few kilometers from the Auschwitz camp?

GALINA: About thirty. Just on the Czech-Polish border.

ELIEZER: Alert to the blind! The time of the dead has returned, you are going to be, once again, locked up in Auschwitz.

*Screams, cries. They drag themselves on the ground.
They hit their heads against the walls. They rend
their clothes. Generalized despair.*

TANTI BACI: All the possibilities united into just one.
The second extermination is being prepared.

GALINA: Calm down!

FOLK STOTSKY: Don't let yourselves be overwhelmed
by irresponsible elements... What do you want?

RANDAL: To go to California.

FOLK STOTSKY (*sarcastic*): The color red was forbidden there (even in lipstick) because it was inter-
nationalist and subversive.

RANDAL: That isn't in California, that's Chicago. Besides that's old: it dates from the White Terror.

FOLK STOTSKY: And you think that it won't start
again?... The American wheel of fortune...

RANDAL: And then?

FOLK STOTSKY: A brigadist is always a native of the color red, and even (let's be precise) blood red.

RANDAL: If the color red has been forbidden it is because an influential politician had some blue dye to dispose of. And if the associate of another yet more influential politician has a surplus of the color red, the color red will come back as that of a Mormon Christ (including on the lips of our women). Don't confuse business and politics. Avoid having it thought that on this train the blind are not necessarily the ones you are transporting.

PIPEL 21: Ask that of those who have two locomotive lamps in place of eyes.

GALINA: All right, if we are going to speak clearly. The tripartite commission of the western allies, in order to see more clearly yet into things, declared that the mental state of the survivors of the camps (that means you) was so abnormal that discriminatory measures were necessary. And you will see completely clearly into things when you have the delousing card.

RITA: Stop! We know only too well what that means.

MECHANIC: And what does that mean?

DJANGO and KORRI: It means: No! to delousing.

FOLK STOTSKY: And will you say yes to General Patton whose three official stars say that it is officially difficult to consider you as human beings.

The pipel applaud.

PIPEL 21: Here you are, all officially pipel.

PIPEL 19: The faithful of the Besht grow in spite of themselves.

SARAH: No! No! It won't happen…

Once again great lamentation, with rage added in this time.

CONCHA: Soledad said it: we should never have gotten on this train.

PIPEL 21: The mechanic must settle accounts with us.

MECHANIC: And why would that be?

PIPEL 19: Because he is a mechanic.

CONCHA: It should be up to the controllers who lead us by a string, with their report, to settle accounts with us.

FOLK STOTSKY: And what are you asking in exchange?

GALINA: To change locomotives?

DJANGO: Let's not get on it any more.

FOLK STOTSKY: You will get tired of waiting.

SARAH: Let's go!

They all run toward the rails.

ELIEZER: We must block all departures.

FOLK STOTSKY: Calm down! Keep your cool.

MECHANIC: Look! They're lying down on the rails.

GALINA: Don't make the situation irreparable.

In the midst of the ruckus, FOLK STOTSKY, GALINA *and the* MECHANIC *have intercepted the Queen,* TANTI BACI *and* PIPEL 21. *Those who are lying on the rails chant "Long riveted to the chain, hunger tormented us, tortured us..."* FOLK STOTSKY *addresses the three prisoners.*

FOLK STOTSKY: The file on the Jew's death is not yet closed... talk to them... otherwise, you will be held responsible, for this rebellion as well.

TANTI BACI: I don't need your threats ... I am against despair (they are in despair, me too). I'll talk to them.

TANTI BACI *addresses those lying on the rails.*

TANTI BACI: The relations of power do not allow us to affront this situation. It is a trial, it merits a response on our part. For the moment, we must go where the rails lead us. Into the breach: our vigilance.

FOLK STOTSKY: Your turn.

PIPEL 21: The rails aren't good for rats.

    Boos coming from the rails.

PIPEL 21: Better the cars.

      GALINA *to* RITA*:*

GALINA: Tell them that we will go no farther than Ostrawa.

RITA: My Gypsies, get on the train. In Ostrawa, we'll chase away the evil eye, and we will give the promised banquet. You are all invited. This will be the end of all the spirits contrary to us.

    DJANGO *is the first to rise.*

DJANGO: I'm coming to prepare the meal.

The others end up following. Only ELIEZER *stays lying on the rails.* GALINA *approaches him.*

GALINA: The siesta is over.

ELIEZER *gets up and joins the others.*

TANTI BACI: Who can go to this meal?

CONCHA: Neither I, nor my dog, I think.

KORRI *laughs.*

KORRI: He's at our place every day. When the convoy stops, there are often dogs around... With this war... They are looking for their masters... You're looking for the one the Gypsies gave you?

CONCHA: No, the one that Randal gave the Spanish women in memory of Madrid. I couldn't (alas!) even tell you his color. But I know that he is very curly and he has hair even in front of his eyes.

KORRI: It's the same one. I know that one... I think it's a bitch... It was visible a few days ago... She must have had her pups and she is hiding them in a corner of one of the cars. Safety among animals (especially the mothers) is very important.

RANDAL: Concha Paris pulled across Europe by ten puppies, what an adventure!

ELIEZER: Will you go to the meal?

TANTI BACI: I don't find in these Gypsies the gitanos we knew in Spain.

RANDAL: Racist… Me, I'll go… For once we escape our image.

Before leaving the MECHANIC *goes to ask* FOLK STOTSKY *who is already in place:*

MECHANIC: The bureaucratic possibility, will it be present at the meal?

FOLK STOTSKY: With the report under its arm… And the mechanical?

MECHANIC: Like all the others, and for the same reasons… Not going means attacking the Gypsy

family directly. Better then to abandon the locomotive, and to continue on foot... Shall we go?

FOLK STOTSKY: Let's go.

ACT VIII

This time the attempt to take over the journey Tatabanya-Ostrawa takes place in the imaginary space of the x children.

PIPEL 21: The deciding battle of the Besht.

PIPEL 19: The future pipel within Train 713 are at war... They know neither which war nor why.

They isolate each element of the train as if they were a mental illness. Each time they sweep with the cane in front of themselves as in a curling match.

PIPEL 21: The increasingly deaf, blind, mute loco-motive no longer has anything but the rails to assure its coherence.

PIPEL 19: A coherence of future pipel (it too!) which no one wants. Car 22.

Car 22 is isolated. Double play. Imaginary and realistic.

DJANGO: You remember the dance of the pipel. What rhythm! … It was as if you could see them… We have reconciled with each other (to tell the truth they took the first steps…). I asked them to come at the end of our celebration to dance like they did when we were on the Yugoslavian border.

KORRI: What's the use if most of the guests can't see.

DJANGO: A dance is to be seen with the ears… Besides, without dancing at the end it's not a Gypsy meal… One of the pipel has already agreed.

PIPEL 21: Car number 7, same game as for the previous car.

ELIEZER: I will not go to the Gypsy meal.

SARAH: A deportee only refuses a meal on the point of death. Are you afraid of discovering things in common with that woman?

ELIEZER: Her impunity of a young wild animal astonishes me… And then, she put her shawl over the body of Moishe Stern the day of his death.

SARAH (*sarcastic*): You could take it back to her without committing yourself to anything. Is she the one who will enter our possibility – or is it you into that of the Gypsies?

PIPEL 21: Car number 15.

Same game as with the previous car, with the addition of CONCHA *to this car.*

CONCHA: You didn't sense Dog, the dog going by? The Gypsy companion said she had seen him.

TANTI BACI: You'll have to look at their place... There's a lot of cooking going on there... The smells must have attracted him. But you can wait for him here. Dog, the dog always comes to our car at the end of the afternoon.

RANDAL: He got into the habit at the time of the brothel. Not that he's a voyeur, but he always got some gratification out of it.

PIPEL 19: Car without number.

Car for the Queen alone (and lonely). Same thing.
RITA *addresses* ELIEZER *(internally).*

RITA: Friend of the lapidated man, this is the Queen
speaking to you. I have the impression that the
possibilities of this story have gotten confused.
A letter of your alphabet has taken my place, I,
who only learned to read and write in order to
survive in a camp. Here I am illegible somewhere
in the pages of your book... Friend of the
lapidated man, I invite you to the meal of reconciliation (only the men, not the women). Tell all
the Jews even if they answer that all the Jews are
dead. Of that, one must not speak. Of course that
other war hurts (my womb was opened by it)
but god didn't want it in the way that a man
could have wanted it. In that war god was a kapo.
Nothing more.

PIPEL 21: Car number 3. Trampled headquarters of
the Besht. In the middle of what remains of the
toys from the Christmas tree... Someone (we
don't yet know who) makes them disappear in
pieces... The meeting of those pieces was, until
yesterday, our summit meeting. Having, we pipel,
something to say (and not to dissimulate) about

Auschwitz and its blind. It was stolen from us. Or destroyed. Or maybe both.

The dispersed cars travel toward Car number 3 and reconstitute the convoy. PIPEL 19 *and* PIPEL 21 *act realistically.*

PIPEL 19: Django killed the dog to serve at the meal.

PIPEL 21: He wasn't big.

PIPEL 19: But it was my dog. He took him from me.

PIPEL 21: It's the American's fault.

PIPEL 19: I think I can do them all in.

PIPEL 21: That's why you're helping them with the meal ...?

PIPEL 19: Yes! ... Do you have the powdered death? (The one you keep in case the Besht needs to commit suicide.)

PIPEL 21: And in exchange?

PIPEL 19: Five watches. The mechanic has a box full of them that he must have filched from other refugees before us... You can be sure that he won't go complain.

Train 713 is back together.

LOUDSPEAKER: Ostrawa! Ostrawa!

Cry from KORRI:

KORRI: The Danube has abandoned the Gypsies!

ACT IX

Loudspeakers once again.

LOUDSPEAKERS: Unlimited stop. The train for displaced persons is requested to park in space number two on the garage track.

The displaced persons (D.P.), that's their new name, get down on the quay of the Ostrawa station and prepare to spend the night. Impression of unease.

KORRI: When the Danube gets farther away, misfortune arrives.

TANTI BACI: That is no reason to bring misfortune. Auschwitz is not far.

ELIEZER: Can things happen twice?

RANDAL: Optimism has never worked for us thus far.

ELIEZER: Maybe our stakes are different.

RITA: I am superstitious ... Not you?

ELIEZER: Maybe by bringing us back to Auschwitz the train wishes to betray something in the balance of the stars.

RITA: Will you allow me? I am intrigued... Can you read his hand?

She is speaking to KORRI *who immediately takes* ELIEZER'S *hands.*

RITA: He must be descended from a Jewish king... A Jewish king, harp player...

KORRI: A king possibly... a harp player certainly.

Intervention by DJANGO.

DJANGO: Me, I play the violin.

FOLK STOTSKY *comes by.*

FOLK STOTSKY: We've been asked to apply a curfew... There is troop movement on the border.

KORRI: Nothing serious?

FOLK STOTSKY: Routine exercises… So we don't forget we're at peace… 'Til later.

KORRI: Difficult… We have to prepare tomorrow's meal.

They all go to bed. RITA *remains alone with her group.* KORRI *plans the seating for the meal then prepares to distribute each one's roles.* DJANGO *takes* RITA *aside.*

DJANGO: In Auschwitz, they would surely have cut you down.

RITA: Most surely.

DJANGO: We are getting a little closer to Auschwitz again each day. Are you blind, Queen? Or did you simulate it so you could take a place in this train and get farther away?

RITA: Only the spirits can decide.

DJANGO: That may be a good answer for the feast, not for Django.

RITA: At the moment only the feast is important. I will sing the destiny of woman as they all invented her there. Their response is the only possibility in which, without seeing it, this convoy lives.

DJANGO: In your place, I would begin the feast relaxed, sprightly, optimistic. I would say what great luck we have... Generally those whose eyes interested Doctor Mengele went up in smoke the very day he had chosen to bottle them. We were lucky. Our eyes are now in the museum of horrors. But we are still alive – and even more – (in a way), in the process of going back up the Danube. We would have preferred to do it behind a horse like mine (may God have his whinny!). But he didn't have our luck. We are forced to follow the belching she-devil of iron whose rails never succeeded in shaking hands if only to say hello to each other. But so the Gypsies are made. They live poorly. No one lives as poorly as they. But they are the luck of this convoy.

RITA: If it is I who begin... I say:
(Sung)
Do you like butchered women?

(Spoken)
And I await the response,
common possibility.

DJANGO: Queen, leave these stories for another time.
They're not meant for a meal.

RITA: It's precisely to be able to tell them that I am
having the meal.

DJANGO: If you want to talk about the womb, I can
sing my mother's. They will think once again that
the Gypsies are folksy. And they'll keep their
good humor. That's necessary.

RITA: No.

DJANGO: You are younger than I. You must listen to
me.

RITA: The right of age isn't enough.

DJANGO: My mother had her womb cut out with a
kitchen knife this long, in front of all the Gypsies together. And you oblige me to sing it.

RITA: We're not talking about the same knife.

DJANGO:
(*Sung*)
He said: She's a whore.
She marries and remarries every night
She brings back food for the children
and money to play cards.
I accept the food and the money but not that
she be a whore.
(*Spoken*)
And the old ones said: Do what you must do.
My father opened
my mother's legs. She was tied down and she
was screaming.
(*Sung*)
It wasn't easy
to remove the womb
(*Spoken*)
The blade worked for a long time... my father,
his hands full of
blood, showed the womb finally cut.
(*Sung*)
He gave it to eat
to his big red dog.

He sits back down. RITA *gets up. Only the speaker is standing. The others are seated at her feet, listening while beating the mea culpa and giving signs of the greatest affliction.*

RITA: Your mother's womb is a story that belongs to us even if it only serves to feed the necessary hatred of woman against man. Since the Queen's womb is a story for them they must dress themselves in it. May this convoy no longer be more than a single story. A single possibility…
(*Sung*)
a womb
…dead and
transfigured.

KORRI: There may be a way of making both of you right, but I have bad feelings… To whom are we speaking?

DJANGO: To those of convoy 713 who condemn the Gypsies to be Gypsies – and not men like my horse, who knew how to read numbers, was able to be.

KORRI: By whose voice?

RITA: The voice of the thousands of guinea pig dead who at night still had the strength to become a brief glimmer above the crematoriums.

KORRI leads RITA and DJANGO'S sticks into the space she creates.

KORRI: So that they pass through us, we must make a triangle... Here the Queen, then the authorities... on her right the mechanic, on her left... the controller... Directly in front ... the Jewish King.

RITA: It's a bad triangle.

DJANGO: It unites all the possibilities of this story around you, Queen.

KORRI: Then the post-triangle where the pipel dance.

RITA: The abortions? What an idea...

DJANGO: They danced, remember, in Terezino Polje on the Yugoslavian border, that memorable evening when we had decided to stop making life unbearable for twenty-four hours.

KORRI: On the program, above all, the camp infirmary…. its image as restricted barracks which all could see – and in which they enclosed the Queen so as to cut her down in the back of their minds… The lapidation of the Yiddish journalist was a mistake. In their hearts, it was the Queen they wanted to get. The hours and understandings got mixed up. For everyone, the Jew must be victim (it's an obligation). Let him try to be one no longer and it's the scandal of all the united good consciences that they all are. The only ones with whom they are not obliged to be victims are us. So the caravan gets itself back on its wheels… They make Gypsies of us – with all the defeats that the errant use of freedom drags with it. That infirmary, that's the hors d'oeuvre that we must serve them. They all saw it. At the entrance, fifty naked women, all alive in spite of the cold. At the exit, fifty naked women, fifty cadavers. Before and after.

RITA *sings the opening.*

RITA: Into that infirmary
    enter my eighteen years.
    Like me, prisoners
    two women twist my arms.
    (It's for a test.)
    Two doctors, two women:
    one Czech, one Jew.
    (*Spoken*)
    Don't complicate life … It's nothing… A shot.

*At each allusion to the women doctors, prisoners
like herself (Jews, Frenchwomen, Czechs, or Poles)*
RITA *will spit them out like so much anathema in
    front of such and such car of the convoy.*
DJANGO *and* KORRI *get up then, turning toward the
    car and pointing to it at arms length as if it were
    carrying the fault in question. After which the
    Queen comes back among them, they sit again and
    continue to show affliction and despair.*

RITA: Another prisoner like me, a French doctor,
    takes me by the ankles, which she twists. I
    scream. The Czech slaps me, the others drag me.
    I struggle, twist and turn. Third degree. Five min-
    utes just to get to the table.

(*Sung*)
I say to myself: don't capitulate…
I scream… I lay myself out on the table.
(*Spoken*)
The ringed fist of the Czech strikes. The ring was torn off one of the women who died during the operation and now, naked in front of the infirmary where the dawn transfigures her exploded face. Now mine explodes. All these doctors have fingers full of rings… The blood … Beginnings of strangulation… I cede little by little.
(*Sung*)
Loss of consciousness
spread thighs
heels stuck to buttocks
they throw me on the metal table.
Leather harness.
Not one more movement…
(*spoken*)
I tightened with all my strength the muscles of my sex. With no illusion other than to constrain them as long as possible. Another doctor arrives. A Jewish woman, prisoner like me. She has a cylinder of shiny steel upon which is fixed a long wire of matte metal. Rage… it's all I have. I tighten

again. The doctor hits me in the stomach with her fists. The others, like woodcutters, hit from each side of the tree, slap, knock my head. The Jew lifts my knees. Her left hand immobilizes my right thigh. Her elbow blocks my left thigh. She introduces the steel syringe. The Czech strikes. I'm still screaming.

(*Sung*)
The table dances.
Suddenly pain
Stabbing.
It burns running
along the thighs
bites into the stomach
makes it a brazier.

(*Spoken*)
I vomit. The Jew smiles, it'll be better tomorrow.
The Frenchwoman… whew,
that's that! The other one smiles too.

(*Sung. She goes and cries against the wall*)
Four stars begin to shine.
It's night, the pallet
and only five survivors…

Confused noises.

234

DJANGO: What's that?

They get up. The two pipel appear.

PIPEL 21: … We came to rehearse for the feast.

KORRI: Not now.

RITA: Devour them, Jackal. They were trying to curse
the parable of the meal…

DJANGO *tries to calm her.*

DJANGO: It's just an inconvenience.

The pipel disappear.

RITA: Go sting them, Spider … poison them.

DJANGO: Gone.

RITA: I don't have the heart to continue.

DJANGO: A queen can't let herself be bothered by
two abortions with whom, in any case, we have
made peace.

RITA: Where were we?

DJANGO: (*sung*) Four stars begin to shine
    it's night and the pallet
    and only five survivors.

KORRI: (*spoken*) Fire in the stomach.

RITA: (*spoken*) A day goes by, and I stay alone, fire
    in my stomach.
    (*Sung*)
    Death, they called for it.
    Not me.
    I don't want to die.
    I resist.
    (*Spoken*)
    Between two crises, I hold on with all my strength
    to what is left to me of the Gypsy. That gives me
    breath. That will give it to me until the time when
    I command all of them. The Frenchwoman who
    studied in the cities, the Czech who studied
    medicine, the Jew who knows books... I will be
    kapo... But I no longer have the heart to con-
    tinue. My inspiration is gone.

    Silence.

DJANGO: And you think that after that they will still want to eat? You'll have to give them something to drink first.

KORRI: We have no time to add a drinking spree… It's already getting light.

RITA: Those pipel made my blood cold. It's a bad sign.

The Gypsy group goes to rest. Everything is silent on the garage track. Through runs and pirouettes the pipel summarize the possibilities where they might find refuge, theirs seeming to be compromised.

PIPEL 21: Possibility of the X children… Car 3… Fallen on the front of the operations… All the toys have been stolen… Disappeared… Turn ourselves in to what other possibility?

PIPEL 19: That of Car 15, the Spanish? In danger… the dog has disappeared forever.

PIPEL 21: That of Car 22, going back up the Danube?

PIPEL 19: Excluded. its days are numbered. The possibility of the Book?

PIPEL 21: In mourning.

PIPEL 19: But not to be excluded … We are entering into comic book time – with a best seller that could be called: The pipel signs his vengeance with a hot dog.

They disappear into their holes.

ACT X

Music of the seven possibilities started up by
DJANGO. KORRI *goes the length of the train,*
announcing:

KORRI: The feast can begin.

RITA DONAU *turns to chasing away the evil spirits.*
KORRI *seats the guests. In attendance,* FOLK
STOTSKY, *the* MECHANIC, ELIEZER, TANTI BACI,
RANDAL. *Each possibility has sent one delegate. At*
the last minute, PIPEL 19 *joins them.* PIPEL 21 *still*
stays behind.

RITA: Abortion! What are you doing here?

MECHANIC: Half a character.

RITA: Disappear! ... (He hurt me).

RANDAL: The two of them always behave badly.

DJANGO: But they have helped a lot for the meal.
They want to help more, and we need them.

239

Sometimes they are like women but they can also be men.

RITA: Men, that!

She laughs. ELIEZER *returns her shawl to her.*

ELIEZER: I thought that we had come to a reconciliation meal.

RITA: Is it important to you?

ELIEZER: Yes.

RITA: Then you may stay, pipel.

KORRI: On the condition that you be quiet.

RANDAL: Why? With them each of the possibilities of Train 713 has delegated a representative to this meal. Each of us is here a possibility of the history we are in the process of living.

RITA: Perhaps the time has come to make only one of them. Until now each of the possibilities of this train has been lived as an illness in which we are condemned to die of solitude.

RANDAL: That depends.

RITA: Garibaldi, does he know what the Rebi died of.

TANTI BACI: Maybe we don't have the same illnesses, you and I.

RANDAL: That a kapo has been killed subjectively or objectively is good for Controller Folk Stotsky's report.

ELIEZER: Not at a meal supposed to be one of reconciliation.

FOLK STOTSKY: What's more, the report says that the one who threw the stones at the rebi is capitalism… The affair, as far as we're concerned, is closed.

ELIEZER: But the dead man remains.

RITA: In which of the possibilities here represented?

FOLK STOTSKY: We are beginning this meal badly.

RITA: Amongst us, the war against an illness begins when we remove the sick person's shirt. We spread it out, we hit at it with an ax then we throw it over the roof… Treating each possibility the way we treat the shirt – and finding it identical for all. Having all the same possibility in order to have the same story.

TANTI BACI: I would like to know… To which same possibility (therefore same story) we are promised in accepting this reconciliation.

DJANGO: In the beginning of time someone wanted to know, and we all lost paradise.

RANDAL: It would surprise me that there be a paradise to be lost on our train.

MECHANIC: Unless that paradise be the garage track. Why not?

TANTI BACI: In that case we ask only its loss.

RITA: Before we begin… may the Gypsies and non-Gypsies hark unto the sign under which this meal is placed.
(*Sung*)
Uninterrupted death
of the woman in you…
The insult to my womb
our humiliation.

They all get up precipitously, astonished by this newly proposed possibility.

RITA: After this evening, the same possibility for all.

DJANGO *and* KORRI *applaud and try to normalize the situation.*

DJANGO: Now that you know, you can drink to the health of each and every.

KORRI: And then eat.

DJANGO: You are among the Gypsies.

MECHANIC: So we see.

DJANGO: The blind will hear it.

He plays the violin.

DJANGO: We are the possibility of going back up the Danube, which is to become this evening that of the uninterrupted death of the woman in you, the insult to your womb, your humiliation.

RANDAL: To be point blank about it, it's a little hard to understand.

ELIEZER: But not to accept. We must enter into the Gypsy way of talking.

RANDAL: The difficulty this evening comes from the fact that we are on both sides of a door, where one awaits the other. Since the door opens both ways, we all have the impression, at the same time, of catching it in the face.

DJANGO: Better to catch it on a full stomach, it will hurt less.

KORRI *has the dishes and bottles brought in, one after the other.*

KORRI: You knew the Gypsies of Dachau, didn't you? They went on a hunger strike to protest. In a camp, it was an enormous…challenge.

ELIEZER: No one (alas!) noticed. The Gypsies of Dachau were ill informed.

RANDAL: The only real challenge was Canada… The possessions of thousands of those selected daily for the gas chamber (a colossal fortune!) were piled up there. Through that, all the givens of the concentration world were upset. Being kapo of Canada gave more power than the SS commandant.

TANTI BACI: It seems that he would even have been your protector (Queen!), the kapo in question.

RITA: Toilet rumors! But like all toilet rumors full of truth. The kapo from Canada was my protector… a melancholy pimp. He came from the distinguished neighborhoods of Berlin.

RANDAL: He paid a percentage to the SS. That was his strength.

KORRI: I'm the one who brought him his coffee, every morning. To tell the truth, at the same time as he was getting his massage.

FOLK STOTSKY: Unbelievable!

KORRI: For his birthday, he had the right to a morning concert, a concert during the day, gifts, flowers...

FOLK STOTSKY: More and more unbelievable!

RANDAL: ...and the congratulations of the notables of all three camps together. The opulent melancholia of the Berliner kapo had become proverbial.

RITA: A proverb is stronger than a law. But he had one weakness, (a real one).

DJANGO: Food (like all of us)

RITA: In the camp, for fear of doing without, he lived amidst a whole pile of kegs of beer, bottles of wine and alcohol, boxes of prepared meats, and especially meat. Bulimia of meat... I said to myself, I can have him. And I had him. With a dog roast to make the acquaintance (a big SS dog who had electrocuted himself pissing on the barbed wire and that I had been able to get hold of under pretext of autopsying it).

DJANGO: Go on! Tonight, it's dog too.

RANDAL: Dog? What dog?

DJANGO *senses that he has made a mistake.*

DJANGO: It's not at all what you think.

RANDAL: How's that?

DJANGO: It's a meat they call Hungarian dog.

PIPEL 19: A meat that gives virtues man doesn't possess…

PIPEL 21: … courage…

PIPEL 19: … endurance…

PIPEL 21: … sense of smell…

TANTI BACI: Must we feel we have the courage all to play kapos of Canada on the day he ate the electrocuted dog?

KORRI: To those who don't like the meat, we will give something else.

RITA: There are evil spirits who, in spite of my recommendations, weigh on this encounter. Will you allow me?

She signals DJANGO *to approach her. While making gestures of exorcism she says:*

RITA: It's ruined. I can't manage to sing the woman's gut before a tribunal. I can't manage to speak the possibility in which we should enclose them for a few moments.

RANDAL: Why are you speaking Gypsy?

RITA: It's the only language the evil spirits know.

FOLK STOTSKY: And what do they say?

RITA: That you would like to speak … to ask me something.

FOLK STOTSKY: What?

RITA: Why I was a kapo.

FOLK STOTSKY: It's true.

RITA: The mechanic would even like to add: why contested? What does that mean, a contested kapo?

MECHANIC: Correct.

DJANGO: Being (or having been) a kapo, is to be contested. To save some people it was necessary to sacrifice others. That was the law.

KORRI: You know how the Queen entered the infirmary? Nude, with four prisoner doctors who twisted her arms. And they responded to each of your possibilities, the ones that at this moment you represent on this train.

RITA: Unfortunately, the dead, when they pass from one possibility to the other, change in meaning. The illness eating at the survivors of the camps is the impossibility of understanding one another. It is so for all of the occupants of Train 713.

MECHANIC: You think it's different anywhere else…

PIPEL 21: We, with our canes, we always understand each other.

The pipel hit their canes together.

RITA: What's that?

PIPEL 19: A dance.

RITA: A dance?

ELIEZER: Why not? The pipel dance very well.

FOLK STOTSKY: Excellent idea.

RITA: Music, Jackal!

DJANGO *plays music.* PIPEL 19 *begins to dance then stops.*

PIPEL 19: Hello! says the dog.

The dance degenerates into the stylized acting of marionettes.

PIPEL 21: How are you? asks a guest of the Queen.

PIPEL 19: Hello again! says the dog.

PIPEL 21: The world is so small and events only remain secret when they don't take place.

THE GUESTS: Bow! Wow! Wow! say the guests.

ELIEZER: But they know that it is the dead speaking in their place.

RITA: Hello! says the Queen.

FOLK STOTSKY: The pages of the report are birds. They fly away.

THE PIPEL: Bow! Wow! Wow! The Gypsies would like to say.

RANDAL: It really is a celebration.

DJANGO: Django's horse is present. And Django is leaving with his murdered horse.

The music stops. The Queen lets out a deadly scream.

RITA: Wahou! Wahou! says the Queen.

She turns and sees DJANGO *on the ground screaming. The guests, in turn, scream.*

THE GUESTS: Wahou! Wahou! say the guests.

KORRI: They've been poisoned!

THE GUESTS: Because they ate dog, explain the guests.

RITA DONAU *kneels, then falls over. End of the stylized acting.*

KORRI: The Queen must not die. She doesn't want to. We don't want…. You represent all the possibilities of this story. Is there just one where the Queen doesn't die? We will abandon ours… of course there is. We will ask asylum of it… Queen, get up!

She helps RITA *to get up.*

KORRI: It's time to go to a different possibility.

RITA *is standing, held up by* KORRI.

RITA: Which one? The abortions who cast spells during the parable?

She shakes her head no.

RITA: The reports of the Soviet bureaucracy.

She shakes her head no.

RITA: Especially not that of the warriors forever tricked by History… Wall Street, the bank on rails.

She shakes her head no … She looks at ELIEZER, *then hesitates.*

RITA: The one of the Jewish king and his book. Yes!

ELIEZER *doesn't move. The Queen lets herself fall to her knees.*

KORRI: Finished the possibility of going back up the Danube!

Helped and held up by KORRI, DJANGO *and* RITA *regroup.*

KORRI: The story of the Gypsies of the train from Auschwitz stops here.

With slow steps, so as not to lose their balance, they leave the playing space. CONCHA *appears, feeling her way with her cane.*

CONCHA: You haven't seen the dog?

RANDAL: He no longer enters into the truth these rails propose.

CONCHA: Why did you all lie to me? I went through the cars one by one. I called him. He's no longer here.

RANDAL: What good to you is a truth which would only confirm that he is no longer here.

CONCHA: I won't leave here until I've found him.

ACT XI

*Whistles. Commissar and controller group the
displaced persons together.*

FOLK STOTSKY: The military maneuvers the other
evening on the border had only one goal...

SARAH: ... not to allow us to enter Poland.

FOLK STOTSKY: Indirectly, not directly.

Sarcasm.

SARAH: Our thanks to the Polish army for indirectly
avoiding Auschwitz for us a second time.

ELIEZER: And maybe a pogrom too. All the surviv-
ing letters of the alphabet owe it their thanks.

GALINA: And now the big news: the West (which
some of you have demanded), you are going to
have it. All of you!

*RANDAL cries out with joy and sings Yankee
Doodle.*

TANTI BACI: Randal and disturbed brigadism – a chance not to be missed for 713.

RANDAL: I'm singing the Statue of Liberty. For everyone.

GALINA: The line of demarcation will be crossed this very day. You are being thrown back on Germany.

SARAH: What does that mean?

FOLK STOTSKY: You will find the Danube again, even if all the bridges have been bombed.

MECHANIC: Defeated Germany will be provisionally confused with your misery. You will hardly see it.

FOLK STOTSKY: The report that we were to make on the trains, we are going to file it in Moscow. Mission accomplished.

GALINA: Maybe we'll meet again.

SARAH: Maybe not… The image of the death train stopped here, this night. Did you know?

FOLK STOTSKY: This time, it was not you that it wanted to join, it was me. That train was one of the Germans of the Volga being deported. End of the autonomous Soviet Republic. It is dying now, all along the iron path.

Arrival of the two pipel, very upset.

PIPEL 19: Do you know what they are saying in the Ostrawa station?

PIPEL 21: The trains dumped five thousand children in the Brandenbourg.

PIPEL 19: No names, relatives, village, language – they are like us! They run in all directions.

PIPEL 21: Poisoned rats like us.

PIPEL 19 *grabs onto one of* FOLK STOTSKY'S *legs.*

PIPEL 19: Let me leave with you, please.

GALINA *shows the report.*

GALINA: This report contains the seven chapters of the story of this journey... From Auschwitz to the line of demarcation. One of them is largely reserved for you.

FOLK STOTSKY: In a way, you will also be in Moscow.

PIPEL 21: The rat will capitulate... He has lost the war... but he doesn't know before whom.

PIPEL 19: Let us come with you.

GALINA: Goodbye to all!

GALINA *leaves looking straight ahead, without a word.* FOLK STOTSKY, *with a great deal of trouble, manages to rid himself of the pipel.*

PIPEL 21: If we had at least given you the clap.

PIPEL 19: That way you would have taken something of us back to Moscow.

Everyone awaits FOLK STOTSKY'S *response. He makes an effort to control himself before responding to the provocation. The pipel themselves are ready to beat a retreat.*

FOLK STOTSKY: That is a desire which is only valid for the possibility of the X children. Not for the bureaucratic. (At least at this time.)… That of Train 713 stops there… To each their world, even if for each one it is habitable with difficulty.

PIPEL 21: Being a rat everyday, you think that's easy…

FOLK STOTSKY *leaves while the loudspeakers announce:*

LOUDSPEAKERS: The union of the train workers of Ostrawa salutes the just return to their family of the combatants for liberty. Good luck. Imminent departure for the line of demarcation.

The MECHANIC *is carried in triumph. Euphoria.*

MECHANIC: We will have the CCT 703 to Regensburg and the NCEL 108 to Dachau. A way of breathing the space which will change all of us.

The MECHANIC *sees* GALINA *return. He steps back down to the ground.*

MECHANIC: Did you forget something?

GALINA: This!

She destroys her notebook meant for the report.

MECHANIC: Is the Ukrainian that you are letting it be known that she wants to cross the line of demarcation?

GALINA: Yes, by entering into your possibility (the mechanic's).

MECHANIC: Passing from the East to the West will be a political choice in everyone's eyes.

GALINA: But necessary to remain in the likelihood of this journey.

MECHANIC: That is not at all given in the common spaces of the times when, in fact, for you, it's only a question of passage between two possibilities.

GALINA: Each death convoy has a correspondence in the story that we are living. Do you remember when the convoy of the Ukrainian women went by and I sang the Manual of Russian grammar?

GALINA *sings a few lines of it which the* MECHANIC *begins to hum with her to show that he remembers.* GALINA *stops.*

GALINA: Already East or West are no longer a problem.

MECHANIC: It is still to the other side that you want to go?

GALINA: No! … It's somewhere else!

MECHANIC: In any case, even if you cut into the mechanical possibility, the Ukrainian convoy will catch up to you. You can't erase your origins.

The MECHANIC *gives the signal to depart. After some hesitation he cries to* GALINA:

MECHANIC: Come on!

GALINA *joins him. Once again departure, toward Regensburg this time.* CONCHA PARIS *refuses to get on the train.* RANDAL *throws his hands in the air in a gesture of impotence.*

RANDAL: I who am at the origin of the dog, I think I understand you.

TANTI BACI: We all think we understand you.

RANDAL: But this convoy can not stand the least distress under pain of giving birth, now that the trial is over, to the fall of all.

MECHANIC: With the dead with which your days and nights are filled (to saturation), crying over a dog seems to me to be in poor taste and, to say it all, a lack of modesty.

PIPEL 21: Dying by procuration is for us. Not for you.

CONCHA: And if over so many kilometers, my neighbor was no longer man?

TANTI BACI: It would be a poor recompense for all those years of militancy: yours, Soledad Bauer's or even Helmuth's. It would mean believing that the orange groves of Spain will give no more fruit.

CONCHA: My neighbor has four legs. And he is no longer here.

MECHANIC: Think that with each hour spent on this train a child dies of hunger in the world.

SARAH: So?... Eliezer, do you remember a certain Weissberger?

ELIEZER: The one from Vienna? He sang the exploits of his crushed dog.

SARAH: To operatic airs. It was his way of making him live again – and of living with him. We should all understand it.

MECHANIC: But to what end?

SARAH: It's easy… Help me… Concha Paris, you are assured of our understanding – but in your interest (and whatever you may think) we will not leave you on this station platform. We are taking you with us.

They load CONCHA *into the car.*

CONCHA: It will be against my will.

Without much conviction, ELIEZER *tries to intervene.*

ELIEZER: If it's against her will, we are committing a kidnapping.

RANDAL: Be happy with thinking, Eliezer.

SARAH: For the moment the line of demarcation is thinking for us.

MECHANIC: Let's go!

ACT XII

Departure for Regensburg. They sing.

COMPLAINT OF THE DOG FOR THE BLIND
WHO IS NO LONGER HERE

With what touch
what smell
what hearing
to follow the dog for the blind
under the stars
that have become
over all of Europe
the dead of the camps?
The trees branch
on contradictory currents.
All around multiply
the signals of the rails.
With what touch
what smell
what hearing
to read them?
On what other arc
have the dogs for the blind
disappeared?

In what way
their universe, does it differ
from the interminable stops in the stations?
Each time the same answer
a horizon
at the edge of a space without bounds
(maybe) brought back from the steppe.
With what touch
what smell
what hearing
to cross them,
We, the blind
of Train 713.

SARAH: Concha Paris, maybe later when we speak
again of this train, your possibility will find its
place again. But today all dialogue with the others is broken.

CONCHA: Am I already a branch torn from the tree?

SARAH: In all other versions, a branch torn from the
tree isn't even newsworthy. In yours it must not,
always, be a scandal.

TANTI BACI: Soledad Bauer was like you.

CONCHA: Sol Bauer was the rifle in the Madrid trenches. She was ten years of militancy, of feminism, of incarceration between the walls of affliction. Soledad Bauer, nothing can destroy her.

SARAH: For us all, events were such that the dog became (alas!) a meat fricassee in cumin. For you he remains, desperately, another way of knowing the stars, and the objects that they light and maybe too, with them, the orange groves of Spain.

CONCHA: Today the orange groves of Spain are dead. Between these rails the Spanish women ground down in the night of the camps will never be able to know if they went forward to meet them or if they turned their backs on them.

Regensburg stop.

LOUDSPEAKERS: Regensburg. Customs formalities. One hour stop.

MECHANIC: Here we find the Danube once again.

ELIEZER: But not the Gypsies to put it to music. Of them remains only the sob of the locomotive. They are gone.

TANTI BACI: But faithful to the laws of the caravan without ever entering into any of the possibilities of the others.

PIPEL 21: What animal ever lived in his own? The hunters are everywhere.

TANTI BACI: Me, I've always lived in my own, precisely because it has never been one.

MECHANIC: Prepare yourselves for the formalities.

They all hurry toward the formalities office.
CONCHA *stays alone.*

CONCHA: Dog? One question which no blind person can answer... Were you black? Were you white? Another color? Or the color of oranges?

Return of control.

MECHANIC: Here, the Soviet stamp suffices. The formalities will be carried out in Dachau where the allied commission is in session. The way is now open...

RANDAL: What a gag for Randal. America awaits him in Dachau.

To CONCHA:

RANDAL: You need a stamp on the Russian let-pass if you want to continue in this direction.

CONCHA: My direction is Ostrawa.

RANDAL: After all, to each their story. Yours is already an Indian story. (My relations with them were rather rare, even when I worked in hotels in the West, amongst the buffalo.)

The others act as if they don't see CONCHA *so as to not pose themselves the problem: ought they leave her or put her on the train against her will?* RANDAL *gets on the train. The convoy leaves.*

CONCHA: Black? White? Or the color of the Orange?

Here you are an Indian now, Dog! I will go back as far as that color which, maybe, is still somewhere that of convoy 713.

CONCHA, *cane in front of her, leaves in the opposite direction as that of the convoy. Alternation between the characters of the two directions now opposing each other. Dachau direction.*

ELIEZER: A blind woman like us walks toward Ostrawa. Why? What makes a blind woman walk toward her dog who is no longer there?

SARAH: Does suffering have a meaning, even if it escapes us?

Ostrawa direction.

CONCHA: Each day the words diverge, they change meaning. Each day I say to myself: this steppe, has he returned to its call, with all its smells? And it is up to these smells (in which he rolled himself) to say, the length of the iron way, if the Spanish women of the Ravensbruck and then Tatenberg camps are still living or not…

271

Dachau direction.

ELIEZER: Wherever you may be in the world, the Book answers you? It is for the others that you walk toward Ostrawa. A blind woman must enlighten the others. In the prayers which sometimes rose from the gas chambers, it is above all, all that the Book could not be that is crying today. If the Book no longer answers, who dies from its silence?

Ostrawa direction

CONCHA: In what moment of the revolution lost beyond the Pyrenees, do the dogs for the blind wait? Under what too narrow star do they await the sunrise?

Dachau direction.

TANTI BACI: Of how many appendices is the war in Spain made. At this moment, one of them is trying to go back up the slopes of the universe to the place of the fatal banquet.

Ostrawa direction.
CONCHA *has stopped, she now tries to touch the sky*
with her cane. She touches it.

CONCHA: Soledad, a water dog (like ours) waits beyond the minefields he just crossed. Soledad, the water dog become dog for the blind waits in each night of the locomotive. Soledad, the dogs who become dogs for the blind still wait afterwards, without illusions. Soledad, if it is without illusion, it is without us. What are we other than an illusion? with an entire opera singing on our heads, Soledad.

Dachau direction.

ELIEZER: Engulfed sister, we hear your opera.

SARAH: It is not true, you hear no opera, Eliezer. We are in Dachau. At the Dachau camp.

Train 713 has, in fact, arrived in Dachau.

ACT XIII

What to do in a supposedly liberated camp?

ELIEZER: Twelve months on these rails ... Always outside the words from which the Book should be made ... Never inside.

TANTI BACI: In any event, entering into the view words have of things is a blind person's practice.

ELIEZER: Why (now that the impasse is on both sides) not continue our journey there?

SARAH: A word seen from the inside, how does that further us?

RANDAL: Do you know that there is a railroad madness where, specifically for the traveler, the journey doubles itself?

MECHANIC: Do you want to travel in the mechanism which makes up the sight of things for a non-seeing person?

GALINA: Don't you wonder if you are in the process of demanding the possibility of the mechanic?

PIPEL 21: A sighted person said so.

MECHANIC: Especially if he is a railroad worker ... when he follows, with a brain made of luminous references and magnetic tables, the pattern and principal lines of our journey... He can even direct a journey without ever seeing it.

PIPEL 19: So?

MECHANIC: Are you asking to travel in a synoptical schema?

GALINA: Do you think you can exorcise the other one?

RANDAL: What is our next step?

Laughter.

PIPEL 19: Inside a (supposedly) liberated camp that can only be going in circles...

SARAH: ... From one formality to another, while waiting to be ourselves a formality.

PIPEL 21: For the allied commission, we already are.

TANTI BACI: Thus the solution of despair.

PIPEL 19 and 21: Long live the solution of despair.

SARAH: Amongst all the madnesses we have lived on this train, are we now going to travel inside the word, formality?

RANDAL: Seeing or un-seeing, the route would be the same.

TANTI BACI: It's not the journey inside the word which will be hopeless, but rather the journey inside what it means.

GALINA: Formality is a customs word which haunts all borders.

SARAH: Inside words, one risks being trapped by what is said.

RANDAL: In Dachau, we don't have much left to lose.

TANTI BACI: Nothing other than a concentration camp.

SARAH: We are entering the unlikely.

TANTI BACI: Since our entry into Auschwitz, our poor truths have always been made of unlikelihoods.

MECHANIC: As locomotive mechanic who must pull all the cars behind him – I begin. To the word formality, which is proposed to the locomotive, I answer – Paragraph I of the synoptic tableau. This is the passage from the CC 703 to the NCEL 108 both with the same wheel rhythm – and the same sobbing whistle to put, if necessary, the countryside to music. There you have it, the synoptic train has started up… Car number 15?…

TANTI BACI: Paragraph II. FORMALITY. A quarter hour of questioning prelude to five hours of resignation… The affixing of finger prints. Anthropometry and in the middle, the idiotic photographic apparatus to take away what was left of you. Preoccupying note: Randal has been dissociated.

MECHANIC: ... Car 3.

PIPEL 21: Paragraph III. FORMALITY. A medical bath and the inevitable fight with those in charge of disinfection who wear the same outfit as the manipulators of the gas chamber... Fight between non-seeing and gum chewing (seeing that you could hear!) Terrorizing note: Pipel 19 has been dissociated

MECHANIC: ...Car 7.

SARAH: Paragraph IV. FORMALITY. The new identity which is still the old one: the delousing card...The enunciation of the former matriculation numbers, the comparison with those the cane carries and the verification with those who have them tattooed on their arms. Alarming note: Eliezer has been dissociated.

MECHANIC: Car without number, previously the commissars'.

GALINA: Paragraph V. FORMALITY. The confirmation of my belonging to the rolling personnel. Which would mean – Line one – either that the tripartite commission recognizes without the shadow of a doubt, my passage from the bureaucratic possibility to the mechanical which gave me asylum Line two or else that the same commission recognizes the bureaucratic as an absolute, defying borders and lines of demarcation.

MECHANIC: Stop! ... Now those dissociated by the word Formality itself. They cannot continue the journey. This second part is the stopped journey.

ELIEZER: Paragraph A. The formality was the disinfection of the hair then the declarations under oath, and finally the story of the most important moment in my life, but here, dressed as a judge, an inquisitor. I must explain that at age fourteen I ran away with my older brother Simon from a transport which was to take us to the Warsaw ghetto. My train story starts there. I found myself, with Simon, in the Polish Resistance (it was made up of two cardinal points – East and/or West) but for two runaway Jews it could only be one more illusion with all the difficulties of the time of finding a place there. The Polish Resistance, like most Central European resistance groups, persecuted the Jews. Why? Because they were Jews. They were not people in space like all those who made their borders sizzle and who confronted each other in the war. They were people of time And time was told by the Book. Simon was sent to his death by the resistance leaders during a Waffen SS attack. He was to slow them down to protect the heavy equipment we couldn't carry away immediately. And I understood that night that the true combatant was not in the insurgent resistance at the gates of Warsaw, but the Just man you would always see as archaic with his beard, wobbling along with, in a child's wagon, his books. A wagon which was multiplied by all the sidewalks of the ghetto. It was he, the Just man, the combatant of this war – and not those whose uncertain ministries consisted of uniting or confronting around weapons (the barking prophecy of stupidity…). Struggling demanded being with them. And I too went into the ghetto. I was with the Just in the deportation trains and in the camps. But by doing that I escaped from their language but not from their vindictiveness. They saw my flight as a desertion – in my return to my own, an adherence to those against whom they were fighting. Through a parabolic effect of the bureaucratic meteorite – meteors leaving Warsaw in the direction of London, returning to Paris, to the Commissariat of returns at the Lutetia Hotel, and sent by way of information to Germany to the tripartite commissions (among which Dachau's). Here are my eyes. Today dead in this story, sought for intelligence with the enemy and liable to a war council...

RANDAL: Paragraph B. FORMALITY. An indignant protest. Because we are blind, because on this train (sometimes without knowing it) possibilities intersect, we have all sought to invent a gaze for ourselves. X child, gaze of the rat... Spanish women from Tatenberg, that of a dog... Django, the gaze of the horse killed in the camp (he left with it...). Garibaldi, the gaze of a goldfish in a bowl (when he had a sense of humor and when he had none). But not Randal. No need for him to try to rival the two lamps of the locomotive, at night. This train in which he was, to pull it forward, he gave it a land, an adventure, a crucible, a future, a civilization in eagle feathers. And if it was necessary to add to this land a gaze, it was that of pioneers, of founding groups. That is what (even if I was mistaken as to the place) led me to the Lincoln brigade, and from the Lincoln brigade to the barricades of Madrid. From my perspective it saw much farther, much wider than all the animal universes in which each group of the train dressed itself as if to prepare for a sand painting like the ones they still do in the deserts beyond the Rocky Mountains (each human adventure has its Indians…). My America saw in a more fertile way than the possibilities of sight given the alphabets. More in germination as well. With that before me, blindness was never a stop before things. In a way, I saw then. Since the formalities, it is blackest night… You know (perhaps) of Everett Hale's lieutenant, dead without country, and submerged at latitude 22 11 South and longitude 15 West after twenty years spent from boat to boat, without being able to enter America, because stripped of his nationality. A phantom … That is what my compatriots of the tripartite commission decided that I would be from now on by virtue of the 1940 Nationality Act. Article 401, Paragraph C, punishing the fact of entering and serving in the armed forces of a foreign country. America being from now on for Randal, Article 401, Paragraph C. In them I now walk true days of the infirm. And that, Randal (phantom or not) has not decided to tolerate. Not even in a synoptic tableau.

PIPEL 19: Paragraph C. The breaker of toys from Car 3 has been raging. Even better... With the formality... The tripartite commission declares that blind Pipel 19 is a faker, and decides to send me to a camp (one more) for reeducation... No commentary... I won't go.

MECHANIC: Paragraph C of Pipel 19 is in the present. The conclusion (unless it escapes into a hypothetical future) will be as well. The journey on the synoptic tableau is coming to an end. On this synoptic tableau the formalities of the tripartite commission sitting in the former SS quarters of Dachau accumulates the despair of two continents... The possibilities of each former deportee of Train 713 (little matter the way they are told and what can be told of them) revolt. Can a mechanic like me, who is not made of political words, imagine cars revolting against the law of the rails? And taking the locomotive hostage? On the level of one of the realities of this camp that is what is happening, under the obvious impulse of those dissociated from the different cars. Train 713 is occupied, like a factory. Everything is blocked. The synoptic tableau and the optical journey are becoming one and the same thing. Galina and I are hostages inside it.

The blind have started in with attack/defense gestures in the construction of a quadrilateral signifying the occupied convoy. In the middle the MECHANIC *and* GALINA.

RANDAL: We are living in the name of a concentration camp – and there we are debating a new identity – refusal.

They sing.

SONG OF THE BLIND REBEL

Revolt due to circumstance
Without sight sly
underhanded or oblique
without sight scowling
without sight point blank
to shoot down with a look

the red, the blue, the yellow
and the white rainbow
of hopes from below.
Revolt of the canes turned
toward the earth – finally lifted.
It will be spoken of in past tense...
(...The Revolt where everyone
was blind,
 you know?)
What alphabet did it want
to read, and did it read?
Wings beat or carry
the gazes of the canes.
Train 713
 arriving
from Auschwitz SEES.

They announce (*the blind and* SARAH).

EVERYONE: The seven days that shook the rails of
the world.

MECHANIC: You're jumping the gun.

TANTI BACI: Before all else, organize. Know what we
have just done... How to name our refusal?

SARAH: A train occupation with the intention of not leaving immediately.

PIPEL 21: We've been occupying it for twelve months, Mama! You're just now noticing?

TANTI BACI: A seeing person who opens her eyes, maybe it's the sign that now, we're talking revolution.

GALINA *demonstrates her disagreement.*

GALINA: For twelve months you've been asking only one thing: to get out of this train.

ELIEZER: Maybe beyond the words it's a way of keeping time.

RANDAL: What are you saying Eliezer? At the very least we're talking about a performance, like we do back home.

PIPEL 21: While waiting to enter the Dachau museum. Maybe the gallows is going to be useful again to punish refusals of obedience.

286

MECHANIC: Here you are in a democracy. And the refusal of obedience is merely the exercise of your contradictions.

TANTI BACI: We are infringing upon the night of the century… We must see with our dead retinas… It will be a revolution.

Murmurs.

SARAH: Calling the occupation of an already occupied boxcar a revolution, (the mechanic is right), you are jumping the gun.

ELIEZER: You are sighted, Sarah! Rebbi Stern said it: for you, this will never be the same thing as for us.

SARAH: For a blind person (even if they are from the international brigades) what is a revolution?

RANDAL: A revolution is a revolution.

SARAH: On the condition that the tripartite commission doesn't cut off provisions.

GALINA: Revolution is too big a word for you.

SARAH: We risk finding ourselves crushed under it. For nothing.

PIPEL 21 and 19: If it is for nothing, Long Live the Revolution!

The combat order for guarding the convoy they are occupying breaks up. After a moment they all announce:

EVERYONE: Later! In the night of the first day!

They are all slumped over.

PIPEL 21: Toothache!

RANDAL: Toothache!

SARAH: Toothache!

MECHANIC: I, who find myself in spite of myself in this empty station which is your refusal, I've got it.

RANDAL: I strongly suspect my former compatriots of having injected truth serum into our last provisions... It's CIA style and it would explain this collective toothache.

TANTI BACI: The problem is not in the underestimation or the overestimation of the enemy. It is knowing if you can make the revolution and, at the same time, have a toothache... In thirty years of militancy, I still haven't succeeded in resolving it.

ELIEZER: For the moment we are occupying our convoy, that's all. And it's fair!

EVERYONE: Second day!

Each new day, the different walls forming the occupied convoy turn in a clockwise direction.

LOUDSPEAKERS: Train 713. The Allied Commission communicates. No one of you is considered to be a mutineer. But you will be beginning tonight at midnight, hour at which the respite the commission is according you ends. After that, there will be intervention. By force if necessary. We are appealing to your reason.

TANTI BACI: Revolutionary democracy. To each to decide. The enemies of our movement, like the others…

GALINA: I didn't think to find myself in a revolution again so soon. (Must I say that my old one was enough for me.)

MECHANIC: Not only do I participate in no revolution, but I consider myself hostage of what just happened. My possibility crosses ideologies like it crosses borders. I too have a toothache, but inside my possibility. And in none of yours. I demand that it be dissociated not from yours, but (you are the ones to show it) from these exercises for keeping time.

TANTI BACI: You want to leave? No one here is keeping you.

The MECHANIC *and* GALINA *go out of the convoy to boos – except for* SARAH *who warns:*

SARAH: Don't you think you are overestimating the situation?

PIPEL 21: I don't want to have a toothache anymore. I ask to leave.

TANTI BACI *brains him.*

TANTI BACI: A rat doesn't have himself cured... You are free now, Pipel.

Neither of the two pipel has reacted.

PIPEL 19: There is one thing (maybe the only one) that the pipel have learned. That is, that a rat never opposes a cat, but always another rat.

TANTI BACI: We are caught in a historical process. It is sometimes difficult to resolve.

SARAH: More than possibilities, these are the impossibilities that you must face up to, that you must revise. What astonishes me is that for two days, I've been making the same gestures as you.

ELIEZER: For Eliezer in search of the Book, revolt is normal. But you? To the appearances of what good conscience are you sacrificing yourselves by revolting?

TANTI BACI: By heredity, maybe… At eighteen I wore the Garibaldian shirt. It was my father's – but it was my grandfather who gave him his.

PIPEL 19: Poisoned rats are rebels without shirt and without good conscience.

PIPEL 21 *finally gets up but doesn't leave the convoy.*

PIPEL 21: And even for your revolution, they could care less.

MECHANIC: Pipel, you're the ones who don't understand. What do you think you are doing in there? Playing bit parts for the Barnum circus? What's keeping you from leaving?

PIPEL 21: Your disappearance! Not from the spot where you are, but from all the sewer pipes of the universe.

PIPEL 19: In any case, in any revolution there are rats… A question of conformation.

EVERYONE: Third day.

Rotation.

RANDAL: Even in a camp a bank has a role to play. Remember Auschwitz with Canada (alas!). One of the great deals of the century (and often in dollars).

ELIEZER: Wall Street! Making us breathe green paper in order to tell us it's a question of revolutionary ecology, don't you find that immoral?

RANDAL: Not if our bank has enough collateral to allow it to be given credit. I add that if the affair in which we are engaged is a revolution (as Tanti Baci says) without a bank we are in the most complete, if not to say the most often repeated, political error. All revolutions which have been smothered up to now, were so for having ignored the Bank. I am not going to tell you the story of the Commune. If we are (which I believe) in a test of force, then, on the contrary, the bank is our salvation.

SARAH: And that's all you've come up with?

RANDAL: We do have a basic guarantee which allows us to discuss.

SARAH: To discuss what. To change who?

RANDAL: Who entirely transformed the days and nights of this convoy? The bank car. (Intended for the group of the alphabet!) For the man on wheels, there is one and only one book: the account book.

ELIEZER: Wall Street! Don't make us fall into mockery.

RANDAL: Might you be a racist (of the written page)?

PIPEL 21: Mocking books are the only ones you can breathe salty. In convoy 713 whatever the possibility being lamented there, the best seller is Hot Dog!

PIPEL 19: Doesn't that tell you anything?

PIPEL 21: The hypocrisy of the convoy told as preface to its occupation by us, today.

MECHANIC: With, in the first instance, the poisoned Gypsies.

ELIEZER: No! With in the first instance a response to suffering (if it has a meaning outside the Book).

TANTI BACI: A revolution can give meaning to suffering. Not a book. Maybe because we are realizing the dream of Helmuth Bauer, at this moment.

RANDAL: He too thought to realize it. In Moscow…As commentator when he announced after the call number of Radio Proletarian: Helmuth Bauer speaking to you live from Red Square. At this moment the glorious parade of the workers' celebration is unfolding… And then?… (You're the one, Garibaldi, who told me about it) … The sun which, on this great day is part of the demonstration, shines on the wall of helmets, ringing them with its rays… And you said to him (undoubtedly because you were still young) …

TANTI BACI: Yes – I said to him... You are lying Helmuth. Look outside, it's pouring... I said it to him because I was young... And Helmuth answered... It's to make the sun come back out... A little magic is necessary in life.

RANDAL: The magic of the militant Garibaldi. As far as we're concerned, it only makes blind people.

EVERYONE: Fourth day.

The rotation isn't finished when GALINA *appears with a white flag.*

GALINA: I am Galina Roubleiva. Do you accept me?

The enthusiasm among the occupants of the train is great. TANTI BACI *abandons his guard position to welcome her.*

TANTI BACI: Our former commissar returns to the revolution.

GALINA *accepts the embraces.*

GALINA: Since we have known each other for twelve months certain ties have formed between us… It seemed normal to the allied commission to send me as emissary. (Between us: A revolution of the blind which you conduct as if you were all sighted is absurd, think about it! …)

Disappointment among all the occupants of the convoy.

PIPEL 21: The convoy of the Ukrainian women has begun going backwards.

ELIEZER *persists.*

ELIEZER: Is that all you have to say?

SARAH: Galina, Ma'am, just between us, you have a face that looks like a behind. Think about it.

GALINA *remains impassive.*

GALINA: The tripartite commission refuses to speak with you. But it sends me to keep contact.

TANTI BACI: We haven't changed. Above all, self-management of the convoy by the blind. Number 185460 (Eliezer) and A 48706 (pipel) will be in no way dissociated. Number 73 551 (Randal) is to receive an official copy of the judgement taking away his American nationality.

RANDAL *insists on adding.*

RANDAL: And subsidies to be determined which the commission must turn over for the running of the train.

Still impassive, GALINA *retorts.*

GALINA: Of course… But the tripartite commission has received a double of the Folk Stotsky report on the death of Moishe Stern on this convoy.

TANTI BACI: We all killed him!

ELIEZER and SARAH: Not us!

GALINA: The report accuses no one but it questions the new (and reactionary) order which was put in place on the convoy starting with the bank.

Because he opposed it Stern is dead. The commission would like to put a few faces on this new order.

RANDAL: I may have stolen the role of usurer from him but not existence.

GALINA: You obviously didn't kill the rebbi just because no one could see.

RANDAL: From the point of view of legality, nothing to say. It was that of the camps, after the liberation… This kind of story, unfortunately, you end up getting used to.

GALINA: Unfortunately…. That's this truth!

RANDAL: I know exactly the same (… and in English) when the brigades were sinking in the mud of Jarama, like the dysenterics in that of Auschwitz, at the time of the interregnum. Garibaldi you remember the Anglo-Irish brigade?

TANTI BACI: Yes… but I think you should have forgotten it.

RANDAL: It's true… A handful of survivors, like here, one having tens of times under enemy fire risked his skin for the other. And yet… (a slightly twisted joke, a slightly heavy Spanish wine…) they fell apart. For the English the IRA was fascist. For the Irish, the royal family, mentally handicapped (true in both cases). Result even more stupid than with Stern: three dead.

TANTI BACI: Must it be added that it was the Americans of your brigade who started it.

RANDAL: They took part, that's normal. America has always been, in a way, the suburbs of Ireland.

TANTI BACI: Objectively, it was you who fired.

RANDAL: And you believe it?

TANTI BACI: Coming from the other side of the Atlantic, I believe everything.

RANDAL: And what's that, everything?

TANTI BACI: Everything.

RANDAL: And then?

TANTI BACI: Everything: the anonymous society for assassinations, the starred Mafia, Al Capone political thinker preaching the anticommunist crusade, worker's bodies in the lakes of Chicago!

RANDAL: Mustn't let the macaroni go down the drain... It's not right to attribute to us these gifts that come from you.

TANTI BACI: The gangsters come from where? From Italy? Or from your ballot boxes?

RANDAL: But... Are you attacking the Democrats?

TANTI BACI: Especially when they are Republicans. Al Capone was what, officially?

RANDAL: Officially it will have to be rectified... First on your face...

Battle with cane blows. The beautiful revolutionary order falls apart. SARAH *intervenes.*

SARAH: There is the memory of Moishe Stern on the end of your canes. Don't mistreat it.

GALINA *thinks her mission has been accomplished.*

GALINA: I will keep you up to date on the evolution of events.

She goes off. No one pays attention.

RANDAL: There is nothing worse than a blind man.

ELIEZER: Yes, two blind men!

Intervention from the MECHANIC.

MECHANIC: Try to find another story than your comics. They don't stand up. Know that, for you, there is only one way out: throw yourselves from the moving train.

PIPEL 19 and 21: For the moment we are the ones occupying it.

The occupants of the boxcar take up their watch again.

EVERYONE: Late in the night of the fourth day.

TANTI BACI *roams alone on the convoy.*

TANTI BACI: Bitterness… To leave the bowl, for a gold fish, is to die. But isn't it the bowl that keeps him from seeing? What to do?

PIPEL 21: The rat is ill… He is shaken by jerks and twitches. He scratches… Can the Besht die?

Rotation.

EVERYONE: Fifth day.

LOUDSPEAKERS: Train 713. The tripartite commission communicates. Following unjustified sabotage, diversions, and work stoppages, the Dachau center for the distribution of provisions is being transferred to Vienna. Our representatives will discuss with yours the best way to face the situation.

RANDAL: They're cutting off our provisions.

SARAH: It was to be expected.

303

TANTI BACI: The revolution begins today.

MECHANIC: Unless it ends… The commission is allowing you to leave Dachau without losing face.

GALINA *appears with her white flag.*

TANTI BACI: You should have brought the black flag.

GALINA: Why?

RANDAL: It's the flag of famine.

ELIEZER: You didn't hear the loudspeakers?

GALINA: (Oh!) a manner of speaking.

SARAH: How's that, a manner of speaking?

GALINA *stops her.*

GALINA: I know. I have a face like a behind.

Return of the word Formality.

PIPEL 19: Yet another formality.

304

GALINA: Exactly. A formality allowing you to leave Dachau (I will be with you...). Whereas on the first day of discussion the commission set no conditions, now it does. In my opinion it can only get worse.

TANTI BACI: What are the conditions?

GALINA: First the pipel recognized to be a faker must put himself at the disposition of the Commission to undergo reeducation in the appropriate institution. Must also put himself at the disposition of the Commission the friend of the rebbi against whom an investigation is underway. Lastly, the fallen ex-American may leave with you.

RANDAL *tries to face up to it.*

RANDAL: I have no desire to take its director and the subsidies it has a right to from the bank on wheels.

GALINA: No mention has been made to either the subsidy requested or the self-management demanded.

TANTI BACI: We note that Randal stays with us, and we refuse the departure of the other two-subject to the discussions and deliberations we are going to have. The response will be given tomorrow.

GALINA *leaves. Rotation.*

EVERYONE: Sixth day.

MECHANIC: So? Are you evacuating the convoy?

PIPEL 19: We have nothing to say to you.

Very touched, ELIEZER *announces:*

ELIEZER: It is time to affirm that the twelve months that Noah spent in the arc have been removed from the calendar. There are only the pipel and I remaining… And, in a way we surrender.

PIPEL 19: The war (ours) is lost.

PIPEL 21: (The Besht won't stop dying of it).

306

PIPEL 19: In a way I give up too. But not like Eliezer. Anyway, what do we have in common? Train 713 ... It's no longer enough.

SARAH: The Formality, journey fragment spent across a synoptic tableau has devastated us (and put some in question). Sarah can not indefinitely play the survivor of the Jewish group. I am leaving with my own. I will belong, finally, to the possibility of the Book.

GALINA: No one will want you.

SARAH: For Sarah, from now on there will only be one journey, that of the Besht (Blessed Baal ChemTov) reading the Zohar. He covered thus creation from end to end.

GALINA: So, canes out. Let's go.

Goodbyes are said with the canes. ELIEZER *slows the departure down to say:*

ELIEZER: Do you know the journey of Rebbi Hananya, wrapped in sacred scrolls and burned alive?... The Romans had condemned him for teaching the Torah in public. During the torment, the disciples in the distance had tried to get some indication from him crying, "What do you see, master?" And he: "I see the parchment burning, but the letters float unharmed... They continue to express themselves..."

SARAH: So catches fire in the name of a camp the possibility of the Alphabet.

PIPEL 21, TANTI BACI *and* RANDAL *prolong the goodbyes by knocking with their canes. From the sound, they recognize that the blind are considerably diminished in number.*

RANDAL: We are no longer numerous.

Rotation.

PIPEL, TANTI BACI and RANDAL: Seventh day.

MECHANIC: The seven days that did not shake convoy 713 are over.

GALINA: Hands behind your heads. Line up in front of the convoy.

They put their hands behind their heads and line up in front of the train.

GALINA: You are going to get reinforcements. Pipel 19 is now definitively blind.

MECHANIC: The faker is not faking anymore. He put his eyes out.

PIPEL 21: How?

MECHANIC: With a nail... Horrible, his empty eyes (they ran all night...)

TANTI BACI: I think that he lost nothing. He was really blind. Like us. And he knew it better than anyone.

PIPEL 21: What he knew is of no importance. He wanted to stay pipel to the end.

LOUDSPEAKERS: Train 713. You are going to leave the Dachau camp to be directed in reduced convoy to Vienna. Before departure, you will receive the medical care required by your condition. A warm meal will be served.

MECHANIC: To get the train rolling again there are three versions left. The mechanical (me), the economic (our unuprootable banker), the political (Garibaldi, defeated yet again). They will suffice.

PIPEL 21: And the X children?

The MECHANIC *finally declares war* (*his war*).

MECHANIC: Graffitis! sprayed on the convoy at the moment of departure from Auschwitz! The journey has already begun erasing them. The pipel are lost to this train story... Before even beginning, they were unlikely. One can not exist solely to destablize. Useless, the lamentation of the pipel over the toys of Car 3, disappeared... I'm the one who destroyed. I'm the one who made disappear rather than endorsing your united illnesses.

GALINA *brings* PIPEL 19 *back.*

PIPEL 19: I need to be consoled by no one.

TANTI BACI: Thanks to you, a blind person's cane has become a reason for being.

PIPEL 19: There are too many rats in the correction house... The blind person's cane got scared.

PIPEL 21: To make its journey amongst the dead rats the Besht is going to need it.

PIPEL 19: It's not afraid any more.

TANTI BACI: Is the new commissar there?

GALINA: I'm here.

TANTI BACI: Why Vienna – and not the Brenner? There is more sun that way.

GALINA: If I answer because of the Danube, would you believe it?

TANTI BACI: It's Italy I need. To see there, me too. Like all of them.

MECHANIC: Departure for Vienna.

TANTI BACI: This train must stop one day. That will be the revolution of the blind... When it explodes...

ACT XIV

The train shudders off in the direction of
Mauthausen.
The MECHANIC'S *song.*

SONG OF THE IRON HORSE

The railway signs
multiply
the challenges of the milky way
suddenly
taken by clock time.
The steam horse alone
fraternizes
on one side and the other
of the lines of demarcation.
The other revolutions
lose
their words and pile up dying
on this convoy.
The versions of their march
contradict each other
destroy each other
their possibilities
disperse

but the train
remains.
Two rails suffice
to write the scripture
in iron
of a flamboyant circus
pushed by the wind
always inspired
which is born
of mechanical brains.

Stop.

LOUDSPEAKERS: Mauthausen… Special train arriving from Ostrawa. Parking beside the river, on the garage track.

The pipel run toward the river.

PIPEL 21: The Danube, do you hear it? It says Gypsy.

GALINA: How's that?

TANTI BACI: We pass from one camp name to another… One way of not disorienting us.

PIPEL 21: Pipel, I leave you my rat.

PIPEL 21 *gives his rat to* PIPEL 19*, then goes off toward the Danube.*

PIPEL 19: The Besht is dead!.. Pipel! Where are you?

PIPEL 21: With the greetings of the X child.

PIPEL 19: Pipel!

PIPEL 21 *jumps into the Danube.*

GALINA: He jumped in the river.

They all hurry behind GALINA *trying find with the cane where pipel jumped.*

PIPEL 19: I have to take his rat back to him.

He dives in turn.

GALINA: They are drowning. They are both drowning.

RANDAL *and* TANTI BACI *yell*:

315

RANDAL and TANTI BACI: Goodbye comrades!

MECHANIC: They found their way out in the Danube.

GALINA: What a cruel fate, that of the X children…

MECHANIC: It bears the mark of the camps.

RANDAL: The hour has come for unexpected summaries.

MECHANIC: All aboard for Vienna. Just between us, Vienna today is in your image. You will not be too disoriented.

TANTI BACI *puts on a face mask.*

GALINA: Are you taking care of your rheumatism?

TANTI BACI: No, I'm opening a new era.

RANDAL: That's what you always say when you put on a new hat… And I know hats. From the parasol-umbrella hat to the ear warmer… I worked for two years in the buffalo state as innkeeper among the cowboys.

316

The locomotive is rolling. MECHANIC, GALINA *and* RANDAL *advance.* TANTI BACI *stays where he is.*

GALINA: Why isn't he following?

MECHANIC: To impress me. I know his version of the convoy. It's the one where the locomotive is tried as a war criminal. The sentence is death.

GALINA: That's one sentence beat... Why, on this train, do they always manage to believe themselves to be on the side of the victors?

MECHANIC: They believe and that's enough... The Garibaldian thinks he can find in one of the quarries of Mauthausen the explosives that were left there before.

TANTI BACI: In the night the locomotive will enter into the world of the stars...

MECHANIC: Even on the convoys returned from chaos, the technical head knows that in spite of hell he will get out.

Explosion. Everyone on the ground. TANTI BACI
salutes with raised fist, and disappears.

RANDAL: There is no more bank… It exploded… The
train has joined the X children… in the Danube.

GALINA: Finished, Train 713. Nothing but pieces.

MECHANIC: It is not a question of knowing how many
pieces are left, it is a question of continuing.

The MECHANIC *tries to gather up the canes he can
still find and leaves again.*

GALINA: Continue with what?

MECHANIC: The locomotive is neither a commentary, nor a textual interpretation, but a song…
The song of space.

RANDAL: There is no more song.

MECHANIC: But there is space, the mechanical possibility continues.

GALINA: After all, the locomotive only exploded in the brigadist possibility.

MECHANIC: We don't need anyone to continue our version. It is enough for us. It is enough for the world. Who can stop it?

He has gone off. One no longer hears anything but the rhythm of the locomotive that he hammers out with his feet.

GALINA: It's true, who can stop progress?

With only the rhythm of the feet, she leaves in the same direction as the MECHANIC. RANDAL *remains alone on the banks of the Danube searching.*

RANDAL: We are characters dreamed by the fake toys of the Christmas tree at Auschwitz... Why did we steal those toys?

*PUBLIC SONG BEFORE
TWO ELECTRIC CHAIRS*

The electric chairs are those in which Nicola Sacco and Bartholomeo Vanzetti died in 1927, in the prison at Charlestown (Massachusetts). Two Italian immigrants, like Auguste Gatti, (the author's father). Two anarchists, once again like Auguste. Upon hearing news of their death, Auguste tied a black scarf around his not yet four year old son's neck. This son was called Dante (he only became Armand later on), Dante like the son of Nicola Sacco. Like this other boy whose father a few days before being electrocuted, wrote: "Dante, my son, my comrade... remember always that you must help those who are suffering and who are calling for help... These are your brothers, those who fight and fall, like your father..." It could have been a letter from Auguste to his son.

Gatti explains all of this during production for the world premier of the play at the TNP (National Popular Theater) in Paris, in 1966. He also explains that the corridors of death, where for seven years the two immigrants waited for their ultimate verdict, are not unknown to him. He too was sentenced to die at seventeen and he understands the weight of this waiting. He also explains the writing of this play, his refusal of any historical reconstitution, his writing in Selmaires.

The Selmaires are extensions and generalizations of structures used in earlier plays to interrogate concepts and representations of reality. Reality only exists as told by this or that character. It only exists in the confrontations arising from various inventions paralleling reality. The question is not how Sacco and Vanzetti died. (Were they guilty? Victims? Who gained by seeing them dead?) "What is important is knowing if Sacco and Vanzetti will once again die tonight."

"Our agony is our triumph," said Sacco and Vanzetti. Writing in Selmaires is the only way to take this statement seriously – to give this agony the possibility of its triumph... in the present of every show.

CHARACTERS

BOSTON:
    BOYD, manufacturer
    EVA, his wife
    GRANT JR., his attorney
    KATZ, businessman
    FARLEY, New York intellectual
    ANNE, his wife
    LAUREEN, usher
    KURLANSKI, extra

LYON:
    DERLINSKI, theater manager
    BONNETADE, assistant stage manager
    VASTADOUR, engraver
    THAYER, actor
    FULLER, actor
    STEWART, actor

HAMBURG:
    ERHMAN KLOSE, law professor
    KASSEL, clergyman
    MULLER, attorney
    VORORTZUG, father of Muller's client

TURIN:
   CERVI, factory worker at Fiat
   PINO, his son
   LETIZIA, his friend
   BOSCHETTO, journalist
   COLEONE, union organizer
   VENTURELLI, anarchist

NEW ORLEANS:
   MANN, political in-fighter
   LITTLE NED, Jack-of-all-trades
   XIOMARA, Mexican immigrant
   CLERK, at the coat-check

CHARACTER-OBJECTS (giant pictures / puppets)
   COOLIDGE, President of the United States
   PRESS AGENT, professional false witness
   OFFICIAL OF DEATH, professional false witness
   FBI AGENT
   UNKNOWN SOLDIER

Setting: *The play takes place in five theaters
in five cities in Europe and the United States.
There is only one stage so that the five audiences
from their different vantage points
are watching the exact same play.*

MEASURE FOR NOTHING

*In the supposed theater, while awaiting
the spectators, the Character-Objects sing
a complaint.*

COMPLAINT OF THE TWO IMMIGRANTS

In the little mortuary parlor
of North End in Boston
two little immigrants
lying disgraced in their
tight Sunday suits,
awaited rigidly
the end of the assassination
of man, and the stars
in which he lives, one hundred times
each hour of his life.

One was a fish merchant
and the other was a cobbler
The cops from the INS
named them Sacco & Vanzetti
and on their pay sheets
they were worth $6.50 a day.

They went off without a Hobo stick
into a grenade's breech
where their ashes could not be
disentangled. They went
looking for work
on other stars, sisters
of those electrocuted
on a night of bludgeons, inside the
world of the prison at Charlestown in
the State of Massachusetts.

The walls and the stage close.

I

BASS AND TREBLE CLEFS
AS PARTISAN SPECTATORS

BOSTON

Stage right. In front of the ticket window of the theater: BOYD, GRANT JR., KATZ *and* EVA *wait to be assigned their seats.* BOYD, *tickets in hand, is restless, looks around for the absent cashier. Meanwhile,* EVA, *his wife, is talking with her husband's guests.*

EVA. Have you heard of this?

GRANT JR. What?

EVA. This case, (Sacco and Vanzetti).

GRANT JR. *vainly* Criminal cases were never my area.

KATZ. It had an enormous impact at the time.

EVA. More than the starlet you talked about at dinner?

KATZ. (Oh!) The one who hung herself with only her g-string from the W of the Hollywood sign?

EVA. It's amazing how well you know the history of our country Mr. Katz.

KATZ. Here, it's only two anarchists who killed the cashiers at Slater and Morill.

BOYD. (Where is the manager of this theater?)

KATZ. That is right isn't it (Mr. Boyd)?

BOYD. I don't know. Some nights killing a cashier is a moral gesture.

KATZ *smiles vaguely to show he understands* BOYD'S *impatience. The latter momentarily exits to look for the manager.* KATZ *continues talking to* EVA.

KATZ. A simple case (unfortunately politics got involved).

EVA. And it happened in Massachusetts?

KATZ. Right here in Boston.

GRANT JR. I even think it happened in the South Braintree district, (if you care to know more).

BOYD *returns triumphant, but not yet calmed.*

BOYD. He's coming, (he's coming). I wonder why whenever it's this type of show they begin by mistreating the audience.

EVA. What are we doing here (my dear)?

BOYD. I wonder.

GRANT JR. I was asking myself the same question.

BOYD. (But?) It was you, my dear, who dragged me to these parts (as soon as we finished dinner). You and our friend Katz.

KATZ *bows.*

KATZ. (I'm confused.) Madame Boyd said (that she loved police thrillers...) I must have misunderstood.

BOYD. Police thrillers – that's not what's lacking these days. Ah! There he is.

Darkness stage right, lights in supposed hall where
LAUREEN, *the usher is talking to* JIM KURLANSKI.
The room is empty.

KURLANSKI. Is this the first time you've ushered?

LAUREEN. Yes – it costs a lot (I paid the old usher to let me work). I am from Wisconsin.

KURLANSKI. Well then, watch out.

LAUREEN. For what?

KURLANSKI. For everyone. – What happens in a theater once the lights go off (is incredible). It's enough to make the American Federation of Labor blush. If you want to hold on to the illusion that the real show is happening on the stage, close your eyes once the curtains go up.

LAUREEN. Are you with the theater?

KURLANSKI. No, (I'm a sailor).

LAUREEN. What are you doing here?

KURLANSKI. (I'm a witness.) For a seasonal worker like me, it's the best kind of work. – I know professional witnesses who earn up to twenty thousand dollars a year. They can testify in any trial.

LAUREEN. Are you making fun of me?

KURLANSKI. Relax, I'm one of the witnesses in the play. – True or false, they're not much more than extras.

LAUREEN. I don't really understand.

KURLANSKI. If you want to know everything, meet me after the show, at the Astoria club. (You'll come.)

LAUREEN. We'll see.

KURLANSKI. I'll be waiting.

Stage left. In front of the theater box office, the attorney MULLER *talks with his client* VORORTZUG, *whose son in prison.*

VORORTZUG. This story about Italian anarchists sentenced and then waiting seven years to be put to death terrorizes me.

MULLER. There's still time to go to the music hall. – You insisted so strongly on coming here, that I would have felt uncomfortable suggesting something else.

VORORTZUG. Excuse me, Counselor, (I don't really know what I want anymore). Since my son's arrest, I can't think of anything but the trial.

MULLER. You shouldn't give a trial more importance than it has. I was prosecuted twice in twenty years (when Rathenau died and during the denazification trials). – Did I give up being an attorney? (If it weren't for fear that you would unreasonably multiply the hopes in what I'm about to tell you), I can assure you that the case is presenting itself rather well.

VORORTZUG. That's the lawyer's point of view. – For a father it's a little different.

NEW ORLEANS

At the coat check reserved for people of color, MANN, *who is black, is upset with the clerk who has disappeared in the back.*

MANN. You're just a negro (don't you forget it).

CLERK. But, where do you want me to hang your umbrella?

MANN. I'm paying – so, I want it well placed.

CLERK. I can't hang it in Heaven.

MANN. Hm! (I hadn't thought of that).

LYON

Theater entrance. DERLINSKI, *the administrator, is pacing back and forth, nervously looking at his watch. The bells announcing the beginning of the show can be heard. The actors playing the roles of* JUDGE THAYER *and* GOVERNOR FULLER *enter quickly.*

DERLINSKI. What's going on? – I just called your houses.

THAYER. We're not late.

FULLER. You're never late – to play a mean governor.

DERLINSKI. Did you bring the President of the United States?

THAYER. The inspector is bringing it.

DERLINSKI. Who?

FULLER. Bock, you know, the person playing inspector Stewart.

DERLINSKI. Where is he? (FULLER *raises his hands to show he doesn't know.* DERLINSKI *yells.*) But it's about to start. (FULLER *and* THAYER *go off towards their dressing rooms.*)

HAMBURG

At the coat-check. MULLER *takes off his coat and continues to give his argument to* VORORTZUG.

MULLER. Compare to our youth. – At sixteen, I was in the Balkans continuing the battle of this German army that the bourgeois world thought it had eliminated.

VORORTZUG. At that time, I was twice your age.

MULLER. You were even (part of the red sailors of Hamburg).

VORORTZUG. We fought (one against the other).

MULLER. But didn't we have in common a rifle with which we thought we could topple everything? – When the Great German Front regrouped across Europe you were at my side.

VORORTZUG. (Under orders.)

MULLER. Together we lost the great battle. (The bourgeoisie was stronger.) And that's what it does to our sons. – It puts them in prison. In what way can you feel responsible? The drama of a young German isn't the struggle against thousand year old divinities – it's in the impossibility of being American. – That's very different from what we were. – Do you want me to tell you something? The fact that you brought me to this show proves to me that (at heart) you refuse the world order of the winners.

VORORTZUG. I'm not sure I follow.

MULLER. What is this Sacco and Vanzetti thing? False accusations thrown out to obtain the deaths of people who want to change the world. – It was a pre-taste of the Nuremberg trials. (A dress rehearsal of sorts, amongst so many others.)

The actor playing the role of inspector STEWART
rushes out stage right in front of DERLINSKI, *just as
nervous. He's carrying on his back an enormous
puppet supposedly representing* PRESIDENT
COOLIDGE.

DERLINSKI. That's the president? – It's enormous.

STEWART. The United States is big. – Michel isn't
coming tonight. An accident, he can't move.

DERLINSKI. An actor can't come – and you tell me
now.

STEWART. I didn't set the time of the accident.

DERLINSKI *holds his head in his hands.* STEWART
drags the puppet backstage.

BOSTON

BOYD, his wife and friends wait inside the supposed theater to be seated.

GRANT JR. Now (of course) there's no usher.

LAUREEN. *Running to them.* Oh, excuse me.

BOYD. I've been in the automobile industry for eighteen years. – Let me tell you, if I treated my clients the way this theater treats theirs, I'd have been in the hands of a psychiatrist long ago.

TURIN

Stage right. The journalist BOSCHETTO, the union leader COLEONE and the anarchist VENTURELLI are having their tickets checked. Their discussion is very animated.

BOSCHETTO. You no longer represent anything but the last remnants (a pathetic party), anarchism died with the Spanish civil war.

VENTURELLI. Don't worry, the very existence of people like you guarantees that it will live on. – Do you know the case of the people who were hanged in Chicago? The event that created May 1st? Throughout the world (in spite of your death certificates) this holiday is celebrated. – Even if people like you pretend not to know what it's about – have we for even a single day ceased to testify (in our way of living or thinking), for or against the anarchists of Chicago and the ideas for which they were hanged?

COLEONE. You might just as well (if you want to go looking in Chicago) testify for or against Al Capone. – That doesn't mean he represents a party.

VENTURELLI. He represents more. – If you mention Al Capone, you mention the founder of a whole continent's union (somewhere midway between a gang and a club). Even you, Coleone (as a specialist in crossing fences), if you don't still bring flowers to his effigy, it's out of pure respect for bourgeois conventions.

BOSCHETTO. Anarchist traditions would have us blow up bombs which, no matter how loud, serve no purpose.

COLEONE. (Our friend) Venturelli's bombs are purely verbal.

BOSCHETTO. What worries me is (his desire for purity), unlike (it seems to me) the actions of certain saints of libertarian martyrdom fighting for freedom.

VENTURELLI. What a pitiful journalist like you will never be able to understand is that in politics, the murderers are not those who dirty their hands – but on the contrary the ones who are constantly making sure they are clean.

NEW ORLEANS

Stage left. While checking her coat at the coat-check, XIOMARA, *a mestiza Indian suddenly feels "white" among all the blacks. She oscillates, like a pendulum clock, from her particularism to her friend,* LITTLE NED, *who is black. The oscillations are disorderly.*

CLERK. Both together?

LITTLE NED. Yes.

XIOMARA. No.

LITTLE NED. (Hey hard head!) You're not going to make trouble.

XIOMARA. I don't like it when people decide for me.

CLERK. Well, what'll it be?

LITTLE NED. (*vexed*) Both together.

Stage right. PAOLO CERVI *waits with his son at the ticket booth.*

CERVI. You're still young. There might be things you don't understand. I'll explain later. Sacco and Vanzetti, that's a case that's always been dear to my heart. – I wanted you to know about it. (LETIZIA *arrives.*) Letizia! – I was beginning to worry.

LETIZIA. I just got your message as I was leaving the store. – You're worse than a husband (you dispose of people's time without the slightest hesitation). Fortunately I always agree with you.

CERVI. Always – that's saying a lot.

LETIZIA. How's work?

CERVI. Eight hours a day, putting together the same parts. – I can work without really being there. (It gives me time to think of you.)

LETIZIA. And your daughter?

CERVI. Ines – she's sleeping. (She's much too young.)

PINO. She wouldn't understand.

LYON

VASTADOUR, *who has a subscription to the theater through his company's committee, talks with* BONNETADE, *factotum of the theater, who for the moment is at the coat check. Their discussion contains a sort of friendly aggression masking much shyness on both sides.*

BONNETADE. A specialized worker and single – at least you Mr. Vastadour, have no worries.

VASTADOUR. What do you know about it?

BONNETADE. Just look at you.

VASTADOUR. What do you see? A man so beaten down – he goes to see creators of illusions to give himself a memory.

BONNETADE. That's what I was saying – you succeeded in life – by your own standards.

VASTADOUR. By my own standards? (They may not be that big) but they're not on your horizons.

TURIN

From the ticket booth. CERVI, LETIZIA *and* PINO *cross the stage to reach the coat check.*

LETIZIA. You have a good job at Fiat (the kids will grow up).

CERVI. They need a mother, these kids.

LETIZIA. One must know how to wait (Paolo).

CERVI. But I spend my life waiting. – At Pino's age, I was waiting to grow up so that I could get out of the rice field. When I grew up, there were no more rice fields but there was the war. So I waited in Africa (then in an English prison camp) for it to finish. The war over, my wife was sick. – So I waited for her to get better (she died). Now…

LETIZIA. You're too single-minded to be happy with what life gives you. Even when the divorce from

my husband is official (even when I'm with you)
you'll continue to wait.

NEW ORLEANS

In the supposed audience, two sets of seats are lit,
MANN'S, *and* LITTLE NED *and* XIOMARA'S.

XIOMARA. Isn't there a program? How can that be?

LITTLE NED. There must be one.

XIOMARA. Where?

LITTLE NED. I don't know, but there must be one. –
Wait a second. (*He goes over to* MANN, *who is
fanning himself with a program.*) Brother, could I
borrow your program for a minute?

MANN. Me, your brother? What's that? Have you
looked at yourself?

LITTLE NED. (It's for the little Mexican girl over there.)

MANN. If the Mexican girl wants my program, let

her come and ask me for it. – I don't need a
middle-man.

LITTLE NED *returns, downtrodden, to* XIOMARA.

XIOMARA. I hate embarrassing situations. This is the
last time I'm going out with you.

HAMBURG

ERHMAN KLOSE, *law professor, and a clergyman,*
FATHER KASSEL, *are at the ticket booth.*

KASSEL. It would be interesting to know what type
of crowd is here tonight.

ERHMAN KLOSE. Probably, full strength, everyone
appearing on stage. – We'll see by the way they
react.

KASSEL. People are never free at a show (they come
to put to death).

ERHMAN KLOSE. I don't think that's true for me.
(Yourself?)

348

KASSEL. Mr. Professor (you're still young). While you were (thank God) studying in the United States, I lived through Germany's Great Passion. In the parades, through the debacles, under the inflammatory rhetoric, I could always recognize in each man, a spectator of the march to the Cross. Whatever their backgrounds, their languages, their purpose, they could only express one desire: "Crucify! Crucify him!" without even knowing to whom they were speaking.

LYON

DERLINSKI *goes over to* BONNETADE.

DERLINSKI. Do you know about the catastrophe? – Michel had an accident. Do you know his role?

BONNETADE. No!

DERLINSKI. Not even a little? You were at the rehearsals.
BONNETADE. That's not enough.

DERLINSKI. In that case you'll read the script on stage.

BONNETADE. Never!

DERLINSKI. We don't have a choice. – Come on Bonnetade, you're not just anyone. You're an accomplished actor.

BONNETADE. That's enough. – I'll go.

DERLINSKI. Anyway you'll begin acting in the audience (it'll be easier).

HAMBURG

In the supposed audience, two sets of seats are lit, MULLER *and* VORORTZUG'S *and* KASSEL'S *and* ERHMAN KLOSE.

KASSEL. The two (sure) victims of this whole affair seem to me to be the two unfortunate cashiers who were shot down in South Braintree. – But no one cares about them. They are (how should I say) acquired victims. It would be better (according to your reasoning) to be more interested in the twisted ones, supposing (of course) they have a right to be considered victims.

ERHMAN KLOSE. Perhaps if you put yourself in the mindset of the White Terror, as it periodically recurs in the United States, in any event as it existed in 1921, you'd understand my point of view. – Supposing, of course, it has a right to be my point of view.

BOSTON

Stage right, FARLEY *and* ANNE *read the poster about the show.*

FARLEY. It's the same story as the execution of Julius and Ethel Rosenberg. – Shall we go?

ANNE. The train for New York doesn't leave until one in the morning. – We have more than enough time.

II

SOUNDTRACK AS CREDITS

An announcement is being made that the show is starting. When the house lights turn off in the supposed theater, three gun shots are heard. From imaginary stage the actors, THAYER *and* STEWART, *erupt into the supposed audience.*

LYON

THAYER. It's the South Braintree crime all over again.

STEWART. There's a second one (Bridgewater).

THAYER. We'll take care of that one later. – Solve South Braintree first.

STEWART. Your ID?

BOSTON

BOYD. That's too much? (*All the spectators of the Boston group look for their IDs.*) Here it is. –

Spencer Boyd, industrialist, 112 Lincoln Road, Boston.

EVA. Eva Boyd. – I'm his wife.

Meanwhile, LAUREEN *seats* FARLEY *and* ANNE *who just entered.*

ANNE. Excuse us, we're late.

LAUREEN. You'll catch up.

LYON

STEWART. Your ID?

BOSTON

FARLEY. Who? – Us?

ANNE. Anne Joyce – 145 First Ave., New York, passing through Boston.

HAMBURG

ERHMAN KLOSE. Doctor Erhman Klose – professor of law in Hamburg.

LYON

STEWART. Your ID?

VASTADOUR. For the moment – I have nothing that would interest you.

STEWART. Your ID?

VASTADOUR. What's it to you?

THAYER. (Refusal to co-operate) a sure suspect. You've got one, Stewart.

VASTADOUR. Pardon me, I'm always very slow to understand. – My name is Vastadour – Roger Vastadour, engraver, 12 Great Hill Dr., Lyon.

TURIN

CERVI. Me, I'm Paolo Cervi, widower, father of two children –assembly worker at Fiat, Turin.

LYON

STEWART. Just looking at you, I'm sure your legal status is murky.

NEW ORLEANS

XIOMARA. My name is Xiomara Reyes, Xiomara Reyes... uh, uh, I...

She repeats it twice then stutters. LITTLE NED *tries to protect her.*

LITTLE NED. She's a little "Wetback". – Why do you want to come and scare her? Get the hell out of here if you don't want the place broken up.

MANN. I hear buzzing in my ear.

LITTLE NED. That's a sign that you're still alive – that could change at any moment.

He approaches him menacingly. The tone rises.
Everyone begins speaking at the same time.
XIOMARA *begins to scream and cry, close to a*
nervous breakdown. The confusion is at its height.

LYON

DERLINSKI *enters the room and addresses the*
spectators.

DERLINSKI. Sit down and quiet down. Everything that happened – was planned (well almost). We wanted to give you a feel for the overall atmosphere in Massachusetts in 1920–1921.

VASTADOUR. In Massachusetts?

BOSTON

Coming from the imaginary stage, Massachusetts
Song *begins to resound. All the spectators from
Boston stand to sing. Each stanza is sung by a
different city. Whatever the city from which we view
the* SACCO-VANZETTI *affair, we inevitably return to
Massachusetts.*

THE MASSACHUSSETS SONG

Massachusetts does not exist
the United States Constitution
made it a State to pay for
rights to the imaginary.

Massachusetts does not exist
on the forty-eight state flag
it was assigned a star
but it is a sick star.

It is a sick star
where Lizzie Borden, the one who killed
father and mother, sings German songs
advertising tranquilizers.

The women of Boston live
they say, with well furnished souls,
they believe in Jesus-Christ
Longfellow and the Happy Ending.

All three dead in action
on the palisades of South Braintree.

LYON

THAYER. Gentlemen – we are once again on the eve
of the battle of Gettysburg. But this time (against
foreign enemies) the rifles of Lee and Grant will
be shooting in fraternal unity.

FULLER. Millions of petitions and telegrams have
swamped my desk this week. May God forgive
me, for the first time in my life (I wished for a
strike), a postman strike. It is April 11th, 1927. (This
case will have dragged on for seven years.)

STEWART. In a few hours, it will be a pardon or death,
according to what your conscience dictates Mr.
Governor.

FULLER. Misfortune has it that conscience often speaks in contradictory languages. *He exits.*

TURIN

VENTURELLI. What's important to know is whether Nicola Sacco and Bartholomeo Vanzetti will be, once again, executed in this room (tonight).

While other spectators are thinking (out loud), two giant portraits of SACCO *and* VANZETTI *are lowered from the flies.*

LETIZIA. (My God! Imagine Rosine Sacco's distress, surrounded by characters who all wear her husband's death on their faces.)

HAMBURG

A single vertical projector on ERHMAN KLOSE.

ERHMAN KLOSE. (It's hard to imagine the details, which at times like this must take on terrifying proportions.)

BOSTON

A single vertical projector on KATZ.

KATZ. Madame, according to the law I must announce to you that tonight, at midnight, Nicola Sacco (will be electrocuted). Tomorrow you can take delivery of his body.

NEW ORLEANS

A single vertical projector on MANN.

MANN. (The execution clothes are very good electrical conductors. They've already been tested. Furthermore every precaution is taken to avoid electrical outages.)

TURIN

A single vertical projector on PINO.

PINO. (Ines stayed home. She's too little to understand.)

The projector on PINO *turns off, the one on* BOSCHETTO *turns on.*

BOSCHETTO. (Once the lights dim, once they've dimmed three times, once three times the electric power of the entire prison has been channeled to that chair right there, everything will be over.)

The lights dims imperceptibly to complete darkness, then shine abruptly on the two portraits and on FULLER, *standing facing them, down stage.*

LYON

FULLER. I've delayed your execution to hear your version of the murder. – I'm listening. First, don't look at me. – Don't look at me that way! (They must not be normal.) Hatred (they're breathing hatred). Don't look at me like that: I've come to hear your version of the murder. – Speak! Speak will you! I am Governor Fuller, and I've come to delay your being put to death (you must realize that I will not do this everyday). – Speak, I am listening. (*He walks back and forth, then not getting any response he painfully turns towards the imaginary stage.*) Alvan T. Fuller, that is – a bicycle salesman to start out, (but currently about to be accepted by the High Society of Boston Brahmins), an income of seventy million dollars – the culture of a businessman bothered by stomach pains (however, put back in balance by daily absorption of bismuth and eating lightly buttered slices of bread). Plus – the responsibility for the destiny of Massachusetts (undermined, it is true, by fears of congestion). All this crossed the doors of this oozing, disgusting, filthy prison to try and save them – and this is the welcome! (*He turns again to the portraits.*) Do you know what you've done to me (a sensitive man)? – You've opened me up to the voracity of petitions, telegrams, cartoons, that arrive in the tens of thousands every day. I fled (to Paris). Seventy-two death threats in five days, I had to leave again right away. – I thought this prison might be the only place I could find respite. Wrong! (Here too, I see only hatred.)

NEW ORLEANS

MANN. I'll pay for both burials, if that will save you a case of depression and sleeping pills. I can afford it. As an infighter I'm ranked number one by the Republican Party (and not just in New Orleans), even the bailiff Magrath told me the other day, "You're no negro like the others. Oh! That no! You, when you lie, it serves the country!"

LYON

STEWART. Isn't it a point of national humiliation, to give even the slightest importance to foreign protests?

THAYER. Or even to certain segments of (our own) population.

FULLER. In that case, may our national dignity decide. – Mrs. Stratton, you who head the Institute of Technology.

NEW ORLEANS

A single vertical projector on XIOMARA.

XIOMARA. (Let's end this evening as quickly as possible.)

LYON

FULLER. You, sir, the dean of federal judges, you have your word on the matter.

BOSTON

A single vertical projector on GRANT JR.

GRANT JR. (Why do people insist on coming back to a case that was settled long ago?)

LYON

FULLER. And you, Mr. Chancellor of Harvard University?

BOSTON

A single vertical projector on BOYD.

BOYD. (In the chaos we're living right now, a man with even any clarity cannot think any more.)

FULLER. Could we not (by some decree) authorize you three eminent people to fill out the official paperwork – in my place – refusing the pardons, as is your wish.

THAYER. We'll waste another year.

FULLER. One year? – With this congestion lurking at every moment.

He falls to the ground. While he's being lifted and carried off stage, BONNETADE *comes onstage replacing the sick actor, and informs the audience of the supposed theater.*

BONNETADE. It happened the night
   of April 11th 1927.
   The entire world cried
   to Boston's governor for mercy.
   Laughter Week opened
   in the state of Massachusetts.

III

VERSES FROM LAUGHTER WEEK
IN MASSACHUSETTS

KURLANSKI, *who is sitting in the real audience, stands and approaches the supposed audience.*

KURLANSKI. I ask you respectfully to take into consideration the fact that I saw with my very own eyes – and I can swear by it – the proof of innocence…

LYON

THAYER *makes an evasive hand gesture to indicate to* KURLANSKI *that now is not the right time.*

THAYER. Laughter Week just began – laughter is a sign of health, which doesn't lie. (*He repeats his gesture, without success.*) Secretaries of State, Representatives and Senators have (unanimously) decreed laughing this week mouth wide open.

KURLANSKI. In that case, allow me to respectfully – yet shaken by a satisfied laugh – inform you that the House of Soft Fabrics, for which I am the retailer in Salem, offers you Rudolph Valentino's smile under a mustache made of authentic camel hair.

LYON

DERLINSKI. Stop! – Excuse this short interruption. But we will ask you at this time, how each of you imagines the rest of the play. – You sir!

VASTADOUR. Me? – I would focus on Sacco and Vanzetti, what were they like, their words, their gestures, their way of life. – In a nutshell, I'd like to meet them.

NEW ORLEANS

MANN, *a microphone in hand.*

MANN. Like my captain (Captain Gustavson) used to say in Okinawa, just before dying from his wounds: You have to be careful. – There's something not straight in all this. You think the past is the past. You are children then! Words run a lot further than you think. – It's like in heaven,

367

the gold digger says for laughs that there's a nugget in hell. Next thing you know, heaven is empty. – So the gold digger says to himself that this joke might actually contain some truth, so he too rushes to hell. Since you're asking me, I'll tell you. – Hell is not made for Mann, and if your show continues like this, in fifteen minutes I'm gone.

TURIN

VENTURELLI, *a microphone in hand, answers in turn.*

VENTURELLI. Myself, before getting to these two men, whom the journalist Boschetto was trying to dirty earlier…

BOSCHETTO. (Hey! That's not what I was trying to say.)

VENTURELLI. I would like for us to immerse them further in the context of the time, to get a feel for the general mood they were up against. My parents were immigrants. Before being deported for anti-constitutional activities, I lived my first

years in America. While you were talking about Laughter Week, a song came back to me.
Laughing at half price
is to laugh twice as much.
The Kiss Me house
offers during
Laughter Week
artificial and false
teeth at half price.

It is paramount because it gives the mood. Advertisement is the adult's baby bottle. Without it, he's cut off from existence (and wastes away). And on the same subject, you haven't yet mentioned the important role played by the American Legion.

BOSTON

ANNE, *with a microphone, speaks.*

ANNE. We all know the Rosenberg case here. Since these two cases have a lot in common, I'd be curious to know how they helped create one another.

SELMAIRE 1:
VASTADOUR'S SELMAIRE

VASTADOUR *continues with his idea, and leads the show in the way he desires it. All lights turn off. Stage left,* VANZETTI'S *head is projected. In front, his body in silhouette.* VASTADOUR *speaks.*

VASTADOUR. I always believed New York was a city like they show it on television, or in airline advertisement (that is no longer true tonight). New York is Lyon. There are details that sweep away such images. Lyon didn't have any lights, when I arrived searching for work. New York did not have any for Vanzetti. – The closet where we washed the dishes didn't have windows. We struggled, all day long, in steam. At night (in the cellar where the employees slept), it dripped drop by drop from the ceiling, and fell on us with the cockroaches. For him (it was New York). For me (Lyon). Has there been any separation since? He with his fish stand and his judges (me with my punch card box and my subscription to the theater). Here we are united under the same load – the weight of a single city (a humiliated world).

LYON

THAYER *pounds his gavel on the judge's podium. Despite the identifications and daydreams of the spectators, the show continues.*

THAYER. This is how we raise Cain from the dead so he can kill Abel once again. This Massachusetts we've inherited from our forefathers can it become a slave camp and one of forced labor? Are our children to be assassinated, like those of Russia's imperial family? It is our civic duty to hate those who sully our country and want to burn and bloody our history.

SELMAIRE 2:
VENTURELLI'S SELMAIRE

On his side VENTURELLI *invents the show as he sees it.*

VENTURELLI. The veterans understand it perfectly. – The American Legion itself wants to kick off Laughter Week by placing a wreath on the tomb of the unknown soldier.

Meanwhile a soldier in agony on a cross lit up in neon descends from the flies. It shines for a few moments giving way to shiny letters: "Given by American Funeral C & C." The lit letters disappear to give way to others: "Embalming is a National duty." The letters turn off, and the soldier re-appears, and so on. THAYER *as he's imagined by* VENTURELLI *stands at attention.*

THAYER. And now we shall observe a minute of silence.

SELMAIRE 3:
ANNE'S SELMAIRE

Everything turns off. A vertical light isolates ANNE *from the others. She attempts to introduce herself into the show through Ethel Rosenberg. Simultaneously a poster in ink is projected which reads: "Comrade workers, you fought in every war. Where are your victories?* BARTOLOMEO VANZETTI *will speak on this."*

ANNE. The search for our victories replaced vacations on the Lower East Side. Especially in summer (when it was too hot to go to bed early).

Ethel Rosenberg sat (between her father's legs) on the stoop and listened to him. It seemed to her that she was in that Europe she had never known, and it filled her August nights. He would say.

FARLEY. Poland, in some ways is like here, with the difference that here we're free (well, what a Jew might demand from the word freedom, not much of course, but enough to escape the pogroms and the daily humiliations). You're lucky, Ethel, to be American. It's luck that your ancestors did not have.

ANNE. (It seemed to her that here everything breathed youth, the youth of the world.)

HAMBURG

KASSEL. (The youth of the world is often brutal.)

LYON

THAYER. To be young is to believe. Everyone believes, except for the extremists (they are not men).

373

BOYD. (Sometimes they don't even believe in advertisement.)

LYON

FULLER. The President of the United States said: "Everyone believes." To this end he had prepared himself, right here in Massachusetts (where he had been my predecessor) by breaking the famous Boston police strike. – This immediately propelled him to the presidency of the USA.

SELMAIRE 4:
VENTURELLI'S SELMAIRE

After being caught up in the show, VENTURELLI *returns to his unknown soldier, which lights up again.*

VENTURELLI. Today he is with us, for the inauguration of the monument to the unknown soldier.

An enormous puppet is introduced of which we see only the shoes of the period, striped pants on a large belly, the rest is lost in the flies.

COOLIDGE. I, President Coolidge, am telling you: – Advertisement created the world. Thousands of people believe that the Earth is round because they have seen at some time in their lives (either in the shape of a pencil sharpener or a lamp) a globe. American Funeral (created by my wife during the only police strike the world has ever known, and which I had the honor of squashing) by offering us this monument allows us to enter light heartedly into Laughter Week. – Our boys are dead, but they are not forgotten.

VENTURELLI. And here an interview never given before – the unknown soldier's. (*He approaches, a microphone in hand the* UNKNOWN SOLDIER *in neon, agonizing on his cross and begins to ask him questions. The neon turns on while the* UNKNOWN SOLDIER *speaks and punctuates his sentences. While* VENTURELLI *speaks, it shuts off.*) Who are you?

UNKNOWN SOLDIER. Maines, – John Maines.

VENTURELLI. Fabulous. – Which corps were you in?

UNKNOWN SOLDIER. I was in the Marines.

VENTURELLI. How many years of service?

UNKNOWN SOLDIER. Twenty years.

VENTURELLI. What were your operations?

UNKNOWN SOLDIER. Mexico, Haiti and Cuba.

VENTURELLI. What did you do there?

UNKNOWN SOLDIER. I made sure that National City Bank held decent positions.

VENTURELLI. Do you believe in National City Bank?

UNKNOWN SOLDIER. I believe in it. (In their own way the Mexicans and the Cubans believe in it too.) I then purified Nicaragua for the Interest Banking House and the Dominican Republic for General Electric.

VENTURELLI. Do you believe in Interest Banking House?

UNKNOWN SOLDIER. I do believe in it.

VENTURELLI. Do you believe in General Electric?

UNKNOWN SOLDIER. No!

VENTURELLI. Why not?

UNKNOWN SOLDIER. It went bankrupt! – I then put Honduras back on the right track of the United Fruit Company, and then I kept Standard Oil in China...

VENTURELLI. Why did you do it?

UNKNOWN SOLDIER. Because of the eleventh commandment. – Good for business, good for the country.

VENTURELLI. What are your future plans?

UNKNOWN SOLDIER. (In the situation in which I find myself) none.

LITTLE NED *laughs uncontrolably.*

XIOMARA. (Little Ned! Little Ned, stop!) (LITTLE NED *continues laughing.*) Everyone's going to notice us.

LITTLE NED. (Excuse-me.) A black man who does not laugh during Laughter Week becomes so suspect that he's got to force himself to laugh conspicuously.

VENTURELLI. This inauguration was organized by American Funerals, Katzmann toothpaste...

KATZ. The – only – toothpaste – that – gives – a – brightness – to – your – teeth – that – will – allow – you – to – laugh – at – any – time – and – any – place.

VENTURELLI. Sabil raincoat...

MANN. The – Sabil – raincoat – against – the – wind – and – the – rain – allows – you – to – laugh – on – the – inside.

VENTURELLI. The tanks from the Ulrick Factory...

GRANT JR. Ulrick funeral cars also sponsor Laughter Week by offering regardless of race or religion a complete funeral service at prices defying all competition.

VENTURELLI. The Company of Hard and Soft Canned Food and Redeemer's Digestive Salts.

COOLIDGE. Make your purchases in the stores that support the unknown soldier.

The president begins as best he can a clumsy dance with the UNKNOWN SOLDIER.

THAYER. So goes Laughter Week in Massachusetts.

Everyone rises to sing The Spectators' and the Parallels' Tin Roof Blues, *which unites everyone.*

TIN ROOF BLUES BY THE SPECTATORS
AND THE PARALLELS

So dances the world.
In Germany workers
march on the Reichstag.
In Argentina, General

Pershing learns the Tango.
In Nicaragua, a second wave
of Marines disembarked,
to name president for life,
a latrine inspector.
In spite of hot muffins, fresh
eggs on top, and
Virginia ham, with which
they surrounded his glory,
the engineer Taylor died
at the very time he usually
wound his watch.
(He had forgotten that day.)

Suddenly blank shots erupt.

THAYER. An attempt on the President!

In the greatest confusion the puppet is taken out.
MANN, trampled, lies on the ground.

FULLER. Miraculous country! – Someone shoots at
the president, and a negro dies.

NEW ORLEANS

MANN *gets up and leaves the show.*

LITTLE NED. We always need a negro like that to end Laughter Week. – At least no one cries on his account.

LYON

THAYER. Stewart! – What do you think about all this?

STEWART. Those are the shots of South Braintree (we haven't finished hearing them).

THAYER. Explain for those covering their ears!

STEWART. The facts are simple – two clerks from Slater and Morrill just got shot down in front of South Braintree's palisades. Their purse containing fifteen thousand seven hundred seventy dollars and fifty cents was stolen. Who did it?

THAYER. (It's clear!) The nation is in danger.

BONNETADE. – So, from laugh to laugh
    you went all the way back to
    1921, the date our week
    of fun ends.
    The White Terror in the
    U.S. has just begun.

THAYER. There's not a moment to lose!

IV

ANTIPHONY OF THE WHITE TERROR IN
PALMER CITY

SELMAIRE 5:
THAYER'S SELMAIRE

THAYER (*the actor*) *identifies with* THAYER (*the
character*). *A picture of the latter is projected stage
right. The actor speaks in front of it. He addresses
the police.*

THAYER. Thayer, according to all the witnesses, was
    "a theater director" (sic), a disagreeable buffoon.
    – According to the play's instructions, I must do

382

the exact opposite. Reality in theater must escape reality in life, in order to aspire to any plausibility. (What a job!) Conforming to Attorney General Palmer's instructions tonight bombs will be placed at the homes of prominent personalities in eight big cities (to bring about a saintly reaction in the population). – In our city, it shall be Judge Nott's home (he has accepted). You will place the bomb in front of the window of his colored domestics. Here is the map of his home. Make sure you don't make a mistake, I would find myself in an unfortunate position in relation to an excellent colleague.

SELMAIRE 6:
BOSCHETTO'S SELMAIRE

Overflowing onto the preceding selmaire, projected luminous letters from a newspaper parade across upstage: "Two thousand steel workers in prison… Twelve newspapers shut down… Molly Steimer, sentenced to fifteen years of hard labor for distribution of leaflets… The leader of the steel workers' union, Eugene Debs, once again in prison with his whole general staff." BOSCHETTO *puts himself in the position of American union members of the time, through an event he describes. He walks in front of the luminous newspaper. When the news about Debs' arrest appears, he goes towards* LITTLE NED *and leans towards him. The luminous newspaper turns off.*

BOSCHETTO. It's the White Terror. – Debs has just been arrested.

LITTLE NED. How many times is that now?

BOSCHETTO. Who knows.

LITTLE NED. Are you armed for returning home?

BOSCHETTO. No.

LITTLE NED. You'd better be careful (with the pigs of the Pinkerton agency lurking everywhere).

BOSCHETTO. They won't catch me tonight.

LITTLE NED. In that case, I'm going with you.

BOSCHETTO. Out of the question, I've got a romantic rendezvous.

He goes to exit. Shots. BOSCHETTO *falls. In front of him the luminous newspaper starts rolling again: "Bombs in Boston, Cleveland, Pittsburgh... an anarchist killed while throwing his bomb... Attorney General Palmer has ordered the mass deportation of suspects."*

SELMAIRE 7:
CERVI'S SELMAIRE

As the show on the imaginary stage is developing, CERVI *begins to think that* LETIZIA *could very well be his wife.*

CERVI. Nicola is a son of the country (of the earth), like me – Letizia, could she ever suffer for a man what Rosine suffered for Nicola? (Maybe in the same circumstances...) (*While a scene of* NICOLA SACCO'S *family life plays out he identifies himself with* SACCO. ROSINE, SACCO'S *wife, becomes* LETIZIA. *This identification takes place inside an apartment, which appears close to their seats.*) May 1ˢᵗ, it's a celebration. – The trees are wearing colors. We ought to wear colors too, Rosine what do you think?

LETIZIA. I already know what you're going to offer me.

CERVI. What?

LETIZIA. Everything (a blouse, fine stockings, leather shoes, a dress).

CERVI. You forget the most important (flowers).

LETIZIA. I don't want flowers. (They're sad.)

CERVI. That's true – in the city, flowers are always sad.

Behind CERVI, *the luminous newspaper reads yet again: "No one yet knows the conspirators. All efforts to track them down are still in vain. Several thousand arrests in extremists circles."*

SELMAIRE 8:
COLEONE'S SELMAIRE

COLEONE *recreates bit by bit the Brokton Street affair, which was interpreted in different ways at the time. He imagines himself speaking to*

VENTURELLI. *They are silhouetted against the projected newspaper stories, where pictures of the assassinated men are reproduced.*

COLEONE. It would be giving in to provocation.

VENTURELLI. Do you think I'm gonna get my ass kicked without doing anything? For once it will be – a bomb – that will blow up a few ugly faces. Tyrannical institutions will crumble in blood. We'll destroy them to free the world.

COLEONE. Be quiet. They'd be too happy to show they've captured one (it'll be an excuse for repression).

VENTURELLI. You think they need an excuse? – Once we touch cops and judges, guys from the Fourth Estate (like you) aren't happy.

COLEONE. Watch it – I'll be for the cops and judges when they're on our side.

VENTURELLI. What's the point of fighting, if it's to put the same things back in place.

COLEONE. The people will need specialized personnel that we'll call police officers to protect its conquests.

VENTURELLI. But with cops, they'll be screwed.

COLEONE. Just look at the Bolshevik State.

VENTURELLI. It's barely been born – but even before reaching adulthood, it'll be wearing a soldier's helmet on its head and a police baton in its hand.

COLEONE. Our methods are still the only ones that have been able to achieve revolutions.

VENTURELLI. Thanks to the black eyes we've been receiving for the last century, we've pulled you out of the fire. – Before you were even born they were executing anarchists.

COLEONE. And what was the result?

VENTURELLI. The result? I'd like to shove it in your face.

COLEONE. Maybe you're right. – We'll talk better later.

They begin to fight. Two gunshots. They fall. The luminous newspaper above them reads: "Two bomb throwers dead by their own device while trying to blow up Attorney General Palmer's house."

SELMAIRE 9:
FARLEY'S SELMAIRE

FARLEY *tries to go into Julius Rosenberg's past, whose life he only knew bits of, to place him during these events. Two pictures: one of Julius Rosenberg behind his seat, and one of* NICOLA SACCO, *behind* CERVI'S, *who answers him.*

FARLEY. Julius Rosenberg's family lived in anguish. The father could only return to his job (at fifty cents an hour rather than a dollar ten) by kissing – he who was Jewish – a Christian bible, and swearing to never again be part of a union. That's how you become a millionaire in this country, he would say.

CERVI. Everyone in this country thinks he'll die a millionaire. That's why they live with a smile on their faces, prospering from all the rights they have.

FARLEY. Like most of them, old Rosenberg benefited from only one right, attending his own funeral.

CERVI. Julius Rosenberg?

FARLEY. They say he really resembled Nicola Sacco.

CERVI. (Maybe neither one of them is here tonight, and what we are saying, is simply the inevitable return of words, looking for one another, calling constantly to one another and meeting only once.)

GENERAL SELMAIRE 1

The characters of the supposed audience, who for different reasons feel closer to SACCO *or to* VANZETTI, *stand to sing the* Round of Deportation. BOSCHETTO, CERVI, VENTURELLI, ERHMAN KLOSE, DERLINSKI *and* FARLEY *for* NICOLA SACCO; KURLANSKI, BONNETADE, LITTLE NED, COLEONE, VASTADOUR *and* ANNE *for* BARTOLOMEO VANZETTI, *will form two groups, which each on their own side walk in circle.*

ROUND OF DEPORTATION

We are leaving you, country
immense and cruel as hope.
Between the docks of Naples,
the lighthouse of Hamburg
at attention in the mist,
and the New York customs
we no longer know to which Atlantic
the immigrants are condemned.
Farewell eleventh commandment
we are the flocks
always passing. Yet
our roots are everywhere on the earth.

THE SACCOS *and* VANZETTIS *line up, backs facing
the audience, upstage.* COLEONE *and* ERHMAN
KLOSE *leave the group and approach the audience.*

COLEONE. Black lists have the force of law. Those
who think they're listed, (and we all have reasons
to think we are) have but one option – to return
to Europe, and as quickly as possible. Useless
sacrifices have got to be avoided.

ERHMAN KLOSE. Up to a certain point.

COLEONE. Is there something new?

ERHMAN KLOSE. Salsedo (our printer) has just been sequestered by the FBI.

COLEONE. Does anyone know where he is?

ERHMAN KLOSE. New York (Park Row).

COLEONE. I'm going.

ERHMAN KLOSE. What for?

COLEONE. To see how we can help him.

VASTADOUR *detaches from the large group and joins the two.*

VASTADOUR. I will go.

Police sirens. VASTADOUR, COLEONE *and* ERHMAN KLOSE *are brought back by the two groups, and begin once again to walk in circles and to sing.*

Our roots are deep
they grow where hunger leads us.
The gassed of Ohio, the children burned alive
by the Arizona cops
the hanged of Alabama and Dakota,
the tortured of Tennessee and Colorado
the caged of Wisconsin, the lynched of Florida,
these are the commemorating monuments
of our passage – farewell.

*Once again they go upstage, their backs to the
audience. This time* VASTADOUR *alone leaves the
group and goes toward stage right, where an
inscription lights up "Park Row" FBI. The voice of
an FBI agent comes from the imagined stage, but
his moving shadow passes back and forth on*
VASTADOUR *as if to erase him.*

VASTADOUR. I'd like to see Salsedo. – Rolando Salsedo.

FBI AGENT. Impossible.

VASTADOUR. Might one inquire about him.

FBI AGENT. Impossible.

VASTADOUR. Send him a package.

FBI AGENT. Impossible.

VASTADOUR. I was told he was locked up in isolation here (at Park Row).

FBI AGENT. Are you family?

VASTADOUR. Yes.

FBI AGENT. Then you can take him away.

VASTADOUR *backs away, afraid, as if he's in front of the printer's dead body.*

VASTADOUR. Rolando… Poor… (poor…)

FBI AGENT. A fit of depression under interrogation. He threw himself off the fourteenth floor. – He must not have had a clear conscience. (VASTADOUR *takes his hat off, lowers his head. Stays a moment.*) You may take him. – Everything concerning him is in order.

CERVI *detaches himself from the group and goes stage left, stands under the lit inscription "Italian Consulate of Boston" which blinks on and off.* CERVI *does the questions and answers.*

CERVI. – SACCO. I'd like a return visa to Italy (Mr. Consul).

CONSUL. What's with all of you, wanting to return?

SACCO. A necessary nostalgia for the country Mr. Consul. My boss warned me that federal agents were conducting an investigation on me.

CONSUL. Just plug your ears and wait until it passes.

SACCO. It will pass over us, and there won't be much left behind. (I have a child and my wife is expecting a second one.) Have the kindness to send me back as soon as possible.

MULLER *detaches himself from the group and speaks as though pleading before the courts in Massachusetts.*

MULLER. (I could have pleaded this case with my eyes closed.) Remember this – the day of the murder, Sacco was at the Italian consulate trying to get a visa to go home. Twenty people who were there for the same reasons could testify.

BOSTON

Everything turns off. One vertical light on KATZ. *He intervenes in the tone of the discussion as though he were convincing himself.*

KATZ. An Italian's testimony doesn't amount to much (the fact that there are twenty of them doesn't change anything). The sure fact is that Sacco did not go to work that day – and if he didn't go to work it was to go kill those poor South Braintree cashiers. Between his visit to the consulate and his return to the factory, he could very well have made a detour by South Braintree.

The lights return to the SACCOS *and* VANZETTIS *who have not moved.*

CERVI. We've got to go to Brokton to put the propaganda material in a safe place.

VASTADOUR. I've got it. – Are you armed?

CERVI. Yes.

VASTADOUR. Let's go.

STEWART *approaches them, a gun in hand. All the* SACCOS *and* VANZETTIS *put their hands up.*

STEWART. I just arrested two armed reds, with a bunch of propaganda material.

MULLER. Not a word without the presence of a lawyer.

THAYER. Ask them how they got into the country? Where does the money come from? How many washing machines and silk stockings have they hoarded at our expense?

STEWART. Do you hear? – They don't want to answer.

THAYER. That's a sign of their guilt. – If they're not talking, it means they're guilty. (*He approaches* VANZETTI.) Your name?

THE VANZETTIS. Bartolomeo Vanzetti.

THAYER. Occupation?

THE VANZETTIS. Street peddler.

THAYER *now goes over to* THE SACCOS.

THAYER. And you?

THE SACCOS. Nicola Sacco.

THAYER. Occupation?

THE SACCOS. Shoe-maker.

THAYER. Inspector Stewart. – What more do you need? Don't forget that other than South Braintree, there's another case that you've never solved (Bridgewater). I hope you understand me.

BRIDGEWATER PARADE

Upstage, STEWART *has* THE SACCOS *and* VANZETTIS *line up, making sure they keep their hands raised, then returns downstage. From the supposed theater, the inspector phones the results of the Bridgewater investigation to his other.*

STEWART. Hello! Inspector Stewart?

STEWART. Speaking.

STEWART. Inspector Stewart here. For the Bridgewater case, Sacco's boss came to tell us that the day of the attempted robbery (Sacco was working at home). It seemed suspicious. But since Sacco's boss is an influential person in Boston, I had to take it. For Vanzetti, it's easier. There is no set schedule for street peddlers. (Unfortunately) the Bridgewater hold-up took place on the evening of December 24th. There are twenty-four witnesses who affirm that they bought eels from him that evening in Plymouth. (That's quite a ways from Bridgewater.) They remember it very well since it was Christmas Eve. If they are to be believed, Vanzetti seems to be innocent.

STEWART. Why do you believe them? That's annoying. Then the South Braintree theory is flushed down the toilet.

STEWART. How so?

STEWART. The chief of the State Police is telling me right now that the South Braintree killers have been found.

STEWART. That's not possible.

STEWART. It's the Morelli brothers. – They're being carefully watched at the Star Hotel this very moment. (Only their accomplice Madeiros is still at large.)

THAYER. I'm not interested in stories of police department rivalries. – What do you want me to do with two or three little gangsters that you catch around the corner? (We have time.) Men who can kill in such cold blood for money have absolutely no morals, they'll do it again – and we'll nab them. (There is no doubt about it), the important thing today is not to find (who killed a man, but) who wants to kill a country? Who is planting bombs? Who murders our children and our cashiers? — The extremists. (We have them.)

Darkness on THAYER. *Projector on* STEWART *at his home, in front of a folding screen of mirrors, that multiplies the* STEWARTS.

STEWART. Stewart: Sacco was at the Italian consulate that day.
Stewart: But to get there, he had to have taken a street. (We could arrange things.)
Stewart: There are twenty witnesses.
Stewart: The judges will take care of them.
Stewart: A whiskey, Mick?

Stewart: Vanzetti was in a train.

Stewart: We'll have to jumble the timetables.

Stewart: There are witnesses.

Stewart: A whisky, Mick? Ice cold, never fails to boost a man.

Stewart: A good cop must always see what's behind what every witness says, to know what they're hiding.

(*He serves himself a strong whisky.*)

Stewart: A cop's job is not always fun.

Stewart: A good whisky always inspires good ideas.

Stewart: Of the four or five Stewarts walking around in this room, which one is telling the truth? Which could really benefit from their innocence?

Stewart: That's where we've got to begin.

Stewart: My God, am I tired – and I still have to take care of the mass deportations.

Stewart: I'm gonna call Bill to give me a hand.

Stewart: No. – He's on vacation.

Stewart: I'm sick of multiplying myself like this – and for what I earn.

Stewart: Well there was a police officers' strike here in Boston. It ended in blood.

Stewart: After all, they're Italian. No one will look into it that closely.

Stewart: In conclusion, I'm sending them before the jury for first degree murder. It's up to them to deal with it.

Darkness. Lights on THAYER.

THAYER. The time has come to nail down some accusations for the South Braintree crime, we've got to get them to take on a case that will buy us time. It will be Bridgewater.

BOSTON

KATZ. (But) I thought I heard that Sacco's boss said earlier...

LYON

THAYER. (I know), in that case, it will be Vanzetti by himself. – Find me a witness. Anyhow, you will issue the subpoena and I'll preside.

We return to all THE SACCOS *and* VANZETTIS,
among which ERHMAN KLOSE *remembers this trial,
which is studied in law school. Gradually* ERHMAN
KLOSE *will speak like a law professor in an
amphitheater.*

ERHMAN KLOSE. This trial (which is a case study for
second year law students) was handled in an
incredibly frivolous manner. You want an
example? – They brought an eight year old
newspaper boy before the jury. The kid got a
case of the jitters and all of a sudden cried: Once
I heard the gunshots I hid behind a pole. I didn't
see anything.

THAYER. What do you mean you didn't see anything?
Mr. Attorney, what does this mean?

ERHMAN KLOSE. Immediately, attorney Katzmann
thunders. (He didn't see anything, but he heard.
Didn't you hear? Well, speak.) And the kid
answers: I didn't see anything but I heard by his
way of running that he was a foreigner.

THAYER. Vanzetti, are you a foreigner? Answer yes or no.

VASTADOUR. Who isn't a foreigner within the confines of justice?

THAYER. You are affirming that you are.

KATZ. (Consequently...)

THAYER. The jury having deliberated, sentences you to fifteen years of hard labor. – Mr. District Attorney, find me some witnesses a little more solid for the South Braintree trial. Keep in mind the unfortunate experience of my colleague who presided over the trial of that tramway agitator (Tom Mooney). Once they got to the sentencing, all the witnesses came forward and admitted they committed perjury. – These people, you've got to manipulate them with great care.

Immediately, THE SACCOS *and* VANZETTIS *start singing the* Ballad of the Industrial Workers of the World

THE BALLAD OF THE I.W.W.

Why did you lead the strike
Tom Mooney? Why did you
lead the tramway strike?

They sentenced you to death
Tom Mooney. Ten false witnesses
testified to seeing you throw
a bomb that exploded.

Because they were not
well paid Tom Mooney
the false witnesses officially admitted
having been mistaken.

They sentenced you to hard labor
to celebrate your innocence
Tom Mooney, your innocence
and the tramway strike.

BOSCHETTO *imagines* THAYER *in front of the press,
trying to justify himself after the Bridgewater affair.*

BOSCHETTO. Mr. Presiding Judge, your decisions are being discussed all over the United States. – Could you tell us why you took this position?

THAYER. Mr. Reporter, could you accept a truth that is not your own?

VENTURELLI. In a newspaper, it's almost an obligation to do so.

THAYER. I see you understand me. – I've been slandered, why? On the one hand, you have the extremists (never mind to whom they belong). What do they want? To destroy us. Why? Because we enjoy certain privileges. Who acquired these privileges? We did, or our parents, by the strength of the fist and the mind. The time has come to accept that the good guys are those who respect work and intelligence, and the bad guys are those who seek to destroy them.

THE SACCOS *and* VANZETTIS *begin to sing again.*

Strange fruits hanging
from the trees of Ohio
whipped to the blood
and complaining
and expiring.
Strange fruits
hanging in clusters
from the trees of Tulsa
Kasprovitz disheveled
Clean, eyes bleeding
Diaz, jaw broken
Fitz, with the look
of an animal at bay
Miller, shriveled
into a smile
that can't find
shelter any more
in this world.
Strange fruits,
oil workers
hanging in clusters
from the trees of Tulsa.

EVA *tries to imagine the relationship that might
have existed between* THAYER *and his wife. Stage
right,* THAYER'S *wedding picture is projected. In
front of it,* THAYER *stands alone.*

EVA. Judge Thayer, your wife must have been
harassed by the telephone calls.

THAYER. Margaret, you're getting soft.

EVA. But a nervous breakdown must have been
imminent at any moment.

THAYER. Here you are, a victim of the circus created
around this affair.

EVA. (Why didn't you resign?)

THAYER. That would be desertion – because, what
are they attacking? God, the family, the good of
others, values that have placed man above
animals since the beginnings of time. – Margaret,
in forty years of marriage, have I once seen your
body? No – I've had to content myself with
imagining it.

THE SACCOS *and* VANZETTIS *continue the ballad.*

THE BALLAD OF THE I. W. W. (*cont.*)

Two hundred strikers
were deported
(Jo-Jo, where are you going?)
In the deserts of Arizona
Two hundred strikers
were abandoned,
without water, without food.
Jo-Jo where are you?

In front of them, death.
Behind them, death
among them, too.
Jo-Jo where are you? Jo.

KASSEL. (Your good conscience) is that of someone
just, Judge Thayer. Will that still be the case when
you appear before God?

KASSEL *imagines what* THAYER *will say after his
death. A catafalque is raised. The coffin is opened.*
THAYER *inside explains his actions.*

THAYER. My God, it is I, your servant, Judge Thayer who is in this box (ah yes, I've joined them). I know very well what's been said. But my conscience is clear. The struggle between Good and Evil, Light verses Darkness has always made victims. (When these victims are your servants, their murderers are made into heroes, justice fighters.) When they are the victims, they declare us executioners (and they pound us with sarcasm). But isn't it true, the moment Evil wants to destroy Good – Good must destroy Evil. They blew up the homes of the jury, the executioner and myself. For years before returning home, I telephoned just to make sure the walls were still standing. Five years after their execution, dynamite once again blew up my house, that is, in a place where your holy name was always revered. Do you hear me, my Lord? My duty wasn't it to hate the servants of the Devil? Are we not in solidarity, my God, in the fight against the Prince of Darkness?

A beat. THAYER *stands up on the catafalque, and authoritatively orders.*

THAYER. And now, to work – the trial may begin.

V

TEST TAKE FOR A FEATURE LENGTH
POLICE THRILLER

LYON

The trial is about to begin. THAYER *sits behind the
ticket window, which now represents the tribunal.*

THAYER. Mr. District Attorney, are the witnesses
present?

BOSTON

KATZ. Past ones (or future ones), the witnesses are
always here.

*The projector searches around everywhere and
finally stops in the real audience, on a man who
immediately rises.*

PRESS AGENT. At your service.

*Same light game a second time, the projector stops
on a woman this time.*

OFFICIAL. At your service.

*These two witnesses will be in charge of all wit-
nesses during the trial. That is to say, that each
time there is a female witness, the OFFICIAL will
speak, and when it is a male witness the PRESS
AGENT will speak. Each time they assume a different
identity they appear in a different place, and each
time the projector will find them, whether they be in
the real room, the supposed audience, the flies,
behind the seats or in the wings.*

SELMAIRE 10:
FARLEY'S SELMAIRE

FARLEY *imagines them as David Greenglass, the
brother of Ethel Rosenberg and Ruth his wife, the
witnesses in charge of the Rosenberg trial. We see
cuttings from American Newspapers with the
pictures of David Greenglass and his wife.*

FARLEY. David, Ethel's brother – and Ruth, his wife.
That's them – it can only be them. So many years
before yet it was already them.

ANNE. They are no longer David Greenglass and his

wife, but simply officers of Death (both desperate and contemptible).

BOSTON

KATZ. Mary Splaine. (*The* OFFICIAL *stands from the middle of the real audience.*) The primary witness. (She worked on the second floor of the Slater and Morill factory.)

SELMAIRE 11:
MULLER'S SELMAIRE

Once again, PROFESSOR MULLER *identifies with the lawyer, he goes to the changing room, puts on a robe and progressively intervenes in the trial.*

MULLER. After the gun shots, she goes to the window. Thirty-five yards from there, a car speeds off, and she can see (only at a distance of twelve yards).

THAYER. Quiet. – Speak, Mary Splaine.

OFFICIAL. The man who was between the back of the front seat and the back seat was a man a

414

little taller than myself. He weighed about one hundred and forty, one hundred and forty five pounds. He had muscles, he seemed like an active man. His left hand was fairly large (a hand that indicated strength).

THAYER. So, the left hand in question, did you see it?

OFFICIAL. It was the left hand that was resting on the back of the front seat. – The man was wearing a grayish shirt, almost dark blue. And he had a rather good looking face. The features were well defined. Around here...

MULLER. (Only at a distance of about twelve yards.)

OFFICIAL. Right here it was a little narrow. His forehead was high. His hair was combed backwards, and it was, I would say, two to two and a half inches long. He had black eyebrows, but his complexion was white, a strange white that seemed olive-colored.

THAYER. It is the same man as Sacco?

OFFICIAL. Yes.

THAYER. Are you sure?

OFFICIAL. Absolutely.

MULLER. Thirty-five yards away in a car accelerating at full speed, you were able to see in the space of a second and a half so much detail about a person in a car with four others?

KATZ. (She's a perceptive witness.)

MULLER. I'm not done with her perceptiveness. – Madame, at the preliminary trial, you formally declared: "I am incapable of recognizing anyone, everything happened too fast."

OFFICIAL. It must have been a stenographic error.

MULLER. After that, the private Pinkerton police, specialized in going after workers, strongly suggested that you recognize the assassin. On the pictures shown you, you recognized a certain Palmesano.

KATZ. It couldn't have been Palmesano, he had been in prison for two years.

MULLER. Finally you were introduced to Sacco, not in a group of people as is usually the custom, but alone. You couldn't make a mistake, yet you hesitated. And today (more than a year later, you are positive).

OFFICIAL. I had a lot of time to think since then.

THAYER. You are now affirming that after thinking about it you are sure this is the man in question.

OFFICIAL. I am absolutely sure.

THAYER. Your definite answer is that you are absolutely sure that it is him.

KATZ. (And to think that out of the sixty-five witnesses for this trial, this is the only one that could be hired as a serious witness.) That says a lot about attorney Katzmann's virtuosity – business, whatever it may be, is business. There is only one law – that the best wins.

MULLER. All right. – Witness Pelzer, do you see in this room the man who fired on the cashiers of the Slater and Morill factory?

The OFFICIAL *leaves the room. The* PRESS AGENT *rises.*

SELMAIRE 12:
ANNE'S SELMAIRE

Once again a newspaper cutting is projected with the portrait of David Greenglass. ANNE *connects the witnesses in the two trials.*

ANNE. David Greenglass, Ethel's brother (an incompetent) has now become the press agent erasing shadows (always the same) because shadows return – in the corridor of the condemned.

THAYER. Answer.

PRESS AGENT. I wouldn't say it's him, but it's his portrait.

SELMAIRE 13:
MULLER'S SELMAIRE

Once again, MULLER *thinks about what he would have said had he been the lawyer of this case.*

MULLER. At the preliminary interview, you denied having seen him.

KATZ. Pelzer is what I would call, the honest witness par excellence. Why? Because he has always denied, and today, he is honest enough (whatever it may cost him) to finally tell the truth.

MULLER. Have you ever been convicted?

PRESS AGENT. No.

MULLER. Lie.

SELMAIRE 14:
ERHMAN KLOSE'S SELMAIRE

One, two, three, four brochures on the debates of the SACCO – VANZETTI *case are projected in the supposed theater, turning on and turning off several times.* ERHMAN KLOSE *rises, goes from one to the next and imagines the role he might have played.*

ERHMAN KLOSE. It's much more serious. When Pelzer refused to recognize Sacco, he was immediately laid off by Slater & Morill. After two months of joblessness, he decided to accuse Sacco. That same day, he found his lost job. He wasn't the only one in this situation. During the entire pre-trial, memory and joblessness were tightly linked.

KATZ. A recent past has taught us that the Jews were sometimes wrong to put themselves forward.

KASSEL. Why are you getting involved? (Be careful.)

ERHMAN KLOSE. I'm getting involved in a legal question.

KASSEL. Those are so controversial.

LYON

A projector searches for the OFFICIAL *who appears between seats of the supposed theater.*

THAYER. The attorney has a big responsibility when he brings in witnesses whose depositions tend to prove a murder. – Here you are responding to his summons, Madame Lola Andrews. Don't be afraid of anything – you are here under the protection of the State.

BOSTON

KATZ. I imagine the enormous Katzmann, the real one, his eyes more blue and transparent than ever – saying: "I've held this position for more than eleven years. I cannot remember during this long tenure of serving justice having ever seen (or lent an ear to) a witness as convincing as Lola Andrews."

In the real audience, KURLANSKI *is restless and once again approaches the supposed theater.*

KURLANSKI. I've known Mrs. Andrews for eight years. I was sitting in front of my shop, at 1466 Hancock Street. It must have been between six and seven a clock. Lola passed by. I said: Good evening Lola.

OFFICIAL. Good evening.

KURLANSKI. She stopped and said: You look rather tired.

OFFICIAL. Yes – they're worrying me so much. It's going to kill me.

KURLANSKI. I said: How so? And she said:

OFFICIAL. I'm just coming from the prison.

KURLANSKI. The prison, what were you doing in prison?

OFFICIAL. The Government wants me to recognize those two men.

KURLANSKI. She waited an instant, then all of a sudden:

OFFICIAL. He wants me to recognize them, and I know nothing about them. I've never seen them and I can't recognize them.

KURLANSKI. Then...

OFFICIAL. Unfortunately, I had to go there for work. So...

LYON

THAYER. Mister witness, I would like to ask you a question. Have you tried to discover this person representing the government who tried to force her to affirm something that was false?

HAMBURG

MULLER. What kind of a question is that?

LYON

THAYER. Did you attempt to discover this person who was representing the government?

KURLANSKI. No.

LYON

THAYER. Why not?

BOSTON

KURLANSKI. Well, uh, I didn't think of it. I wasn't sure, you know. I didn't...

LYON

THAYER. And did you think the public interest would be served by someone who represented the government, and was trying to make a false witness out of this woman?

BOSTON

KURLANSKI. I didn't think anything at all.

LYON

THAYER. Identify anyone?

BOSTON

KURLANSKI. I didn't think about any of this, only about what she told me.

LYON

THAYER. Don't you think it would be a good idea to discover him, if you could.

BOSTON

KURLANSKI. I do think so.

LYON

THAYER. Then why did you not do it?

BOSTON

KURLANSKI. Why do you want me to get involved?

425

THAYER. You don't want to get involved? Then what does your deposition mean?

SELMAIRE 15:
ERHMAN KLOSE'S SELMAIRE

Once again the brochures about the SACCO – VANZETTI *case are projected.* ERHMAN KLOSE *rises.*

ERHMAN KLOSE. Before the arrest of Sacco and Vanzetti, Mrs. Andrews was assaulted in her home. The inspector in charge of the investigation wrote the following report. – Read the questioning, Stewart. It's signed by you.

LYON

STEWART. By me?

STEWART. (*He reads.*) Question: The man who attacked you, wasn't he one of the gangsters from South Braintree?

Answer: It's impossible to answer. I've never seen the faces or even the bodies of those men.

426

BOSTON

KATZ. All of this reinforces what I was telling you. – Never ever have I during my career found a witness as convincing as Lola Andrews. Last witness against Nicola Sacco. – The honorable Carlos E. Goodridge.

HAMBURG

MULLER. No one knows him.

LYON

THAYER. All the more reason to meet him. Speak, Mr. Goodridge.

BOSTON

PRESS AGENT *is discovered this time, coming from back stage.*

PRESS AGENT. I'm playing billiards. Bam… bam… three shots. I hurry to the site of the accident. A guy turns a gun this large on me. Why are you sticking your nose in here, he tells me. Put that sneezing contraption away I answer. He didn't seem to want to continue the conversation. – I understood. I went back to the bistro and continued my billiards.

KATZ. The man with the gun, who was it?

PRESS AGENT. Nicola Sacco.

SELMAIRE 16:
ERHMAN KLOSE'S SELMAIRE

For the third time the brochures are projected, but open this time. We see entire passages underlined in pencil.

ERHMAN KLOSE. The only inconvenience is that Carlos E. Goodridge doesn't exist. On the other hand a certain Erastus Corning Whitney does exist, an arsonist and check counterfeiter. – Fleeing the State of New York, he was arrested for robbery in Massachusetts. Two days before the opening of this trial, Mr. Erastus Corning Whitney had to (he pleaded guilty by the way) appear here. After an interview with you Mr. District Attorney, the case was classified closed, and Erastus Corning Whitney became Carlos E. Goodridge. After a year of pressures and blackmail, these are the types of witnesses to which you've reduced yourself.

BOSTON

KATZ. You have no right to try to influence the jury.

LYON

THAYER. Not to worry. The jury has too high a conscience of its duty to stoop to these types of considerations. – The witnesses against Vanzetti.

HAMBURG

MULLER. Thirty-one people have declared that Vanzetti was not one of the men in the car with the gangsters. Thirteen others officially saw him in Plymouth that day.

LYON

THAYER. I asked for the accusation witnesses.

BOSTON

KATZ. (Why is he insisting? Luckily there's the bulldog, Katzmann): It's hard to have them utter three words that aren't contradictory. – Justice is very frightening for some people. But all of this is of little importance next to the witness who's a ballistics expert.

LYON

THAYER. Captain Proctor.

PRESS AGENT. Present.

THAYER. As an expert, did you examine the bullets recovered from the bodies of the unfortunate victims? Could you tell us if these bullets belonged to the revolver of Nicola Sacco?

BOSTON

KATZ. Allow me, for the clarity of the debate, to pose the question differently. Bullet number 3, in your opinion, was it fired from this revolver?

PRESS AGENT. My opinion is that logic would have it that it was shot from that revolver.

LYON

THAYER. You may step down. – Thank you, Mr. Expert.

BOSTON

BOYD. We have the essential.

LYON

THAYER. Mr. District Attorney, you have the stand.

BOSTON

KATZ. (Katzmann, at fifty was still ashamed of his name, too German sounding for his taste, of the Harvard degrees he hadn't gotten, of the poor neighborhoods of Hyde Park from whence he came.) If he won that day, he knew that at the end he would have a membership in the golf and tennis clubs, the title of Council to the

431

Boston Family Association, and above all, an imposing Victorian House on River street.

MULLER *takes charge again. A picture of Mrs. De Falco is projected. In front of her the* OFFICIAL.

MULLER. There is also Mrs. De Falco. Madam, you went to see the Sacco and Vanzetti Defense Committee, and you asked them:

OFFICIAL. I'm here on behalf of attorney Katzmann's brother. If you give him fifty thousand dollars, everything will work itself out.

THAYER. I don't know this woman. Furthermore, I believe you've taken advantage of her, by taking disloyally and without warning, the stenographic suggestion of an attorney with the only purpose of blackmailing.

MULLER. The brother did admit...

KATZ. But he wasn't charged. As for Mrs. De Falco,

432

she was declared not guilty by the honorable Judge Murray who deemed her actions "imprudent but not criminal."

THAYER. You dare attack the decisions of justice? – Where are we headed?

BOSTON

KATZ. Two deserters who fled to Mexico to avoid the war. Two murderers, two anarchists, do they deserve so much literature?

LYON

THAYER. Since you've started your summations – continue.

SELMAIRE 18:
LITTLE NED'S SELMAIRE

In light of what he has just heard, LITTLE NED *imagines what the requisitions might have been.*

LITTLE NED. (I know this type of summation), if Xiomara decides to go to a white neighborhood in New Orleans tomorrow and claim she's been raped, they would do the same to me. – The prosecution testimonies are obviously contradictory. Some pretend to have seen the gangster car at two PM, others at five – and when they finally agree on the time, it's to identify the car in completely different places. I understand that no one agrees on where in the car Vanzetti was seated. Sometimes in the same testimony we find him both in the front and the back seat. What do we make of all this? Do you throw it all out if you think all these people had the honest intention of telling the truth? – Sometimes possibilities outweigh plausibility and probabilities outweigh possibilities. True or false, you must accept as the simplest common sense that Vanzetti was in the car, and Sacco being his partner, you'll have no trouble associating the two men.

HAMBURG

ERHMAN KLOSE. May I ask you a question?

BOSTON

KATZ. Everyone is free to express himself as he likes.

HAMBURG

ERHMAN KLOSE. Why is it that every, (I insist), every witness for the defense, or for the prosecution who refused to formally identify the accused lost their jobs from one day to the next?

BOSTON

KATZ. Because everyone is free to act as he likes.

LYON

THAYER. In any case, the Court refuses to use the identification of Sacco and Vanzetti as a basis for any verdict in the trial. The alibis that you produce will only confirm this, and prove the same thing. The testimony of Captain Proctor, expert in ballistics, could suffice. However the verdict will under no circumstances rely on the eyewitnesses. The proofs that condemn the accused are circumstantial. The only law that will count is the feeling that I have, me, of their guilt.

VI

INTERMISSION WITH THE EIGHTEEN CHOIR BOYS OF DISTRESS OF MAY 1st

It's intermission. Everyone gets up, blows his nose, talks, smokes or freshens up, except VASTADOUR *in Lyon and* CERVI *in Turin. They remain seated in their chairs, and relive what they have just seen. They find themselves, from the point of view of the show, in a parallel situation to* NICOLA SACCO *and* BARTOLOMEO VANZETTI *when isolated, alone with themselves they hear sounds of the May 1st parade. As the relived tragedy gradually takes the place of the real tragedy, the spectators from intermission replace the walls of the Charlestown prison. Around two central thoughts, pushing* VASTADOUR *to identify more and more with* BARTOLOMEO VANZETTI *and* CERVI, *with* NICOLA SACCO, *are added, in minor mode, other thoughts of others affected in more diverse or more superficial ways by the show.*

BOSTON

Once the intermission is announced, GRANT JR. *holds* EVA *back and lets* BOYD *go off talking very warmly with* KATZ.

GRANT JR. Honey, it's our day today.

EVA. How do you want to do it? My husband is here. The evening is lost.

GRANT JR. Pretend you have a violent migraine.

EVA. It won't help. All he wants is an excuse to leave.

GRANT JR. He can't leave Mr. Katz – the deal they're working on is too serious. (Do you think Spencer can ruin, or risk ruining this deal?) Come on! ... When you tell him that you want to go, he'll become very embarrassed, and at that moment I'll offer to take you home.

EVA. Making love in the car – has always left me unsatisfied.

GRANT JR. In the car, we don't risk any surprises –
we'll take care of the rest.

TURIN

VENTURELLI. Replace the names of Sacco and
Vanzetti with German names: Spiess, Fisher,
Lingg, Engell. Replace the electric chair with
gallows and you have the story of Chicago.
Bombs explode, some think they were planted
by anarchists, others by cops. They hurry to
arrest the most visible union leaders of Chicago
in their homes. They were demanding one day
off per week with loud protests – they sentence
them to death – and they hang them.

LYON

To keep the mood, DERLINSKI *plays through the
speaker,* the Country Where the Month of May Dies.

There where the month of May passes
our brothers' heads fall
in the guillotine's basket of bran
there where the month of May passes
their bodies grill under the straps

their lungs explode before the flowers
of cyanide rising from the gas chambers.
But in the morgue's coolers
their eyes continue to ask
why the month of May dies
there where the month of May travels.

VASTADOUR. It was the same record (but muted) that must have been playing in their heads, we've only added the lyrics.

BOSTON

EVA. Honey, I have a terrible migraine. Do you want to stay to the end?

BOYD. I just invited Mr. Katz to my club after the show. I've got to be there to introduce him.

KATZ. Please, Madame's health first.

BOYD. Since you are making such a big deal of it, dear Mr. Katz, my consulting attorney will have the pleasure of taking my wife home – won't you, Grant? Eva will be ever so grateful for your sacrifice for her, and I can assure you that my wife's gratitude knows no boundaries. Goodnight. (*He turns his back to them and takes* KATZ *by the arm.*) My dear Katz. – What do you say to a glass of champagne? It'll put us in an excellent mood. Don't feel bad, (Eva is a child, don't take her headaches too seriously).

LYON

Where the Month of May Dies. (*Cont'd.*)

Here the hanged of May 1st. Here Chicago.
We call those shot down in Barcelona,
the caged of Rome, the garroted of Xérès
the grass revives on the plot of the executed.

TURIN

CERVI. Basically, the verdict was in long ago. (It was already pronounced in 1886 in Chicago.)

LYON

VASTADOUR. Our celebrations are hard. They take you from the parades of the streets of Plymouth to this sinister corridor (without any transitions).

CERVI. (Drunken solders, dressed in skirts, danced while two houses were burning. – It was May 1st. Your May 1st.)

A sentence of COLEONE *speaking with* BOSCHETTO *and* VENTURELLI *is isolated.*

COLEONE. It's still a celebration (we don't have any others).

A sentence from LETIZIA *speaking to* CERVI *is now isolated.*

LETIZIA. If Nicola was showering Rosine with gifts that day – it was to hide an apprehension he couldn't quite understand.

A sentence of BOSCHETTO *is isolated.*

BOSCHETTO. This fear, he tried to turn it into a celebration. When I was reporting on the Amazon, I found the exact same thing among the Indians.

BOSTON

We isolate what FARLEY *is saying to* ANNE.

FARLEY. How many people have an appointment
with only one day. – They know it (and do
everything to transform it), but when the
moment arrives, they find themselves naked
before it. (I always have the example of my uncle
Joseph before me.)

TURIN

We isolate this time a group made of LETIZIA,
CERVI *and* PINO

CERVI. Who are you arguing for right now? For
Rosine Sacco or for Letizia?

LETIZIA. Hurry up. – Pino is thirsty (the intermission
is almost over).

CERVI. You want me to give up my seat to mingle
with some of the people I saw out there while I
was waiting for you?

LETIZIA. Of course – it would be deserting your post.

CERVI. You don't realize how right you are.

LETIZIA. Fine, stay then. (Come on Pino.)

NEW ORLEANS

We isolate the conversation of LITTLE NED *and* XIOMARA.

XIOMARA. Why didn't Sacco want to learn English?

LITTLE NED. (What a question!) Because he didn't want to!

XIOMARA. The other one, Vanzetti (the one with mustaches like Zapata) is constantly studying it (he says it'll help him someday).

LITTLE NED. You didn't speak English when you met me. (Did that prevent you from having Little Ned?)

XIOMARA. In prison it's not the same thing. – The guards (if you don't understand) hurt you. I stayed in jail three days when I crossed the border (I know).

LITTLE NED. Don't worry, what (Nick Sacco) said, all alone, for days – there's no need for words to understand it. – It's the discussion of an unemployed negro with the boss of the Johnson plantation.

HAMBURG

The conversation between the professor and the clergyman is isolated.

KASSEL. The language of the victims, whichever one, is always simple…

ERHMAN KLOSE. At the risk of contradicting you – I would dare say I'm convinced of the opposite.

KASSEL. What would you have them say?

GENERAL SELMAIRE 4

This selmaire corresponds to reading the program, (for those staying seated), and (for the others),

walking through the halls of the theater where a
whole documentation: pictures, writings, quotes
about the plays are posted. Pictures of Spiess, Fisher,
Parson, Lingg and Engel are lowered from the flies.

CERVI. Comrades of Chicago (have you found a piece of land where you won't have to die everyday, like men?) You've left us May 1ˢᵗ (what a terrible inheritance), it was already made of the same sentences, the same words, Nick and Bart spoke.

FARLEY. The same as the Rosenberg couple would utter.

ERHMAN KLOSE. (Can the house of the dead give birth to any others?)

COLEONE. "My defense is your accusation, the causes of my alleged crime, your history. In the case you've built, there are neither witnesses nor evidence." Thus spoke Spiers.

ANNE. "Your sentence is nothing more, nothing less, than premeditated murder. Before this court and before these people, I accuse the prosecuting attorney and his noble colleagues of premeditated murder." Thus spoke Parson, son of an American general, who came out of nowhere to turn himself in, to share the pain of his companions.

VENTURELLI. (Already the same words.) "To subdue the people who believe that eight hours of work a day is sufficient for the salary they receive – you've cut the throats of its union leaders." Thus spoke Engel.

CERVI. "May 1st prefers our ideas to our lives." Thus spoke Fisher. When these words can no longer be spoken – May 1st will no longer exist.

ERHMAN KLOSE. Spiess, when they put the rope around your neck, you said: "The voice you are about to strangle will be more powerful in the future than all the words I could pronounce now." – You said it, Spiess. And now we have nothing to say.

COLEONE. Let it be known, that in 1886 in Chicago, five men were killed because – because (because...)

BOSTON

ANNE. (They are two blind cats. They walk through the memories we create of them. Bart, Nick, two blind cats.)

LYON

VASTADOUR *speaks with* BONNETADE *who came to ask his advice.*

VASTADOUR. Do you understand? – At the very moment I finally connect with them, it's only to realize: they will never know me. So I have a sort of feeling (like distress) invade me. – I say to myself that's only because I'm a good audience. (It's not true.) This distress comes from them – their solitude at times is frightening.

BOSTON

KATZ *and* BOYD *drink champagne. Noticeably* KATZ *is trying to distract* BOYD, *whose face is somber.*

KATZ. To have the ballistics' expert say the exact opposite of what he's thinking – that's

Katzmann's masterpiece – the expert later cried out to the whole world that he was sure of the innocence of the condemned, (too late!) The two rabbits were in the bag, and Judge Thayer (even dead) wouldn't have loosened the hand that was holding it tight.

TURIN

LETIZIA *alone with* PINO

LETIZIA. We're gonna buy some candy for dad.

PINO. He doesn't like candy.

LETIZIA. What does he like?

PINO. Flowers, trees and bell peppers.

BOSTON

KURLANSKI *has found* LAUREEN.

LAUREEN. If they were guilty – why weren't they executed right away?

KURLANSKI. It's not about innocence or guilt (but about grandeur). The grandeur of our legal system, is to make available to each condemned an arsenal of procedures so that in the end only those who want to serve their punishment do so. The risks of a judicial error are practically reduced to zero.

TURIN

COLEONE *continues his discussion with his two friends.*

COLEONE. And what about the incidents with Joseph Ross, the interpreter for the trial, who falsified the translations to the detriment of the accused.

VENTURELLI. It's typical of bourgeois justice – the interpreter barely knew any Italian, but he was wanted for bribing judges. His son had the same name as Judge Thayer, and attorney Katzmann was his godfather. – That's what you call competence.

Backstage the actor playing THAYER *asks the actor playing* FULLER *to help him rehearse some lines.*

THAYER. Painful revelation you're admitting to. – No! Doesn't work. Give me the cue.

FULLER. Attempting to bribe judges – that's your case, Thayer.

THAYER. Painful revelation you're admitting to. Since I'm the only judge in the last instance, given this, Judge Thayer will be judged by Judge Thayer. – What will I tell him? Judge Thayer, with the damaging letters you receive everyday, with the filthy words with which your cabinet is described, you drink the chalice to the dregs. Even the Protestant newspapers (your own faith) are attacking you. You are becoming an old man, and I'm noticing with regret, that pity for old-timers disappeared from this world.

FULLER. What will you decide?

THAYER. I'll decide what Judge Thayer decided.

FULLER. It's in the bag (you've got nothing to fret about), it'll all work out.

STEWART. Ten minutes, we're starting again, guys.

HAMBURG

MULLER *is smoking a cigar in the company of* VORORTZUG.

MULLER. The most interesting aspect of this play isn't in the ideas (rather basic) that these two unfortunates were defending (no!) It's the role of the lawyer. – A role in solid gold. Yet the lawyers kept changing, without ever finding a good one. And the saddest thing is that everyone knew (more or less) the guilty parties, the Morellis' names were on everyone's lips.

VORORTZUG. And were they arrested?

MULLER. Only the boy that was doing the lookout.

VORORTZUG. Young?

MULLER. (A certain Madeiros.) He must have barely

been twenty… (the age of the warrior that democracies transform into the age of the degenerate outcast.)

VORORTZUG. Did he confess?

MULLER. He tried to clear Sacco and Vanzetti. (He was a poor boy.) Nothing like the messianic spirit German immigrants brought to the U.S., and maintained all the way to the gallows of Chicago. (MULLER *points to the portrait of Lingg.*) Look at that one.

VORORTZUG. What?

TURIN

LETIZIA *and* PINO *return to* CERVI

LETIZIA. Did you know that German (Lingg)? I've rarely seen such a good looking man.

CERVI. They say that on the eve of his execution – he put a stick of dynamite in his mouth and approached a candle's flame. But what no one mentions is (who brought the dynamite to the cell of someone sentenced to die?) With half his face blown off – he agonized for more than twelve hours.

LETIZIA. That's too bad (he was very good looking).

CERVI. Women's taste will always surprise me.

LETIZIA. What else can I say about him (that's all I know of him).

CERVI. Don't get upset (all roads lead to Rome).

GENERAL SELMAIRE 4 (Cont'd.)

CERVI *will be the start man of the general selmaire. He tries to imagine all the roads leading to Lingg.*

CERVI. (Lingg?)

ANNE. The best looking kid in Chicago – Lingg (might this be the present, this ever visible face of all those we've never met?)

VENTURELLI. Your coffin was nonetheless there at the meeting – Lingg.

COLEONE. At the meeting with the four hanged brothers. A coffin all covered in red, in wreaths, in flowers. Behind him, wagons hung with grief for the widows, delegations, corporations, the clubs, eighteen choir boys constantly relaying each other, three hundred women standing, forming squares, wearing black crepe on their arms, and six thousand sad workers (bare headed) with a rose against their chest.

FARLEY. At the head of the procession a mad soldier was making the starry flag dance.

ERHMAN KLOSE. You are gone, Lingg.

COLEONE. Just like Spiess, Fisher, Engel and Parson, who was the son of an American general, are gone.

KURLANSKI. Just like Joe Hills is gone, the songster at the prohibited meetings (sent to the gas chamber).

VASTADOUR. Just like Vanzetti is gone.

CERVI. Just like Sacco is gone.

ANNE. Just like Julius and Ethel are gone.

CERVI. Among which crowds are you moving now? We hear lots of news from the living, but none from the dead. – Only the eighteen choir boys continue to sing. For whom? We still don't know.

HAMBURG

VORORTZUG *tries to speak to an imaginary Madeiros, as he would with his own son. He does the questions and the answers.*

VORORTZUG. Madeiros, why'd you hang out with the Morelli brothers?
  – What's it to you?
  – Two human beings were just killed.
  – What do you think? For the Morelli brothers, it was just business. Me, I was just the look out, if they hadn't fired, they wouldn't have had the dough. (Dough, once you have it, everyone respects you.) The amount the Morelli brothers got in five minutes, a poor

guy would have to sentence himself to hard labor his entire life. And for who? For what?

– What about the families of the two victims, that you plunge into misery?

– My parents, grandparents, great-grandparents, they've been there for centuries. They left Portugal for a better life, (it hasn't changed). When they lynch a negro, or when the cops charge on workers and wipe out a few, everyone congratulates themselves. How were they different from Negroes or workers these two guys that were killed? (You can be sentimental some other time.)

MULLER. You're not too tired?

VORORTZUG. No. I was speaking to this young Madeiros, to understand the reasons that pushed him into this awful path.

MULLER. Beware my dear Vorortzug, it was your son with whom you were talking. It's just one small step from there to take on Madeiros' punishment later on.

VORORTZUG. Anyhow, it'll happen deep within myself. (No one will see anything.)

MULLER. Is that good?

VORORTZUG. You said it yourself, he was a poor boy.

LYON

Once again DERLINSKI *is struggling against the unexpected.*

DERLINSKI. Bonnetade – the record.

BONNETADE. But (that's after the intermission).

DERLINSKI. During! – Hurry up !

BONNETADE. Give me a second, I've got to connect the wires.

DERLINSKI *addresses the three actors who see him full of stress.*

DERLINSKI. Hurry (give me a hand) bring the rails!

BONNETADE, THAYER, FULLER, *and* STEWART *exit.*
DERLINSKI *talks to the crowd, explaining:*

DERLINSKI. Here it is. – Sacco and Vanzetti were in
different prisons. It took seven years for Vanzetti
to be transferred to same hallway as Sacco. (*He
places the railings that the three actors bring him,*
(*one per person*) *and he continues with his explanation.*) From where he was locked up, Sacco
could not see Vanzetti arrive. – Once he learned
of the transfer, he waited behind his door to greet
him. Vanzetti arrived (in the middle of the night)
and was locked in a cell where Sacco could neither hear nor see him. (He had to yell to be heard)
and that would draw an immediate punishment
from the guards. Sacco still found a way to greet
Vanzetti. – He sang. Once he heard him, Vanzetti
understood. The song became a duet. Neither
the guards nor the other prisoners dared inter-
rupt them – it was the first time that a song rose
from the corridors of death (on Cherry Hill).

DERLINSKI *turns to the wings to* BONNETADE.

DERLINSKI. Bonnetade – are you ready?

BONNETADE. (*Off.*) Ready.

DERLINSKI. The song – here it is!

All listen to the song that NICOLA *and* BARTOLOMEO *sang in unison that night:* E lucevano le stelle…

TURIN

The song ends, CERVI *repeats the last two verses.*

CERVI. I die hopeless. – And yet, I've never loved life as much.

VENTURELLI. Be careful (companion), once you commit to these stories (you get caught up in them).

LYON

VASTADOUR. Was that part of the show too?

DERLINSKI. That depends for whom.

HAMBURG

VORORTZUG. I've got revelations to make.

459

MULLER. This probably isn't the appropriate place.

LYON

DERLINSKI. (Intermission is over.) Bonnetade – turn off the house lights.

Bells indicating the end of intermission are heard.

HAMBURG

Lights off.

VORORTZUG. (I've got revelations to make, and I will make them.)

VII

SOUTH BRAINTREE PARADE

*Three spectators will assume an increasingly
complete identification with the characters on the
imaginary stage. They are:* CERVI, *in Turin,*
VASTADOUR, *in Lyon, and* VORORTZUG, *in Hamburg.
The Charlestown prison is now in the middle of the
seats where* CERVI – SACCO, VASTADOUR – VANZETTI,
and VORORTZUG – MADEIROS *are living, and the
grids are placed around them. They are living the
passion of the three condemned men.*

HAMBURG

KASSEL. Above all, we must be (impartial), even if
it's hard.

ERHMAN KLOSE. Impossible. (That would be capitulation.)

KASSEL. Why is that?

ERHMAN KLOSE. You can't withdraw your adherence
to something that concerns you.

KASSEL. I analyze first (then I adhere).

ERHMAN KLOSE. Illusion! – Consider this, Sacco and Vanzetti never knew South Braintree, the site of the crime, in their life. (For them it was something abstract.) Tonight however, they know it through us (or at least the idea that we have of it). We are the site of the crime – and through us Sacco and Vanzetti will once again be sentenced (and executed).

KASSEL. I refuse to follow you there.

TURIN

CERVI. Yet, we do wear this sentence – a uniform – short of rejecting it when (tomorrow at the factory), it simply doesn't fit anymore – but tonight we are wearing it, (that's for sure)…

SELMAIRE 19:
CERVI'S SELMAIRE

CERVI *relives all* NICOLA SACCO'S *distress when*
ROSINE, *his wife and his son Dante come to visit*
him in prison. BONNETADE *goes to the dressing*
room and puts on a guard's hat.

BONNETADE. (Nick) you have visitors!

CERVI. Who?

BONNETADE. (How about that!) What's going on? Are
you sick?

CERVI. No! I am very well.

BONNETADE. Mrs. Sacco!

LETIZIA *and* PINO *go towards* CERVI *who they see*
behind the bars.

LETIZIA. Nick!

PINO. (Daddy!)

CERVI. How beautiful you two are! You're really magnificent. You smell of trees (you smell of grass). You've come from far away haven't you. I was just talking about that with the comrades. We have many comrades.

LETIZIA. That's true (there are a lot of them)! Ines wants to know why you never come out with us?

A picture of Ines appears on one of the panels, stage left.

CERVI. (This "us" comes from me) and it goes far beyond this mortuary hall. It forces me to listen to myself alone – yes alone, still alone – through these voices that I believe come from somewhere over the ocean. Do you hear the ocean?

LETIZIA. We hear it, Nick (we hear it very well).

CERVI. You do hear it, don't you?

LETIZIA. Nick, (we brought you flowers).

CERVI. Flowers? (Give them to me.) Once again the question: is it me who is dying? Is it you?

INES.(*Off.*) (Dad!) You promised last time – that you would play with me – the white horse running in the fields.

CERVI. That's true! – the horse.

He kneels.

PINO. Dad!

LETIZIA. (Are you tired?)

CERVI. Dante! (*He reaches for him at a distance, arms open.*) Where is Ines?

PINO. She stayed home (she's too young to understand).

CERVI. Take Ines and your mother (to visit Bart). He doesn't have any visitors. His family is far away.

LETIZIA. Of course, Nick, (we'll go see Bart).

465

CERVI. You too are his family.

SELMAIRE 20:
FARLEY'S SELMAIRE

This visit of SACCO'S *children reminds* FARLEY *of the two Rosenberg children's visit to their parents, locked up in Sing-Sing.*

FARLEY. Playing with his children in this hallway to give them a carefree moment, Julius Rosenberg had never known anything more terrible. (Even if you can hold out to the end of the visit, you never get over it.)

BONNETADE *escorts* VANZETTI *out from behind his bars. Immediately he goes down on all fours and begins to run.*

VASTADOUR. Going from Plymouth to Boston,
through the bitter air of
Massachusetts Bay
the horse dreamed of a world
without fences, because he did not
want to jump any more.

But the District Attorney and the college president said:
this horse wants to drink the whole ocean
and the horse went back
in the opposite direction. Having
run around from Plymouth to Boston so often
the horse could no longer find the way out.

He falls in front of Ines' portrait.

ANNE. What terrible benchmarks. (Can such moments remain sterile?)

The family imagined by CERVI *leaves. Ines' picture stays, but no longer lit.*

LYON

VASTADOUR. Nick! – Your wife has only one fault, being beautiful. Behind your peep-hole, you think (that she consoles herself with someone else). Then you're upset with yourself – and you grant her all the agonies of a wife forced to mourn a living husband.

TURIN

CERVI. Since you understand everything, you know that I'm a burden on them. – They should forget about me and go on with their lives.

LYON

VASTADOUR. They are struggling, and you have no right to abandon them. – Nick, I know what's in your silences. You've abandoned us (you're already living with the others) those of Chicago and those already fallen at the four corners of the world.

TURIN

CERVI. (And how are they disgraced?)

LYON

VASTADOUR. They're not. But you're forcing me to go to war against them. (And it's painful for me.) Anyhow, our dead are so numerous they don't need you. You shouldn't turn towards them anymore – do it at least for Ines. We were already in prison when she was born. For her, a father represents the house of the dead, or a home for the criminally insane.

TURIN

CERVI. Bart you too were with the criminally insane, yet you still lived in the present.

NEW ORLEANS

XIOMARA. (But he didn't have any children to appear in front of.)

TURIN

All the lights focus on Ines' picture.

CERVI. I would love for you to understand me. I want so much for you to hear your father's heart beat for you, (I love you so much)! It's hard to understand at your age. But the words, all the words I'm telling you cannot be lost. They will reach you, through the years, and you'll feel how much affection these narrow walls can hold. The most precious, the softest aspect of my life as a militant (yes, I am one), is the hope of living with you (of living, do you hear?), with your mother and your brother on a small farm, and of listening to you, of feeling you. (*He imagines* NICOLA *the day of his liberation from prison, speaking to his daughter. He leaves the grid he's in, and prowls around her picture.*) It's over. Come, come Ines, let's go sit under a tree, and we'll learn English, (it's about time I learn). After that, we'll race in the forest. And when you're tired, I'll sing to you, *E lucevano le stelle...* We'll come back through the prairies and pick wild flowers (the ones your mom likes best). Then we'll play hide and seek in bushes. Then we'll go swimming, then – then – then – then. (*His imagination can't go any further, he goes towards his grid.*) You are in my heart, in my eyes, in each corner of the cell, in the little bit of sky I can glimpse and everywhere my eyes set. It's your father Ines! Your father, can you hear him?

HAMBURG

Behind his railing, VORORTZUG *calls.*

VORORTZUG. I wrote to the *Boston American*, to reveal what I know of the South Braintree case. The police must have tried to destroy the letter. Try to get this magazine to Sacco. There's a note for him inside.

LYON

BONNETADE *has a magazine in his hand; he opens it, folds it and says:*

BONNETADE. Sacco, take this magazine, there's a note for you in it.

TURIN

CERVI. Bart! Bart! "With this letter, I confess having been in on the South Braintree crime. Sacco and Vanzetti were not involved. They ought to contact their lawyers." Signed, Celestino Madeiros. I have in my hands the confession that proves our innocence.

VASTADOUR. We'll have waited six years for that. We
made it.

GENERAL SELMAIRE 5

All the VANZETTIS *rise.*

THE VANZETTIS
The sinister immigrant barracks
scream victory from Plymouth and from Boston.
They will be filled with golden crabs
they will be filled with bountiful fish
to celebrate the founder of Massachusetts
Bartolomeo Vanzetti.

The SACCOS *now rise*

THE SACCOS
Two school children said
to a child who could not attend
anymore: you have a famous
father, they gave him five marbles
and one in glass. Inside
twelve colors spelled the name
Nicola Sacco.

THE SACCOS *and* VANZETTIS
    The judges and cops
    will protect the offices of the corporations.
    From behind his pushcart, Bart
    will speak again of a world
    without fences. And Nick
    will nod in silent approval
    in the city of red bricks
    with his antiquated look of a copper engraving.

SELMAIRE 21:
VORORTZUG'S SELMAIRE

VORORTZUG *continues to identify with* MADEIROS
through the pressures he is being submitted to after
his confession.

VORORTZUG. Now, I stand waiting for you on firm
    footing.

STEWART. Madeiros, since you participated in the
    murder, do you know your accomplices?

VORORTZUG. I know what I did. – I don't need to
    worry about anyone else.

STEWART. Keep quiet then. – If you want to save your skin, keep it shut permanently.

VORORTZUG. You can check all the details I gave you. – There are twelve pages, handwritten.

STEWART. Do you think I have time to waste reading your literature?

VORORTZUG. The Committee for the Defense of Sacco and Vanzetti also have a copy. There are writers over there – they know how to read.

STEWART. You're wrong to want to defy justice.

VORORTZUG. On the contrary, I'm assisting it.

STEWART. Which gang, according to you was behind the South Braintree hit?

VORORTZUG. I won't give a name.

STEWART. Your confession is worth nothing.

VORORTZUG. Saving two innocent lives and ratting are two different things.

STEWART. Which means your two accomplices were those two anarchists, and you're gonna burn with them. – As you wish.

SELMAIRE 22:
ERHMAN KLOSE'S SELMAIRE

ERHMAN KLOSE *feels the need to hurry things forward. Once again, flashing on and off, the images of brochures on the case are projected.*

ERHMAN KLOSE. My testimony can confirm Madeiros'. Everyone knows the names of the accomplices. They're Mike, Joe and Patsy Morelli.

STEWART. That's enough! (We didn't ask you.)

ERHMAN KLOSE. That's true. – Nonetheless, according to your law, a motion was adopted on this point.

STEWART. (It's Judge Thayer who's going to be surprised.)

ERHMAN KLOSE. One way or another, innocence always triumphs in the end.

VENTURELLI. One way or another, (you were right to mention it).

LYON

Two shadows appear from the imaginary stage hands up, it's the Morellis. In front of them, STEWART. *The roles of the Morelli brothers are played by the* PRESS AGENT *and the* OFFICIAL OF DEATH.

STEWART. Are you the Morelli brothers? – Lower your hands, someone's gonna notice.

PRESS AGENT. What do you want then?

STEWART. Move out of the state, and in a hurry. – Get the hell to New York.

PRESS AGENT. Are you serious?

STEWART. Dead serious. But first, sign this affidavit saying you never knew Madeiros.

OFFICIAL. He squealed!

PRESS AGENT. The fucker! We'll be waiting when he gets out.

STEWART. Don't worry, he won't be out anytime soon.

PRESS AGENT. Why the affidavit if we're done for?

STEWART. The judge asked for it.

OFFICIAL. Hey, we're okay with it.

STEWART. Now scram!

At the ticket-counter / tribunal, THAYER, *alone gives his opinion on Madeiros' affidavit.*

THAYER. Beyond the shadow of a doubt Madeiros is a crook, a thief, a liar, a rum smuggler, a nightclub employee in shady places, a counterfeiter, and a man sentenced for the murder of a cashier of the Wrentham bank. An affidavit from such a man must be closely scrutinized and dissected with the greatest care, wariness and reflection before a jury's verdict, confirmed by the Supreme Court of this country can be set aside. Two irrefutable arguments come to mind. Why would the Morellis, who are capable of acts, very virile to say the least, burden themselves with a youth, incapable of handling a gun, unknown in the gangster world and on top of all that, he's shy. Furthermore, a definitive argument corroborating the former theory, the Morellis have signed an affidavit stating they never knew Madeiros. Consequently...

FULLER. (Good, everything is going according to plan). The important thing for our electoral campaign, is that someone other than me take the responsibility for their sentencing or their acquittal. – This trial has stopped being a friendly poker game where winners and losers leave the table without grudges – it's entered an intellectual phase and we've got to treat it like live dynamite. – Let Harvard University issue an opinion.

BOSTON

BOYD. In that case, it will be death – our great discovery is pragmatism, don't you think?

LYON

THAYER. The problem is that this death, these two damned anarchists want it. They want it to promote their dark ambitions.

FULLER. I'm not sure I follow.

THAYER. They want to die so that all the subversives and anti-American elements can dirty our country with impunity.

FULLER. Then we need to pardon. – But do it yourself (don't drag me) into activities incompatible with future elections.

BOSTON

BOYD. I don't understand anymore.

HAMBURG

KASSEL. It would perhaps be doing a favor for Sacco's children, who I admit sometime keep me from sleeping.

LYON

THAYER. Do you think their father is a good example
for them? Believe me, it's better that they're apart.

The courtroom. CERVI *and* VASTADOUR *are brought
in front of the public, one on each side.*

BOSTON

KATZ. (I like the archaic yet terribly efficient style of
judicial language . If it please the court, the cases
in question are accusation acts # 5545 and 5546,
confederation against Nicola Sacco and
Bartolomeo Vanzetti. It appears that according
to the trial in this Court and, if it pleases your
Honor, and concerning accusation acts 5545 and
5546, that the accused were convicted of murder in the first degree. The trial was clear in this
matter and we request the Court executes the
sentence.

LYON

THAYER. (Bring me flowers.) Judge Webster Thayer
was seated surrounded by flowers that the people

480

of Boston gave him in a gesture of gratitude by way of the four police and army detachments surrounding the Hall of Justice. – Nicola Sacco, do you have anything to add that may oppose the execution of the death sentence pronounced against you?

CERVI. Yes sir. I am no orator. After seven years, you still consider us guilty. Our friends and companions here in this room, and in the name of millions of friends and companions around the world, are then also guilty with us. The sentence is the rich class against the oppressed one. You are the oppressor, judge, and you know it. You know my life, it is clear. Yet you're persecuting my wife and children – me, you're sending me to death. Should I speak of myself now?

GENERAL SELMAIRE 6

VENTURELLI *identifies with the condemned man and wants to speak in his place. Since he has too much to say, his intervention turns short.*

VENTURELLI. What's the use? – Nick's last words cannot be about himself – but rather for the legions of known and unknown people who gather around him during his torture.

All THE SACCOS *rise.*

THE SACCOS. Here's to you comrades, thank you!

LYON

THAYER. Bartolomeo Vanzetti, do you have something to add?

VENTURELLI. Yes, judge. – I have to say that I'm innocent of all the crimes imputed to me, and what's more I have spent my whole life trying to eliminate crime in this world – not only the crime that official and moral law punishes, but also the crime that official and moral law permits and justifies (especially the exploitation of man by man)! If there is a reason why I'm here considered guilty, if there's a reason that's pushing you to annihilate me, it is nowhere else. – There is a man, the best I've ever met in my life, a man the people will cherish more and more, as kindness and a sense of sacrifice are more and more accepted. I'm speaking of Eugene Debs. This man really experienced the courts, prison and the jury. It's because he wanted a world a little better that he was persecuted and defamed, from his youth to his death.

Stage right side, Eugene Debs' picture is projected.

SELMAIRE 23:
BOSCHETTO'S SELMAIRE

Under Debs' picture, BOSCHETTO *tries to imagine an encounter between Debs and* VANZETTI, *without knowing for certain where it might have happened nor what was said.* BOSCHETTO *speaks as if he were Debs.*

BOSCHETTO. And the sun, where does it get its light from, Bart?

FARLEY. From us, Eugene, from us.

BOSCHETTO. And the sky?

FARLEY. It's our solitude, that we're trying to eliminate.

VASTADOUR. They said the defense raised all sorts of obstacles to prevent this case from happening. (That's an insult) because it's not true. The prosecution needed a whole year to gather its evidence (that's one of the five years the case lasted) before beginning our trial, and before getting to our first appearance in court. – Then the defense appealed, and you waited. I think that from that moment you were determined to reject any appeal on our part. You had everyone wait several weeks to announce your decision (the night of Christmas).

SELMAIRE 24:
COLEONE'S SELMAIRE

COLEONE *evokes that winter.*

COLEONE. It was very cold that Christmas. (Boston is a northern city.)

LETIZIA. The children were well covered.

COLEONE. It was the workers' solidarity that clothed them.

LETIZIA. But they were still cold – on the inside and the outside.

ERHMAN KLOSE. (They've been cold for more than seventy years.)

ANNE. There's something obvious here that we can't quite name. Sacco's two children were already the two Rosenberg children, destined to die from that Christmas, everyday of their lives.

VASTADOUR. I don't even wish a snake to suffer what I've suffered for the crimes that I am not guilty of. But I did suffer for others who exist only in your mind – because I'm an extremist, that I am! – I suffered more for my beliefs than for myself. But I am convinced, that if it were possible for you to kill me twice (and me to be born twice), I would live my life the exact same way. I've been talking about myself a lot, and I've almost forgotten Sacco. He too is a worker that sacrificed everything for the cause; his money, his ambitions, his wife, his children, his life. (Neither he nor I) have ever eaten a piece of bread, from our childhood to today, that the sweat of our brow didn't earn – never! So many times, listening to him, him the worker, the one who always sacrifices standing up, I felt very small. I had to fight not to cry in front of him, in front of this man that is now treated like a thief and an assassin and who is sentenced to die. But the name Sacco will live in the hearts of men and in their gratitude – while your bones, and those of the lead attorney will be reduced to dust by time – and your name and his, as well as your laws and your institutions (and your false god) will be a vague memory of a cursed past in which man was a wolf for man. (VASTADOUR *stops speaking and the greatest silence reigns. He looks at the judge who grabs the gavel*). I'm finished. Thank you.

THAYER *bangs with his gavel repeatedly even though there is no noise or disorder.*

THAYER. In accordance with the laws of Massachusetts, the verdicts of the jury are valid. The objections are rejected. Consequently, Nicola Sacco will be punished by death by electrocution in the week beginning Sunday July 10th of the year of the Lord 1927. It is ordered by the Court that Bartolomeo Vanzetti, on the same date…

VASTADOUR. (One minute please.)

THAYER. (*screaming.*) Will be punished by death by electrocution.

VIII

HYMN FOR AN ASSASSINATED CHILD

HAMBURG

VORORTZUG. All is not lost. The governor is an honest man (he can still pardon).

BOSTON

LAUREEN. Everyone who knows him well says he is a courageous man, straight forward and who fights for what he believes to be just.

487

LYON

VASTADOUR. Those who know him and think highly of him are just like him, they resemble him. – I know Governor Alvan T. Fuller better than they do, because I was exactly like they are. Today, I have changed completely, and that's how I realize what I used to be. (My defense attorney, Master Thomson told me…)

HAMBURG

MULLER. The average American, whose will is law, thinks very little of you. – They are convinced of your guilt.

LYON

VASTADOUR. It's natural that we have so many enemies who feel solidarity with rogues and criminals (who testified against us), with the jury, with Thayer and the executioner. I understand them because I was one of them, and I thought like them. – Today I am ashamed of it.

SELMAIRE 25:
BOSCHETTO'S SELMAIRE

BOSCHETTO *imagines what could have happened at* PRESIDENT COOLIDGE'S *that day. The puppet is being used again.*

BOSCHETTO. Mr. President, the Italian government is requesting clemency to calm the agitation in the cities.

COOLIDGE. Mr. Mussolini who managed to make the trains arrive on time can't keep his citizens at bay? Come on!

BOSCHETTO. The U.S. embassies in Germany, France, Belgium, Holland are continually swamped in protests.

COOLIDGE. Is that all?

BOSCHETTO. In Japan, India, China and South Africa, there are bomb threats.

COOLIDGE. That in no way concerns my administration.

BOSCHETTO. In Latin America, buildings where our representatives live are being attacked, even destroyed.

COOLIDGE. You're so naïve! Can't you see, that's only Russian propaganda.

BOSCHETTO. The British embassy has asked for a pardon.

COOLIDGE. I don't take orders from His Majesty.

BOSCHETTO. The Chief Justice is here.

COOLIDGE. Let him come in.

ERHMAN KLOSE. The defense has just asked for a stay. (The arguments are well presented), but since the Court is on vacation, the defendants will die – before the Court has heard their petition. The case seems of such magnitude that I decided to ask your opinion on a possible stay.

COOLIDGE. I don't have one.

THE SACCOS (*except* CERVI) *and* THE VANZETTIS
(*except* VASTADOUR) *rise to sing* And His Five
Pennies of the New World.

America (which America?)
folds beneath the bludgeons.
America (which America?)
assembles in school
yards on Salem Street
and descends bent in two
from meeting rooms.
America, (which America?)
searches for her lifeline
through the scars
of the old fighters gambling
heads or tails
for soup-line tickets.

THE SACCOS *and* VANZETTIS *split into the four
corners of America to try desperately to obtain a
stay of execution for the condemned of
Charlestown. They are in New York, at a union
meeting.*

491

COLEONE. (*Construction*). Ten thousand people protesting at Union Square.

XIOMARA. (*Food*). That's incredible.

BOSCHETTO. (*Defense committee*). If we can get the backing of the American Federation of Labor, (we'll save them).

LITTLE NED. (*Shoe industry*). The backing of servants and sell outs.

BOSCHETTO. (*Defense committee*). Everyone knows that. – That's why we need them.

DERLINSKI. (*Railway Brotherhood*). The American union movement is dying in the Charlestown prison with our two brothers.

VENTURELLI. (*Jewelry*). To save them we need to start a mass strike.

LITTLE NED. (*Shoe industry*). Are you dreaming, comrade? We'll cut ourselves off from the masses without saving anybody.

KURLANSKI. (*Metals*). The men capable of organizing a mass strike have sold out to the bosses. The unions that could possibly start a mass strike were squashed, destroyed in blood. Remember Chicago.

DERLINSKI. (*Railway Brotherhood*). Ever since Chicago, we've been beaten down so much.

VENTURELLI. (*Jewelry*). Aren't we going to wind up bowing our heads.

LYON

BONNETADE. Are you doing well, Bartolomeo?

VASTADOUR. Perhaps better than I think.

BONNETADE. No one would feel well in your shoes.

VASTADOUR. (You think so?) It'd be hard to complain, we're housed and fed for free, we don't work, we don't produce anything. We are real capitalists.

BONNETADE. Today, you can ask for whatever you want to eat, (and the priest will come whenever you want him.)

VASTADOUR. My only desire is to see Sacco. For seven years we've only had one difference. He always thought we'd be executed. I thought the working class and men of good conscience would end up saving us. – I've got to tell him that today, that difference does not exist.

HAMBURG

VORORTZUG. (*Screaming*). A priest! – Right away. – A priest!

LYON

BONNETADE. (Madeiros is going off again.) Morphine for cell 3!

TURIN

CERVI. Madeiros, I'd like you to be courageous.

HAMBURG

VORORTZUG. They're testing the electric chair.

*The lights dim throughout the prison, indicating
that they are making tests.*

TURIN

CERVI. Don't give up.

HAMBURG

VORORTZUG. That's a good one.

GENERAL SELMAIRE 8

THE SACCOS *and* VANZETTIS *sing the* Muskrat
Ramble of the Indian Leader.

The Indian leader of the I.W.W.
has a body completely swollen
he moans on his bed
with a broken leg.

He should have kept quiet the Apache
what did he know
of Sacco – Vanzetti, foreigners
of the Charlestown prison
and the corridor of the condemned.

They pulled him from bed
and forced him to walk
to speak of Sacco – Vanzetti.
He should have kept quiet the Apache.
Because he wouldn't move,
they hung him from a beam
on the railroad bridge,
in case he had any thoughts
of traveling.

He should have kept quiet the Apache.
And now he swings
he swings the Apache,
He swings with the wind
with his swollen body
and his broken leg.
He should have kept his mouth shut
the Apache, he should have.

THE VANZETTIS *continue their conversation in Colorado.*

ANNE. (*Defense Committee*). How are people reacting in the mines?

LITTLE NED. (*Miners*). Crushed and starved. Just read the papers. We've only got two options – shut our mouths or be Russian spies.

COLEONE. (*Copper*). In the copper mines, we launched a strike. Some struck (others didn't). Those who did paid a heavy price. For them Sacco and Vanzetti have become the scolding wife – and the children asking for something to eat.

KURLANSKI. (*Bakery*). If we had syndicates or powerful organizations like in Europe, we could act, but we don't have any, (it's useless to pretend otherwise).

COLEONE. (*Copper*). The American Federation of Labor does have one good syndicate, but they're having a good laugh about the whole thing. "Those damn macaronis are getting what they deserve."

ANNE. (*Defense Committee*). What are the dock workers in the big ports doing? If they slowed a little it would help.

THE SACCOS *are meeting in the Chicago region.*

VENTURELLI. (*Slaughterhouses*). So, what do we do?

FARLEY. (*Defense Committee*). Meetings are forbidden in the whole Chicago area.

VENTURELLI. (*Slaughterhouses*). It was the same thing for our own hanged ones. Remember the old bearded guy – what he said to the fifty thousand comrades, who carried the five corpses into the earth. "Me, I don't accuse the executioner, I don't accuse this country who sang (for mercy) in churches, because these men were hanged. I accuse the workers of Chicago who allowed the assassination of five of their companions."

FARLEY. (*Defense Committee*). What's the point of marching right in front of machine guns ready to fire?

VENTURELLI. (*Slaughterhouses*). So we're going to sit quietly and wait for them to be electrocuted?

ERHMAN KLOSE. (*Manufacturers*). That's no longer the right question. Are they dying for nothing? That is more important to know. Are we beaten?

VENTURELLI. (*Slaughterhouses*). Yes we are, and for a long time.

They all gather around PINO *who is crossing the supposed stage, and from there, through the streets of Boston. Each one adding a sentence to the debate.*

THE SACCOS *and* VANZETTIS. Who, the white eye of the lighthouse,
Who is he looking for in broad daylight
in the port neighborhood?
Why are the streets of Boston
angled?
Why do the gaze of people
close these angles?
Why is the controller of public transportation
pulling on the alarm?

499

Why is private transportation
insulting,
and why does light act
like an angry schoolteacher?
Why are the good mornings-goodnights
a conspiracy
as incurable
as the third graders
plans
for recess?
Why, when the sirens
scream
does the child feel this scream escape from within.
It's the anarchist's son
(it gave him teeth, said the syndicates).
He's the product of the Italian
(it gave him feet, said the clear consciences).
It's little Dante Sacco
(it'll give him character, said the well-fed).
He's white, but a contagious white,
thought the blacks,
who were snacking on ginger
in milk bars on Lincoln Street.

Three merry-go-round horses
encircle

a barely started school notebook,
at bay
it's little Dante Sacco crying.

SELMAIRE 26:
LETIZIA'S SELMAIRE

As he ends his march through Boston, PINO *huddles
in* LETIZIA'S *arms, who imagines what* ROSINE
SACCO *might have said in such a situation.*

PINO. I can't, Mom (I can't anymore).

LETIZIA. (You must.) Dad is doing better. He stopped
his hunger strike. Bart intervened. It was about
time, (last time I saw him, he was barely alive).
He sent us a note, as if to apologize to us. – He
said that if he went on this strike, it was only to
protest (against death).

TURIN

From behind his grid, CERVI *calls to his son, and Dante at the same time.*

CERVI. Dante, my son, my comrade – between Friday and Monday (they will electrocute us) just after midnight. I will be with you, just as I am now, with all my love and my heart open. – I am for life Dante, so must you be (don't cry). Rediscover happiness the three of you. – But remember, you must always help the weak who are calling for help, the victims, the persecuted. They are your brothers, those who fight and who fall, like your father and Bart. Love (the true one), you will find it in the struggle for the humble, and you will be loved. – From the heart of the house of the dead, I scream towards you Dante, (my Dante) because of the kids' voices, playing on the sports field. Life is dancing, jumping, having fun, singing a few feet away from the walls where the secret agony of three buried souls are locked up. And I want to see you, and I want to see Ines, and I am comforted thinking it's better for you not to see the sad image of three men who are waiting to be electrocuted, (because I don't know what kind of an effect that would have on you at your age). But on the other hand, if you weren't so sensitive, this humble memory could be useful to scream to the world about this persecution, this death. They may annihilate our bodies, but not our ideas, and the young generation that follows us will continue to defend them. Love, Dante. Stay close to your mother and to those who are dear to us in these difficult days. Don't forget to love me a little, I love you so much. Dante! It's your father calling you. Dante! Dante! it's your comrade Nicola – do you hear me?

GENERAL SELMAIRE 9

All gather around Dante. THE SACCOS *and* VANZETTIS *backs to him, the others facing him.*

LITTLE NED. It's the little guy from South Braintree.

XIOMARA. There isn't an inch of his clothing that wasn't given to him – his father had a bank account though.

THAYER. It's the Italian's son! What arrogance! Walking around the streets of Boston like that with a father like his.

From behind his grid, VASTADOUR *yells.*

VASTADOUR. We will fight, Dante, we will fight until the last moment, and even afterwards.

BOYD. Is he defying us? (Or is it simply failure to understand.)

MULLER. Is it you Dante Sacco? – My, have they talked about you in the papers!

KATZ. Our future is in the bag, old buddy. The South Braintree crime benefited the whole family.

VASTADOUR. Remember why they're executing us, Dante.

FARLEY. He's nervous, sad, closed. Not fun at all.

BOSCHETTO. He has people to blame.

LAUREEN. (It's because foreigners never wash themselves.) Have you heard of soap? Tooth paste? Shaving cream?

VENTURELLI. Kid – you see what crazy ideas have done to your father. You'll have to really behave from now on.

FULLER. And walk straight, like a metal ruler.

ERHMAN KLOSE. Smile! Well, smile! – America is optimistic. She needs happy people.

ANNE. Is it you, Dante Sacco? – How do you feel about all this?

VASTADOUR. Later, you'll understand better your father's and my principles. You are like a son to me. A hug from your two fathers.

THAYER. What do you feel, when you sing *Yankee Doodle*?

STEWART. Your name please?

THAYER. Answer yes or no.

STEWART. Your name?

SELMAIRE 27:
KURLANSKI'S SELMAIRE

KURLANSKI *imagines Dante's future.*

KURLANSKI. He has two possible answers.

PINO. I am the son of Nicola Sacco and Bartolomeo Vanzetti.

KURLANSKI. Or?

PINO. Smith. Harry Smith.

STEWART. Black? Italian? Jew?

PINO. Pure American.

From behind the grids, CERVI *asks:*

CERVI. Bart! Bart! – What day is it?

HALF-NOTE AND QUARTER-NOTE
ON A TRIPLE AGONY

LYON

Ines' portrait reappears. FULLER *at his desk.*

FULLER. Excuse me – the doctor forbade excessive work. (For a man of my age, you must understand.)

He turns a gramophone on.

GRAMOPHONE. For seven years and with extraordinary patience I've listened to everything. Despite all the measures taken, all the possible appeals, all the ways of adjourning, the guilt of these two men has remained unshaken.

FULLER *turns off the gramophone.*

FULLER. Should I start it again.

ERHMAN KLOSE *imagines he is intervening with*
LOUISE VANZETTI. *He pushes* LAUREEN *in front of*
him.

ERHMAN KLOSE. Louise Vanzetti, Mr. Governor, the
sister. She came from Italy. A man with white
hair (like yours) sent her.

LAUREEN *kneels and takes out the rosary, and runs*
them through her hands.

LAUREEN. Our father is Catholic. (He rejected his
son because he was red.) For six years, he forbade
us to speak about him. Last month he told me:
"Cross the ocean to the place where my son is
held prisoner. Introduce yourself to the ruler of
that country and ask grace for my son."

FULLER *starts the gramophone again.*

GRAMOPHONE. I am sorry I am unable to do anything.
But all the defense witnesses told me stories that

seem much more like a rehearsal than the product of memory.

FULLER. Maybe you don't understand English well enough? (Certain nuances might have escaped you.) Should I play it again?

LAUREEN. I don't know.

FULLER. Mr. law professor, would you like anything?

ERHMAN KLOSE. To leave.

LYON

VASTADOUR. Nick? (The only thing left for us is to console ourselves.) When I arrived in this country, I worked like an animal, and all I saw around me were walls. Today (when we are definitively) confined within walls I can glimpse the crack.

HAMBURG

VORORTZUG. And how does that help you, Mr. Vanzetti?

LYON

VASTADOUR. Electrical currents are the answer to a lot of things, but not to everything.

HAMBURG

VORORTZUG. I don't know how you'll settle your affairs, but for me at midnight, it's over.

LYON

VASTADOUR. That's not it.

HAMBURG

VORORTZUG. I know what I'm saying Mr. Vanzetti. – Listen, Sacco had a garden, he'd wake up at four in the morning to work in it (solely for pleasure). Tomorrow morning, after the execution, he'll probably get up and work in it again. – Me, I won't get up, (because behind me there are only the alleys of Providence, Rhode Island, that is, misery, rottenness, darkness). After my death, those are the alleys that I'll return to.

LYON

VASTADOUR. We too are carrying all the misery we've known, (and from Turin to Boston, there's quite a bit of it). What I want you to understand, is that we're approaching the day when, through others like us, people will ease it for us.

HAMBURG

VORORTZUG. But there is a difference – you can croak in peace, you're innocent. Whereas me, I'm dying because it's just, it's the price for what I did. – I'm telling you, when you raise yourself as best you can, in the filth of New Bedford's school, there are no honorable jobs. It's always the same garbage, seen from a different angle. The – same – garbage – it – doesn't – change.

VORORTZUG *swells his voice, the* PRESS AGENT *enters.*

BOSTON

PRESS AGENT. What's wrong with you, yelling that way?

HAMBURG

VORORTZUG. I'll – tell – you – tomorrow – morning!

BOSTON

PRESS AGENT. Be careful – or else!

HAMBURG

VORORTZUG. What else can you do to me?

LYON

VASTADOUR. Please, leave us.

BOSTON

PRESS AGENT. What do you want?

LYON

VASTADOUR. Leave us.

BOSTON

PRESS AGENT. You think it's fun hearing you scream like that. (*Leaves.*)

TURIN

CERVI. Celestino? – When you want to say something, if you yell it, only the prison guards will hear it. If you say it quietly – then the entire earth will listen.

HAMBURG

VORORTZUG. Do you believe in God, Mr. Sacco?

TURIN

CERVI. No, but I believe in a tree sap that links us to one another (to yet a million others). That's why Bart said earlier that we are not dying.

HAMBURG

VORORTZUG. The story of your garden, I understand. But this – no.

LYON

VASTADOUR. Celestino. – When you admitted to the South Braintree crime, was it for revenge on your partners who abandoned you?

HAMBURG

VORORTZUG. Revenge? That had nothing to do with it. It's not because of you either. It's because of Mr. Sacco's children. When I saw how furiously they were bent on killing you, I thought it must have been some sort of pay back between the judges and you. (I didn't get involved.) But when I saw those two kids walk into this prison – it simply overwhelmed me. (At the same time, I had the feeling that if I confessed to what happened in South Braintree, all would be lost for me and I would die.) But I couldn't have done it any other way.

LYON

VASTADOUR. That's big what you did there, Celestino. (You don't need anyone now.) Your sacrifice puts you in a place where the justice of this country can't reach you. Sacco and I, we give our lives for the oppressed. You – you give yours to erase the sadness on the face of two children. We are three peas from the same pod, Celestino. It's impossible to shake your hand now. But after our execution, while Nick returns to his garden, I'll come and shake it.

HAMBURG

VORORTZUG. I can't find words to answer you. – Thank you Mr. Vanzetti.

GENERAL SELMAIRE 10

THE SACCOS *and* VANZETTIS *sing* And His Five Pennies of the New World, (cont'd.)

SACCOS *and* VANZETTIS. Night will come to Fall River. Night will come to Boston a night of sweat and agony

the sweat and agony
of the two condemned
from Cherry Hill where all
the trees are cut down.
America, (which America?)
folds beneath the bludgeons.

SELMAIRE 29:
LAUREEN'S SELMAIRE

LAUREEN *tries to imagine the reaction in the streets*
of Boston. She talks with potential reporters who
appear indifferent.

LAUREEN. If we kill these two men – that means
there will never be justice again.

BOSCHETTO. My poor lady. – Has there ever been? If
you weren't fresh off the boat, you would have
heard of Tom Mooney, Joe Hill and a few hundred
others.

BONNETADE. Whoever saw them in their cells would
feel such a remarkable sensation that they could
do nothing but take off their hat and say – these
are a rare breed.

BOSCHETTO. In that case, it's becoming incomprehensible that they haven't been executed sooner.

LAUREEN. That's because the peoples of the entire world did not permit it.

BOSCHETTO. Stop gargling with useless words. – Isn't it the people who take the most pleasure in the torture and execution of its best? If I may and if it's not stretching too far into history, who asked for the execution of our friend Jesus – Christ? (Should we still to this day accuse Pontius Pilate and blame him for bowing to the popular will?)

GENERAL SELMAIRE 11

And his Five Pennies of the New World (*cont.*)
Sung by the SACCOS *and* VANZETTIS

America is bellowing, from the cry
of all its slaughterhouses.
In Chicago, meetings
are prohibited. And the police
watches, because it knows
it is about the sweat

and agony of America.
and that once this night over
its head bowed
on school benches
of Pawtucket and Boston
listening to words
seven year old,
this is its last night.
She will never again be reborn
America, which (America)?

SELMAIRE 30:
KASSEL'S SELMAIRE

KASSEL *follows Reverend Michael Murphy who enters the Charlestown prison on Cherry Hill, preceded by head guard Hendry.*

BONNETADE. I'll go in with you (even though this walk is a real punishment for me).

KASSEL. Strong heads?

BONNETADE. Madeiros bawls for nothing. – But the two Italians are people who teach you about human kindness. (Sometimes it's unbearable.)

KASSEL. Damn! (Can't we try one more time) since they're so well disposed?

BONNETADE. You'd be wasting your time. You'll have enough on your hands with the hysteria, which by itself, will demand of you (body and soul). (*They arrive in front of the three cells.*) Celestino, your priest is finally here. You have all the time you want to prepare your end with him, since it must come.

VORORTZUG. Thanks to you both. – But I don't need anything.

BONETADE. Hey! Celestino! Wake up now.

VORORTZUG. I am perfectly awake.

BONNETADE. (*To* PRESS AGENT.) Did you give him too much morphine?

PRESS AGENT. No. He stopped yelling an hour ago.

KASSEL. Your decision is serious.

VORORTZUG. Take it as it is.

519

BONNETADE. Why don't you want a priest anymore?

VORORTZUG. Now I've got two friends.

KASSEL. For which I congratulate you. But they cannot ever give you the Lord's absolution.

VORORTZUG. They've given me another.

KASSEL. Pray! Celestino Madeiros, pray with me.

VORORTZUG. I'm no longer afraid, why do you want me to pray?

HAMBURG

KASSEL *is again a spectator, praying by himself.*

KASSEL. I can ignore their innocence (if it exists) but not their suffering. – Lord! (Still You, Lord!)

TURIN

BOSCHETTO. Now that once more their last night on Earth begins again
we become visible and palpable

and the tributaries of a body
more than is possible.

NEW ORLEANS

LITTLE NED. So much so – that some of us can only
bear it, by recreating everyday of our life (the
march through the corridor of death).

HAMBURG

KASSEL. All the prisons, or beginnings of prisons
Will do at this moment.
They will reconfigure as if around
A golden number.

BOSTON

FARLEY. Four steps forward-backwards
(and we'll see the electric chair).

ANNE. Three steps left-right
(and we'll see the electric chair).

LYON

BONNETADE. Tonight, like every night – for more than seventy-four years – Rosine Sacco and Louise Vanzetti will cross the river that separates Boston from Cherry Hill.

HAMBURG

KASSEL. You are dead without hope (still You, Lord)? I won't be able to tell them anything, (I won't be able to tell You anything).

LYON

BONNETADE. The house of the dead is on Cherry Hill. – Tonight, like every night (for more than seventy-four years) Rosine Sacco and Louise Vanzetti have an appointment.

TURIN

LETIZIA. The four of us love one another infinitely, Nick.

CERVI. Then, there is no need to be sad. If Ines asks where her father is, tell her: (in the forest). Let her lie down among trees and watch the grass stir, and the leaves, and she will find me again. (Paradise was there, I'm sure of it, but it is forbidden for me.) You, maybe you won't find me there. But the essential will be there; the love that binds the four of us. Hug my son (and companion).

BOSTON

ANNE. (The bars are an inch and a half thick in the house of the dead. Faces push up against the cell doors without being able to touch.)

LYON

VASTADOUR. Louise, the hardest time of these seven years (wasn't the sentencing) no – it was father's abandonment.

BOSTON

LAUREEN. He doesn't understand (these leftist things) very well. We would have been so happy to put you back on the path of faith.

LYON

VASTADOUR. Tell him to redo the roof of the house. Already in my time the central beam was weakening. In the stable, one day the foundation will have to be rebuilt. The animals are always more comfortable when the straw doesn't get wet so quickly. Louise – the last memory you take away of me is this prison. I wouldn't want this corridor to cross the ocean with you, for it to dirty everything at home.

SELMAIRE 31:
COLEONE'S SELMAIRE

COLEONE *sees himself powerless in Salem where a train of protesters is stopped.*

COLEONE. The Diamond Black train won't get to Boston. The best (of those who should be at our side tonight) are left littering the tracks. – The train of railway brotherhood has stopped.

SELMAIRE 32:
MULLER'S SELMAIRE

MULLER *tries to imagine the discussions that could have occurred that night in Boston.*

MULLER. Five hundred thousand petitions arrived again today.

ERHMAN KLOSE. What does that change? At Bunker Hill, they had rifles, and the rifles crackled.

LITTLE NED. There are no just causes without rifles.

On the projected newspaper, news headlines are being shown: "American Corporation is gaining with every hour. Strong rise of Anaconda, Tell & Tell and General Electric. AGFA Motors doubled. Boom in canned liquids.

TURIN

VENTURELLI. They're trying to take refuge in their homes (they're already burning).

LYON

STEWART *calls* THAYER

STEWART. Hello! Stewart speaking. – Everything is shaping up nicely. Wenthrop Square and Austin Street are calm.

THAYER. Lawrence Street?

STEWART. Also calm.

THAYER. Rutherford Avenue?

STEWART. Traffic seems completely jammed.

THAYER. Hello! Stewart! Hello! You haven't told me about the bridge leading to the prison.

STEWART. For now, the troops are in place.

The toiletry ritual begins in the cells. In turn, the barber who shaves the heads and legs where the electrodes will be placed, the dresser who dresses the condemned in their execution clothes, the electrician who cuts the clothes where the wires will pass, the doctor who checks the health of the condemned visit the three men. The spectators, as is their role at the theater, participate in the death of the character. DERLINSKI *becomes the barber in* VASTADOUR'*s cell.*

DERLINSKI. Do you understand? (It's dreadful to work here.)

VASTADOUR. It's your job, you do it – there is nothing more to say.

The barber enters CERVI'S *cell, who stares at him.*

DERLINSKI. I would like to be helpful. (CERVI *doesn't answer. The barber hurries his work.*) Say something (speak). Speak! – That'll do.

He enters VORORTZUG's *cell, who doesn't say anything either. While he is being shaved, the dresser dresses* VASTADOUR *in the execution clothes.* LITTLE NED *fills this role.*

VASTADOUR. The bride-groom is getting dressed. (A solicitous State is giving me warm clothes and entrusts me to the expert hands of a barber to shave me.) As strange as it may seem, the fear is gone, (only the hatred remains).

The dresser goes to CERVI *while the barber finishes with* VORORTZUG.

DERLINSKI. You're so calm! – It's great. You are very calm.

VORORTZUG. Does it bother you?

DERLINSKI. (It's frightening.)

VORORTZUG. Because you think – we're the ones who are frightening!

The barber leaves and talks to the electrician and the doctor who are in VANZETTI's *cell. The* PRESS

AGENT *is playing the electrician and the* OFFICIAL
the doctor.

DERLINSKI. Vanzetti is nice, (but the two others have
gone mad).

The electrician pricks VANZETTI *while cutting the
pants.*

VASTADOUR. Be careful.

OFFICIAL. If he pricked you, it's because you moved,
you're not going to act frail are you?

VASTADOUR. It's not the prick that's the issue, but
your role. If there were a God, he could not have
pity for eunuchs who turn themselves into vile
servants of Death. My only desire was to die
standing, among my peers – and this is what I
get (beings like yourselves). What's worse is that
in every age you'll have your like. – Don't touch
me with your filthy hands anymore, (they're
covered with the grime of the masters you serve).
(VORORTZUG *is steaming.* CERVI, *standing up, pulls
on his clothes.* VASTADOUR *rebels for the first time.*)
(My work is only beginning.) The struggle

continues. – I must live and take part in it. Comrades! Don't cry! Keep your chin up. – Comrades!

SELMAIRE 33:
FARLEY AND ANNE'S SELMAIRE

FARLEY *and* ANNE *try to recreate what the Rosenbergs were doing that evening.*

ANNE. Bart?

VASTADOUR. Ethel?

ANNE. Yes.

VASTADOUR. Do you remember that evening?

ANNE. I was sixteen.

VASTADOUR. It was raining in the Lower East Side.

ANNE. I was sixteen and Julius was fourteen.

FARLEY. There was a cloudless sky over Boston, the same one as over Sing-Sing prison, twenty-five years later. – But on the Lower East Side, it was raining.

CERVI. Julius – you were going to night school to become an engineer, weren't you?

FARLEY. (During the day) I worked in a little tailor shop, repairing sewing machines.

CERVI. That evening, you had an important appointment, and you knew it. – Your whole life would depend on it (and you were late).

FARLEY. I went to City College, (the poor person's university) where the classes were paid for by good grades. – I was very focused so sometimes I would miss the bus.

VASTADOUR. You (Ethel), that evening, you were waiting for Julius in front of the clothing factory where your parents worked.

ANNE. I had written (a poem).

CERVI. It was raining, Julius, and you arrived drenched.

FARLEY. Ethel, I had known her since my childhood. – That evening, it was the first time I looked at her with love inside of me.

ANNE. The poem I wrote, I realized that it was for him.

VASTADOUR. So you decided to go to Carnegie Hall the following Sunday. – Ethel loved music so much.

ANNE. That's all we were able to say to each another that night.

FARLEY. But we had written both our names together for the first time.

ANNE. That's true. – We wrote with chalk on the walls: "Julius and Ethel Rosenberg."

FARLEY. Julius and Ethel Rosenberg, for the first time, united on the walls of New York.

CERVI. And you left (together forever).

VASTADOUR. That night – life belonged to you.

ANNE. Only until three minutes to midnight (except we didn't know it).

COLEONE. At three minutes to midnight – the cops were beating the protesters all around the Boston bridge.

LITTLE NED. Millions of batons were crashing down on the misery of the world (and its raised fist).

VENTURELLI. (Fists and batons), these were the only flowers that, spanning the Earth, surrounded the funeral vigil of Charlestown.

GENERAL SELMAIRE 13

It's Madeiros' hour. BONNETADE (*chief security guard*) *goes towards the real audience.*

BONNETADE. Every night, when Massachusetts' talking clock points to three minutes to midnight – on all the clocks of the world, the official witnesses arrive. They walk across the prison and sit facing the electric chair – and watch the hallway from where Madeiros will come.

OFFICIAL. Madeiros!

VORORTZUG *rises and while the head guard speaks,*
he goes towards one of the seats in the audience,
followed by the OFFICIAL *and the* PRESS AGENT. *He*
sits. A hood is put on him, he waits.

BONNETADE. Madeiros was ready. – Without
anyone's assistance, he went to sit on the chair
and let himself be attached. The silence was so
great we could hear him breathe under the hood.
At five past midnight, the electrical current was
contorting the chair. At nine past midnight,
Celestino Madeiros was declared dead.

All the electrical current being concentrated on the
chair, the lights flicker, then shut off. When they
come on again, VORORTZUG *is a spectator like the*
others.

SELMAIRE 34:
ERHMAN KLOSE'S SELMAIRE

ERHMAN KLOSE *imagines the defense attorneys of*
the two men being executed walking defeated in
the streets of Boston.

534

ERHMAN KLOSE. What will die in us when these two men have been killed?

MULLER. Evaluating it in words would be impossible. Anyhow, we have a living role to fill.

ERHMAN KLOSE. Remember John Donne: "Never ask for whom the bell tolls, it tolls for thee."

GENERAL SELMAIRE 14

In the prison it is now SACCO's *turn.*

OFFICIAL. Sacco!

CERVI *goes towards one of the seats in the supposed theater. The reporter witnessing the execution is commenting.* BOSCHETTO *will be this reporter.*

BOSCHETTO. This pale face, furrowed by seven years of agony, this look that pierces you to the deepest reaches of yourself, Nicola Sacco cannot detach himself from it. He takes these things with him in the hallway of death. – The last twenty-six days, he staged another hunger strike. But he doesn't need anyone to sustain him. In seventeen steps (Sacco is in a hurry), he crosses the distance that separates his cell from the electric chair. – What he possesses he puts between himself and the executioner – his party, his family, his companions, (it's enormous but it's fragile).

The OFFICIAL *and the* PRESS AGENT *put the hood on* CERVI *and tie him to the chair with the straps.*

BONNETADE. I'll wait for him to finish speaking to give the signal. – If he talks until morning, I'll wait until morning.

CERVI. (Goodnight, gentlemen.)

BONNETADE. Thus, (every night) Nicola Sacco dies.

The lights flicker and shut off. When they turn on again, CERVI *has become a spectator like the others. In the streets of Boston, where he is still wandering,* ERHMAN KLOSE *comments.*

ERHMAN KLOSE. The moment they open the door, Vanzetti will be the size of a tree planted on the hills of Montferrat .Even as he greets the guards and regains the size of the hallway, Vanzetti will still be a tree.

The OFFICIAL *and the* PRESS AGENT *went to bring* VASTADOUR, *who greeted them, then went ahead of them. Arriving before his chair, he grabs* BONNETADE'S *hand and shakes it firmly.*

ERHMAN KLOSE. In twenty one steps, (always the same, worn by two thousand six hundred and seventy eight days of prison and two thousand six hundred and seventy eight nights) he will reach the chair. Before sitting down, he will grab the hand of the head guard Hendry and will thank him. – Calmly, slowly, he will speak once more of his innocence. – The hatred that sustained him during his last hours will disappear at that moment. The sparks of the chairs and the contortions of his body will not re-animate him. – At fifty-five minutes after midnight, every night of the world, Bartolomeo Vanzetti will have lived.

The lights flicker and turn off.

BONNETADE. At this moment, I should be declaring him dead (but I will not be able to). My voice will choke as usual (the official witnesses will pretend not to notice).

The lights turn back on. VASTADOUR *becomes a spectator like the others.*

BEL CANTO

During this time, two giant pictures of SACCO *and* VANZETTI *are lowered from the flies. We hear* VANZETTI'S *voice coming from the supposed theater.*

VANZETTI. This is Bartolomeo Vanzetti speaking to you. – If it had not been for this thing, Nicola and I might have lived our lives out talking at street corners to scorning men. We might have died unmarked, unknown, failures. Our condemnation has become our career. It will be our triumph. Never in our life could we hope to do such work for tolerance, justice, for man's understanding of man, as we now do by accident, in this corridor… our words, our lives, our pains, nothing! Only the taking of our lives, lives of a good shoemaker and a poor fish peddler, will count! That last moment belongs to us – that agony is our triumph.

During this time, the supposed audience leaves. In the darkness, LAUREEN *inspects with her flashlight the seats of* CERVI, VASTADOUR *and* VORORTZUG, *as if they had forgotten something. After which, she turns her flashlight towards the audience and keeps it pointed on them.*

GREEN INTEGER
Pataphysics and Pedantry

Douglas Messerli, *Publisher*

Essays, Manifestos, Statements, Speeches, Maxims,
Epistles, Diaristic Notes, Narratives, Natural Histories,
Poems, Plays, Performances, Ramblings, Revelations
and all such ephemera as may appear necessary
to bring society into a slight tremolo of confusion
and fright at least.

Books Published by Green Integer

History, or Messages from History Gertrude Stein [1997]
Notes on the Cinematographer Robert Bresson [1997]
The Critic As Artist Oscar Wilde [1997]
Tent Posts Henri Michaux [1997]
Eureka Edgar Allan Poe [1997]
An Interview Jean Renoir [1998]
Mirrors Marcel Cohen [1998]
The Effort to Fall Christopher Spranger [1998]
Radio Dialogs I Arno Schmidt [1999]
Travels Hans Christian Andersen [1999]
In the Mirror of the Eighth King Christopher Middleton [1999]
On Ibsen James Joyce [1999]
A Wanderer Plays on Muted Strings Knut Hamsun [2001]
Laughter: An Essay on the Meaning of the Comic
Henri Bergson [1999]
Operratics Michel Leiris [2001]

Seven Visions Sergei Paradjanov [1998]

Ghost Image Hervé Guibert [1998]

Ballets Without Music, Without Dancers, Without Anything
Louis-Ferdinand Céline [1999]

My Tired Father Gellu Naum [2000]

Manifestos Manifest Vicente Huidobro [2000]

Aurelia Gérard de Nerval [2001]

On Overgrown Paths Knut Hamsun [1999]

Displeasures of the Table Martha Ronk [2001]

What Is Man? Mark Twain [2000]

Metropolis Antonio Porta [1999]

Poems Sappho [1999]

Suicide Circus: Selected Poems Alexei Kruchenykh [2001]

Hell Has No Limits José Donoso [1999]

To Do: Alphabets and Birthdays Gertrude Stein [2001]

Letters from Hanusse Joshua Haigh [2000]
[edited by Douglas Messerli]

Suites Federico García Lorca [2001]

Pedra Canga Tereza Albues [2001]

The Pretext Rae Armantrout [2001]

Theoretical Objects Nick Piombino [1999]

Yi 羿 Yang Lian [2002]

My Life Lyn Hejinian [2002]

Book of Reincarnation Hsu Hui-chih [2002]

The Doll and *The Doll at Play* Hans Bellmer
(with poetry by Paul Éluard) [2002]

Art *Poetic'* Olivier Cadiot [1999]

Fugitive Suns: Selected Poetry Andrée Chedid [1999]

Across the Darkness of the River Hsi Muren [2001]

Mexico. A Play Gertrude Stein [1999]

Sky Eclipse: Selected Poems Régis Bonvicino [2000]

BOOKS FORTHCOMING FROM GREEN INTEGER

Three Haitian Creole Tales Félix Morriseau-Leroy
O, How the Wheel Becomes It! Anthony Powell
Stomping the Goyim Michael Disend
Letters to Felician Ingeborg Bachmann
Romanian Poems Paul Celan
The Church Louis-Ferdinand Céline
Victoria Knut Hamsun
The Sea Below My Window Ole Sarvig
Traveling Through Brittany Gustave Flaubert
Gradiva Wilhelm Jensen and *Delusion and Dream in Wilhelm Jensen's* GRADIVA Sigmund Freud
Amour, Amour Andreas Embirikos
Selected Poems Else Lasker-Schüler
The Piazza Tales Herman Melville
Island of the Dead Jean Frémon
After Spending a Night Among Horses Tua Forsström
If Only the Sea Could Sleep Adonis